VOLUME II OF THE GLASTONBURY CHRONICLES

THE SWORD OF THE KING

S.P. HENDRICK

Volume II
Of The
Glastonbury Chronicles

The
Sword
Of
The
King

S.P. Hendrick

Pendraig Publishing
Los Angeles, CA 91040

Volume II of the Glastonbury Chronicles:
The Sword of the King
by SP Hendrick
First Edition © 2010
by PENDRAIG Publishing

Cover Design & Interior Images,
Typeset & Layout: Jo-Ann Byers-Mierzwicki

Sword, Crown & Shield Line Art: Jay Mayer
Crown Color: Jim Davis

PENDRAIG Publishing
Los Angeles, CA 91040
www.PendraigPublishing.com
Printed in the United States of America

ISBN: 978-0-9827263-2-7

To Peter Gabriel,
whose "In Your Eyes" became the soundtrack of this series.

And to James Thomas Michael McMahon,
Barry Sanders and Arthur E. Lane
who taught me the magic words:
"What if?"
and that the pen is the most magical wand of all.

Chapter One

Kieran and I have always been together. Within our mother's womb we swam together, sharing the same blood, the same comforting heartbeat, the same spark of life for seven months before we were brought forth simultaneously by a surgeon's laser knife, separated by it first from our mother and then each other. We had sprung from the same seed, Kieran and I, the same egg, and as that gamete divided our oneness became two, yet not completely separate, for we were born quite literally joined at the hip.

The surgery itself was quite uncomplicated; even the fine scar we bore for the first few months of our lives vanished before we were of an age to walk. We were perfect and unblemished as it had been called upon in the distant past for us to be, and that further complicated our lives and the lives of those around us, for there was not one mote of difference between us, not even the instant of our birth to distinguish which twin was which. In some families this would have been a mere inconvenience, a curiosity, but in ours it was a matter of vital importance, for our mother was Queen Katherine and our father King Geoffrey of England, Kernow and Mannin, and we were both the firstborn sons and heirs to the throne and the crown.

It did not matter to us at the time, as we railed against the harsh brightness of the world of the living in our separate incubators. All that mattered was the horrible void of aloneness. As strange as it may sound to one whose memories begin no earlier than the age of a toddler, I remember quite clearly those first few days of life, and even before. The isolation from my brother was more painful than the laser blade had been. We reached out to each other beyond the physical and once more found the link. We would never be entirely apart again.

Alike? Even beyond childhood there was no way to tell us apart. Our hair was the same shade of raven black, curling in precisely the same way around our faces when it was not held back at our necks by ribbons or clips, for we always wore it long. Our eyes were the same blue of a stormless summer sky, our skin the same pallid shade as our mother's. Our manner was the same, our gaits, our voices, in tone, timbre and inflexion, our loves, and our hates - all identical. We were, as one of our nannies used to call us, "The Kieran-Neil Unit".

For a long time there was some uncertainty as to which of us should be Kieran and which Neil, but we agreed between ourselves that it didn't matter. He chose to answer to Kieran, and I to Neil, and so it was settled in the only way it could be. From that day forth I was Neil Andrew Edward George and he Kieran David Geoffrey Charles, both of the House of Windsor, and until the courts could rule otherwise should they choose to do so, both first in line to succeed our father.

In olden days there never would have been a problem; we never would have survived. By the year of our birth, however, such surgeries, though rare, were no difficulty. There had been some increase in the instances of conjoined twins due to higher than normal radiation levels in the early 22nd century, but it had usually occurred among the lower classes, those who lived nearer the sources of the radiation, such as an old nuclear plant which had been cemented in after a fire ninety years or so before our birth. The major earthquake we had suffered just prior to our nation's Millennial Anniversary had unseated part of the cement, and the floods of 2110 had done the rest, seeping into the toxic contamination and polluting the waters of several small towns nearby.

If our birth had been a scandal and the dream of every cheap form of journalism known to man, the birth of our sister Gwenna Alexandra Margaret at Windsor Palace seven years later was a chance for the best of the press to rejoice. Blonde and beautiful and perfect in every way was the first princess born into the family since our great-great aunt Anastasia. Gwenna became the darling of our nation, our parents, and her big brothers, yet our delight in her could not bring her the bond we shared with each other.

Even as we grew we could see the difference: she was fair and filled with sunlight; we were dark and told our secrets to the moon. Still it was her curls and laughter we sought for approval, far more than our nannies or our parents, and it was for the joy in Gwenna's eyes that we played the roles of shining knights, jousting with lances made from Father's old fishing rods, and fencing with measuring sticks, until father decided we were old enough for masques and foils. Oh the feats of bravado and gallantry we'd offer for her entertainment, risking all to see her little hands clapping in excitement, and oh the flourishes and the bows we made to our little Queen of Love and Beauty, for was there ever such a perfect pearl of delight as our sweet Gwenna of the laughing eyes?

One day her eyes ceased laughing and she screamed in terror at what she saw.

Kieran and I had long since given up on foils. We were seventeen and reckless with the immortality of youth. Rapiers and daggers, very real, very sharp and very deadly, had become as toys to us. The danger had only made the contest sweeter. We wore no protective clothing, only black leather pants and boots and blousy white shirts we had copied from a painting at the Tate Gallery, and for the purpose of practicality our long hair was bound behind us at the neck with ribbons of silk.

Our eyes locked as we fought, as perfectly matched to each other in movement and skill as were our weapons. Like panthers we moved, silently stalking each other, now a flash of steel and a counterflash as the other parried, the sound of the impact of metal upon metal ringing sweetly in our ears. How long we paced each other that way I have no way of knowing, but it seemed to go on forever as if in a dream, each movement precise and unplanned, until suddenly and without warning the world around us changed.

It was as if somehow we had merged once more, an effect dizzying at first, powerful and strange. Our minds were one, our thoughts, our actions, as if that gamete had never divided at all and we were once again united, whole and complete, looking through one pair of eyes into a mirror image of ourself, only it was not a mirror, for the sword was not in the place in which a reflected sword would have been. The time it took for the message to transfer from one body to the other was less than a second, yet the body through whose eyes we both saw had that tiny advantage, and without meaning to do harm, used it.

There was a searing pain which ripped through me white hot as Kieran's rapier went into my chest just above my left nipple and I found myself quite suddenly back in the body in which I belonged, bleeding heavily and crumpling to the floor. I lost consciousness as I fell.

No, that's not totally true. I was aware of Kieran's arms around me, lifting me, carrying me somewhere, and Gwenna's hysterical screaming at the sight of my blood, but I was not totally there. All around me was darkness and the whole of my being was a mote of brilliance trapped inside the darkness somewhere within my head. I could hear all. I felt nothing, yet I knew it was Kieran who carried me, for a part of him struggled to break through that darkness to find me.

I heard our Father bellowing commands to the doctor and roaring at Kieran for his foolishness, and I longed to scream out that it was my fault too, that Kieran should not take the blame, but I was too small a spark to be heard, even in the mind of my brother. At least they knew I was alive.

And then the doctor did something to me and all was blackness.

Out of that blackness arose colour and sound, and I saw and heard within them the images of two other men who duelled with rapiers and daggers, but from the clothes they wore and those of the others who gathered around them in the torchlight on the lawn of some fabulous mansion, the period was several hundred years before we had been born. One man was dark of hair and one had hair of a sandy hue. Both had eyes the colour of mine, the colour of Kieran's, and they fought as we did, eyes locked, never looking at the crowd or even the hands or weapons the other wielded.

There was the slightest smile, the slightest nod of the head from the man with the dark hair; I realised I saw it through the eyes of his opponent, the same as I had seen myself through Kieran's eyes. The adrenaline pounded through his system, each muscle alert and quick in action and response. I heard it; I felt it. There was a thrust, but no parry, and I felt the rapier in his hand slide through the ribcage of the other, vibrating slightly as it passed the bone, meeting little resistance as it pierced the heart, passing cleanly out again through the back.

The perspective changed and I watched through the eyes of the other man as he was slain in what seemed to be slow motion, felt the sword from the other end as it invaded the body, cold and filled with the brilliance of lightning as his consciousness and mine fell into the eyes of the man who had slain him.

There was no pain this time. Pressure, yes, and the coldness of the steel. I had heard that mortal wounds are painless because the body goes into shock, and considered that and the sharpness of the blade to have been the reason, but I could find no reason for the immense emotional feeling of well-being, joy, and peace which had accompanied the act. But then why was I trying to rationalise a dream I had while unconscious from my own rapier wound?

Had it been a dream? I wasn't certain. It had been dream-like, almost surreal in parts, yet within it was the essence of something else. There had been faces there I should have recognised, and the whole scene had seemed strangely familiar to me, almost a memory. The colours had been so vivid, so real, and the sounds, and the other sensations - why all had been profoundly clear, and I remembered all of them, even as I struggled to find consciousness once more.

It was a long struggle. The doctor had decided at the beginning to keep me sedated for as long as possible, figuring that if I were asleep my breathing would be slower and more shallow and I would do less damage to the wound and reinflated lung than if I were awake. What he had not counted on was Kieran's need to have my companionship and the communication skills of twins. It took three days for the doctor to realise that the dosage of mandrisine would have to be increased to dangerous amounts to keep me under any longer; somehow Kieran's metabolism was affecting my own and he was throwing it off as fast as I was getting it, but not before he had some very strange dreams of his own.

Upon the return of consciousness we spoke in detail of these and found his experiences identical to my own, down to the feeling of the blade both in the hand of the slayer and the body of the slain, and to the euphoria which had engulfed the whole scene. It had been too real, he thought, to be just a dream. A memory fragment, perhaps, of a life and death before this, or a vision of something of historical importance. Besides, he had been wide awake when I was having this "dream", and he had seen it too, sitting in a catatonic trance just beyond the bed in which I had lain, feeling guilty for almost deciding the issue of the succession for once and for all, wishing it had been my body to whom the consciousness had fled and his which had taken the blow.

He was terrified of having to face life alone, and vowed that if I should die he would take his own life, for there was no meaning to a life in which he was only half of the person we had been when it had begun.

We kept this discussion secret in the way that twins do, not believing we would be understood by anyone else. We spoke of it in shadow whispers the others could not hear, in codes they would not recognise, for a word alone was sufficient between us to stimulate a conversation in which no words were spoken. We had found the telepathy between us had strengthened since the incident; the idea of being isolated within separate minds and bodies had seemed unusual to us even as children; now it had become frightening.

How did they do it, we wondered. How did people tolerate the isolation? Our parents had a communication of their own, based on more than twenty years of marriage, but it was not the same as ours, and Gwenna...

Gwenna had changed. She grew silent, serious for a ten year old. She seldom smiled that radiant smile which before had lighted the world around her. Her smiles instead became thin and all too knowing for one of her years. Within the Maiden the Crone had taken residence and peered forth from her eyes. That, and something else, something all too familiar to us. Something we couldn't name.

Chapter Two

*W*ith the appearance of the first blooms in our garden things suddenly seemed normal again. My wound healed, the scar grew less tender with each day, and Gwenna seemed to throw off the aura of age as the sky threw off its cloak of grey. Summer Solstice was upon us before we knew it and with it came the National Ritual, officiated by our parents at Stonehenge, and this year with Kieran and myself taking the part of the Holly King and the Oak King.

We worked on the choreography for a week, for quarterstaffs, though weapons of our favourite period of history, were not our greatest skill, and the BBC planned to broadcast the ritual via satellite live to the English speaking world. By the time the day arrived for us to do our part we were ready, although we were both a little nervous about the final blow which was supposed to kill me.

Kieran asked several times if I didn't want to be on the other end of the quarterstaff, but I insisted I was more likely to do him injury than he to me, as the injury he had already given me might, by the end of the battle, become irritated enough to hinder my pulling the blow at the last second. Though I had recovered on the surface, his reflexes were still a wee bit faster than mine. Reluctantly, he agreed.

Thousands surrounded Stonehenge, many arriving days before and camping on Salisbury Plain, awaiting the event and keeping a vigil through the final night before the ceremony until the first rays of the sun rose above the heelstone. The main ritual was not until noon, but there was celebration in the air as each group represented there observed the day in its own way, according to its own tradition. Out of the differences between them they found new wisdom and other facets of the Lady and Lord they served.

When the sun reached its zenith King Geoffrey and Queen Katherine cast the circle wide around the henge, using the grave of the martyred King Stephen II and Kevin, Duke of Cornwall as its centre. The quarters were called by the High Priestesses and High Priests of the major covens of Northumbria, Yorkshire, Somerset and Cornwall, the first three areas drawn at random for the honour, the last a tradition in honour of the Duke buried with his King.

While all this went on, Kieran and I stood motionless upon the grave, back to back, our quarterstaffs in our hands. I could feel my brother's thoughts and joined him as we reached beneath us to the bones of our illustrious ancestors, to touch that part of them which we had inherited and invite them, wherever they were, to enjoy the ritual and the festival. After all, our great-grandfather and uncle had themselves done in life and in death what we did only in token, although their lives had not been taken in a duel between them, but had been given freely as a gift to the Land. We thanked them for it, for the Land had indeed prospered and flourished thereafter, recovering from the natural disasters it had experienced, and becoming the financial hub of the world as the Swiss banking scandals of 2067 had emerged. During the Pan-American War our isolation became an asset, and our neutrality as the European Commonwealth fractured into its natural ethnicities assured us a favoured nation status with all those who survived the break-up, for polyglot as the world had become, there were repositories of England in every culture on Earth, left there from our days of Empire.

Yes, our ancestors had served Lady Sovereignty well, but perhaps we should not have invoked them so clearly within our hearts, for as we began our part of the ritual it seemed to us we had disturbed their sleep a little too effectively.

Perhaps it was mere imagination, perhaps it was a peephole into another time, but as we began to circle each other and trade carefully rehearsed blow upon blow with the quarterstaffs I was taken with that same dizzying effect I had felt when last we fenced with rapier and dagger. I watched Kieran, but it was not Kieran whose face I saw, nor mine. It was Stephen's face; I should know it well enough; his portrait hangs prominently in every home in which I've been throughout my life, usually with a candle burning nearby. It could have been an odd angle of the light, I expect, as we do in fact both resemble him a bit, but that wouldn't explain why his face changed again and it became that of Kevin, Duke of Cornwall, grinning as he fought with me, staff against staff. Then the immersion began.

I was sucked into his eyes, looking back at my own body. It was Stephen. It was Kevin. It was Kieran. Finally, it was me again, and I snapped back into it just as my quarterstaff snapped in two, as it had been designed to do.

"What was that?" I asked my brother as we picked up new staffs from the pile, making certain his was the one partially sawn through this time.

"Our ancestors checking up on us," he whispered as he passed.

"Shouldn't they be back by now?" I answered.

"Perhaps they are. Perhaps it's telepathy from someone in the crowd."

We circled each other again, smashing and bashing the wooden poles together, longing for the sound of steel instead of the cracking, thwacking sound they made. The choreography was perfect, every swing, every motion of foot and hand, as the bright side of the year and the dark side vied for control.

This is the anniversary of their death, I thought, visualising my ancestors falling through the sky, arm in arm, to their deaths upon the stones below. I hazarded a quick glance at the stone which had broken their bodies and their fall, where now a camera took in every nuance of our actions for the world to see.

Focus. Not the camera, me. High and low, and a mighty swing slightly to the left side in the centre and...

Just as it was planned, Kieran's staff was in two pieces. Best two out of three. We met in the middle for our new staffs.

"I don't think it came from the audience," I said to him, "but I know they're here, if only in spirit."

"You think they're watching us?"

"More like through us."

We went back to the battle, moving around between the stones this time, around the henge so all the people gathered there could see us in the longest portion of the killing dance. He swept downward with his weapon; I leapt over it. I swung at him from above; he ducked. Some of the actions were almost like fencing, but most were different; blocking required two hands on the same weapon, with the impact coming near the centre of the staff. It was possible to block as a sword might block, or to thrust in the same manner, indeed, the final stroke was to be like that, but for the most part it was awkward, for the balance point of a sword and a staff were by no means comparable.

After several minutes of this performance we found ourselves a bit winded and decided at my nod to go into endgame. My nod. That almost imperceptible little nod and the faint smile of the man in my dream as he had opened the way for the sword to find him.

Something within me responded to the action, resonated to the meaning of it, and I felt the most wonderful rush of warmth flood over me as my own head bobbed ever so slightly and I smiled at Kieran, holding my staff for him to break with the sharpest crack I had heard all morning. I was still smiling as I saw the end of the staff coming for my head, and in that instant of my yielding to him I wanted more than anything for it all to be real.

Kieran's eyes locked again on mine and I felt the rush surge into him as well, yet he resisted it with all his might and stopped the blow from more than grazing my forehead. It did not matter, for once again I had fled my body as it crumpled to the ground. Fortunately for the ritual, my feigned death had been called for and I was supposed to remain inert upon the ground until after the circle had broken and the cameras were off.

The view from above Stonehenge was exhilarating to be sure, and I longed to call for my brother to join me in my flight, but the ritual continued as he was asked to consecrate the cup with our mother. Token incest, I mused, deciding I must joke with him about it when I returned, but at that moment I did not wish to return. The camera stared through me as I flew by it, determined to get a better look at where we'd hit the stones so long ago. Yes, there was still traces of our blood there, yet I doubt either of us had even noticed the impact, so great had been the ecstasy of the moment, even as it had exploded into brilliance and darkness which were one and the same, and here we were again...

And I was back in my body, too shaken by the thoughts which had filled me an instant before to pay any attention to what was happening around me. I was not afraid of it, far from that. I was excited, dazzled at the prospect that I had actually touched the mind of one of my ancestors, thrilled that although I did not know exactly which of the two of them it had been, their essences were even now close by, taking notice of us in the here and now, celebrating with us the turning of the sun.

I longed to call out to Kieran with my voice, but only dared to seek him in thought, for the circle our father had cast from within the circle of stones still stood, and the world watched a celebration which dated back as far as the memory of man.

Not now. It's almost over. Don't break my concentration, Neil.

His answer was wordless and for the first time I could remember he had disappointed me, refused to link. If I could only make him feel the reason I needed to communicate...

But no. It didn't matter. He was right. We were in the middle of sacred theatre and the show must go on as it had down the millennia, although the Gods no longer required our blood on an annual basis, only when the need of the Land was great, as it had been with Stephen. Kevin of Cornwall, who had slain him by cutting off his parachute as they fell to earth from an ancient aircraft, had decided to join his *anmchara*, his soul-friend, in death. It was one of the great heroic legends of our nation, greater still because it was a piece of documented history, and the greatest to me because the blood of the Sacred King flowed in me.

I lay there on the ground, deathly still, fearing that even the shallow breathing of which I was capable would be picked up by the camera and sent to millions, showing them what a bad actor I was, showing it even as far away as Mars Colony, for they would be receiving a transmission of the event as soon as ComSat 23 was in line with BBCSat 6 to boost it along. From there it would go on to who knew where, perhaps all the way to the Sagan Colony. As my face pressed into the grass I thought instead about Stephen and his sacrifice and what I had felt moments before, and I prayed with all the ardour of my adolescent soul that I might be called upon to do the same. I was his spawn, as was my brother. I had felt the sword in my chest and had no fear of feeling it again.

Suddenly I was stricken by remorse; it was not a selfless, but a very selfish prayer I had made, for my death would make life intolerable for Kieran, as he had already told me, and yes, the same exact blood flowed in both our veins. What if it were to be Kieran chosen and not me at all? How would I live? He was more than *anmchara* to me, he was flesh of my flesh and blood of my blood, and most of the time it seemed we shared a single mind as well.

I could tell by the sounds that the pages outside the Aubrey holes had passed the red wine and barley cakes to the faithful who waited patiently for their turn, singing songs of the Lady and the Lord, and of the turning of the Wheel to another season, and heard above it all Kieran's thoughts.

Soon, Neil. A few more minutes and you can get up. What was it you wanted?

I went to the top of the henge, Kieran, and I was not alone.

Crows? Ravens? They seem to fancy this place almost as much as they do the Tower these days.

No, Kieran. King Stephen or the Duke. I don't know which. Maybe both. No, I think just one. One of them was into my head. I shared his thoughts, remembering how it was that day they died.

Ghosts?

No, more like essences.

That's what ghosts are.

No, these, or he, rather, didn't seem to have a physical form at all. Just thoughts. Memories. We saw the blood on the stone they hit on the way down. It's still there.

You don't know which one it was? Nothing in his thoughts?

Kieran, from what I felt there was no difference between them by that time. They had merged, the way you and I...

"Oh Gods," I said out loud, hoping the grass beneath my mouth had muffled the sound so no one heard it with physical ears.

What Neil? No, don't tell me. Father is motioning the quarters to revocation.

Kieran, it can't wait.

What?

I've just had a thought which may explain everything.

What?

What if I'm not seeing these things through someone else's eyes? What if we are Great-grandfather Stephen and his Duke, back again for one more round?

Chapter Three

I could feel Kieran's stare burn into me from across the henge and hoped the camera hadn't picked him out as his head turned from the attention he was supposed to be giving as all assembled bid farewell to the Goddesses and Gods called upon to bless the elements of Fire, Earth, Water and Air at the four cardinal directions. Fortunately for him the lapse had occurred with the Goddess Elen; she was much more forgiving than the Morrigan would have been, and as a representation of Earth in all Her fecundity was well aware of how easily men's minds were turned from purely spiritual matters.

Hush now. Wait until we're alone. We need to talk this through as well as think it.

I agreed.

I waited for what felt like another twenty minutes, my body aching and stiffening in the position I had assumed as I had fallen, longing for one good deep breath to fill my lungs with something like life once more. The pink knot on the left side of my chest began to pain me, and the scar tissue beneath it made its presence known. I meant no disrespect to the Gods, but I wanted this thing to be over with so I could once more be a living prince and not the dead icon of a king. Yet a part of me longed to be lying in perfect peace beneath the marble slab at the centre of the henge, my task finished, my life fulfilled. Dangerous thinking from one who had already taken a sword between the ribs once in this body.

Finally came the words I had waited for.

"May we merry meet and merry part...."

And the voices of thousands joined in the last phrase...

"And merry meet again."

The cameras were off and the people dispersed in merriment, glad of the warmth promised by the change of season, most of them forgetting that in the old days this had been known not as summer's beginning, but its midpoint. I mused upon that fact for a moment as I tried to move and found myself stiffened into the position I had held for so long.

"Come on, old man. Need a hand up?"

It was Kieran, a smile upon his face and more serious thoughts behind his eyes. His hands took mine and helped me slowly leave the position of a somewhat freshly fallen corpse and assume the pose of a reasonably dignified heir to the throne.

"God's antlers but you're cold."

It was the one thing I hadn't noticed until he mentioned it.

"I've been dead. What do you expect?"

"Let's get you out of here, into the airbus and home."

I nodded.

"But there's something I want to do first. Come with me."

I led him back to the marble slab.

"Concentrate on them below us."

"All right."

"Now hold my hands and look into my eyes."

The sensation was almost immediate. It was not hands we needed to clasp but elbows, and our hands found the correct positions. We were flying, falling through the air at great speed, toward the stone circle below. We had only seconds of life left, but it didn't matter. We would not be separated this time. We were one in a way only twins have a chance of knowing, but it went beyond that, two halves of the same soul, united after years of separation, and finally free of anything which bound us to anything but each other and the Godhood we had touched. The bodies were no longer needed; nor would they hold us apart much longer. Their blood would redeem the Land. That which was of Earth would be reclaimed by Earth and we would be free...

We felt the release, saw the brilliance explode as we joined with it and knew only the ecstasy of that instant in which light and darkness and matter and energy all converged into one emotion - love - and after that nothing mattered.

I don't know which of us was the first to let go of the other, but I'm sure I heard Kieran breathe before I remembered to.

"That was only a part of it."

"There was more?"

"Yes. Much more."

"How did you survive it?"

"We didn't, Kieran. That's the point. We died. We're under this stone. And we're standing above it, remembering where we left off."

We hadn't noticed Gwenna until she spoke.

"What are you two doing on the grave of the Sacred King? Don't you know it's time to go home?"

There was something in her eyes when she said those words, "Sacred King", something that was not reverence at all, and it gave us both a chill, but when we looked at her again we saw only our loving little fair-haired sister, eager to get home so she could play.

We climbed aboard the airbus in silence, not wanting to speak until we could be in private, hesitating even to communicate by thought in case there was another telepath around. The area between Salisbury and Avebury was reputed to be populated by several of them who used the energy of the ley lines and the vortices at the stone circles to amplify their abilities. Perhaps that had been all we had experienced.

Perhaps not.

Settled in back at home we were less on our guard. We had barely shut ourselves up in the library when Father tapped at the door and made his grand entrance, the antler crown still upon his head.

"Don't you think you could take that off now?" Kieran asked.

"What? Oh this," he laughed as he removed the crown.

His face was burned from standing so long in the sun and having forgotten, as usual, to wear screen. His skin was quite weathered for a man of his age and status, for he was barely fifty. As a King he was a very good and well-loved ruler. As High Priest of England he was even more effective, giving the different traditions our people observed a common focus. Even the monotheists respected him, and the Archbishop of Canterbury praised his book on Jesus Christ as the Sacred King of the Near Eastern people.

"You two did a really splendid job today. The fight was marvellous. I'm proud of you."

Kieran gave me an odd look.

Neil, I think we should tell him what happened.

No, not till we've worked it out between ourselves.

No, Neil. Now. He's High Priest of the whole bloody country. He's got Stephen's blood in him too. He'll know.

Kieran, please...

"Father, something odd happened today."

Traitor!

Trust me. It will be all right.

"Odd? How do you mean?"

I wanted to keep this just between the two of us until we knew more.

We're too close to it, Neil. We need someone who didn't experience it to tell us what happened, from an objective point of view. Besides, its not outside the family.

I don't trust all of the family.

"Under the Rose, Father. All of this is under the Rose."

He looked from Kieran to me, then back again and raised an eyebrow in interest.

You trust Father, don't you?

Yes.

Then who, Neil? Who?

He saw the image in my mind of Gwenna, that strange look in her eyes.

"Under the Rose, then, Kieran, if you believe it to be necessary, although I'm curious as to where you picked up such an archaic phrase."

Gwenna? She's just a child. But you're right, of course. For one thing she's too young to know any of this.

Don't be so sure. There's something very old inside that child's body, but I'm not sure she knows it's there yet, not consciously at any rate. Go ahead with Father. I think you're right about him after all. He knows something of this; I can hear it in his voice.

"Is it? Perhaps I've been doing too much reading. Anyway, it started with Neil actually. I only fell into it later. Let him tell you."

Oh thank you so much. Talking to him was your idea. I'm not certain I can describe it to him in words, and he can't read me the way you can.

You can do it, Neil. I'll fill in where I need to.

Slowly, almost painfully the whole story poured forth, leaving out only the bits of Kieran's inattention to duty...

You owe me for that

...and my suspicions that something more than they comprehended was going on with our sister.

Neil, just remember that glorious instant of totality and don't bicker. You are arguing with yourself, Anmchara.

Father listened carefully to the whole story, cocking his head to one side when a point interested him as I have seen him do so many times before, scowling here and there, arching an eyebrow now and again, until the entire incident had unfolded carefully before him for response and criticism. He was silent a long time, thinking carefully before he spoke.

He believes you.

Perhaps. Perhaps he only believes a part of it.

Do you think he had any idea of how close we really are?

I don't think he does, even now.

"You've been through rather a lot today."

"Yes."

Another pause, as he looked back and forth between us.

"Have you ever been through anything like this before, either of you?"

We looked at each other.

The fencing accident?

Yes.

Shall I tell him or you?

You only saw it second-hand. Let me.

I filled in the entire sequence of events, from the time we first became disoriented until the time I was allowed to remain conscious, including Neil's ability to somehow assimilate and throw off the effects of the mandrisine, which raised both of Father's eyebrows.

"Does anyone else know about any of this?" he asked.

"Not anyone in the flesh at least, unless one of those telepaths has sorted us out."

He shook his head at my words.

"Not likely. Gentlemen, for I can no longer call you boys, gentlemen, I think I need to send you on holiday to Glastonbury. There's someone you need to meet, and several things you need to discuss with him. Not everything comes down to us in the form of historical records. Why for a long time it was assumed that the death of Stephen II and the Duke of

Cornwall was a tragic accident. Only after your Grandfather celebrated his Golden Jubilee did the truth come out, from records in the Archives in Glastonbury."

"Why did it take so long?" I asked.

"Times were different. The Monarchy was not yet firmly re-established. Stephen had died before his heir was born, and the prospect of an infant on the throne made everyone a little nervous. Fortunately the Dame Protector was quite proficient in politics and between her and Princess Anastasia, the Duchess of Cornwall, the country was able to bridge the gap in years until Kevin was old enough to rule on his own.

"Christianity was still the dominant religion at the time, and for so long the Church of England had been the State Religion that it was difficult to accept the fact that the King was not a Christian, although followers of the Old Faith had been in prominent positions for years. When your grandfather not only admitted in public that he was Pagan but began to celebrate festivals on the Tor, at Avebury, Stonehenge and other such ancient places there was no more than a ripple of reaction from the populace; he'd already proven himself in their eyes. A year later the truth of the "accident" became known and Stephen and the Duke were all but canonised in the eyes of the nation.

"The romantic notion of that kind of self-sacrifice which had held so many to the Christian faith led them away from it to something more immediate. The various traditions of Paganism were explored by an overwhelming amount of the population, and most of them found the transition exceedingly simple."

"So," I ventured, "is there any relationship between these Archives in Glastonbury and the fact that you want to send us there?"

Good point, Neil. Glad you caught it.

How could I have missed it? Father broadcasts almost as well as you.

Perhaps that's where we get it.

You mean it's in the blood? Well, yes, but I still think it's a couple of generations further back.

"As a matter of fact there is. He's a distant cousin of yours, actually, and mine on the Tyrell side, not the Windsor, called Derek Watson. He's an old man now, nearly eighty. He pretty much runs things in Glastonbury, at least with the Order."

Something sent a chill through us both.

Why does this sound so familiar?

I don't know Neil. It does to me as well.

"Which Order, father?" asked Kieran.

"God's Hooves, what have they been teaching you? The Order of the Sword and the Rose. I thought your Uncle Julian would have filled your heads with it by now."

Ring a bell?

Yes, from somewhere, but certainly not all of it came from Uncle Julian. I have a feeling it has to do with whatever I touched when I was... wherever I was.

We nodded our heads in unison. That Order. The most ancient Order of the Land. The Order in which the Knights had the double duty of guarding with their lives the King and his heirs, and if it became necessary, of killing the King to ensure the survival of the Land. It was not a matter of regicide, but of sacrifice, for to have any effect at all the King must consent to the act and go to his death willingly, as did our great-grandfather Stephen. Our great-great uncle Kevin, Duke of Cornwall, had been the member of the Order chosen for the duty.

"Hmmm. I thought he would have by now. You have as much Tyrell in you as Windsor, you know, and you'll both be expected to go through the ritual sometime before your next birthday, the same as your grandfather and I did. You won't be expected to go through the various steps to knighthood, though, unless you want to. You are heirs to the throne, after all, but it honours the Tyrell blood in your great-grandmother's line, and your great-great-uncle Kevin Windsor-FitzWalter's as well."

Do you want to go to Glastonbury?

How fast do you think we can pack?

Chapter Four

Glastonbury. I don't think Kieran and I had visited there more than a handful of times since our father's First Coronation there ten years before. The tradition of the Double Coronation, first at the Tor, then at Westminster Abbey, had begun with Stephen and had been observed by both his son and grandson. When the time came for us to succeed our father, we would follow in the same fashion, although we had discussed one of us being crowned in the first and the other in the second. No matter. Father was young and healthy and we were in no hurry to take on the burden of the Crown.

Arrangements had been made by Father for us to stay at Tyrell House, the headquarters of the Order of the Sword and the Rose, and home to Sir Derek Watson and Sir Robin Watson, a cousin of some degree of both Derek's and ours, and Archivist of the Order. To be sure, there was a certain resemblance to our grandfather in Robin's eyes, and the shape of his face, a resemblance which was utterly lacking in Derek. The two of them, we learned, shared the same Imbolc birthday, the same year and all, and though they were only cousins, they had grown up together in a family so closely knit they also might have been twins. Their mothers had been Ladies-in-Waiting to Queen Emma and Anastasia, Duchess of Cornwall, our great-great-aunt, and they had spent a good deal of their youth at and around Court, playmates of our grandfather King Kevin and great-uncle Stephen of Cornwall. They had both become widowers in the same year, and were glad to have us in residence, for we were a fresh audience for their tales, and the stories they knew between them were more than they could tell in the lifetime remaining to them. Fortunately, most had been written down and preserved in the Archives of the Order, even the more risqué ones, as it was another purpose of the Order to maintain the truth from which history is often fabricated.

We lived in the main house, a lovely old piece of Victoriana which had been built to replace an even older building consumed by fire in the mid-1800's, the result, it was rumoured, of an exhausted scholar burning the midnight oil too late and with too high a wick. At any rate, Sir Rodger Tyrell did lose his life in the blaze, and his son Graham succeeded him as head of the Order, expanding the underground chambers, tunnels and library, and adding a second antechamber to the Temple in the course of reconstruction.

We spent the next six weeks there, studying by day in the "catacombs" as Kieran insisted in calling the subterranean classrooms, and by night socialising with our elderly cousins and learning of such prosaic family traits as our grandfather's uncanny ability to eat green peas with a knife, much to the disconcertion of his nanny. By Lammas we were ready to perform the coming of age ritual each male member of the Watson family of the Tyrell line had performed for uncounted generations. We spoke the poem in unison from memory, learned not by rote, but with full understanding of its meaning, and together we beheaded the barley sheaves and spilled the wine, holding the image of our great-grandfather in our minds as we did so, until other images arose to displace that one.

Neil, what if it's to be Father, and what if we're to kill him?

I tried to visualise it but could not.

No, Kieran, it doesn't feel right. Father is, well, Father, and I don't think we'd be asked to do it. Besides, killing him would put us on the throne, so we'd be going from Tyrell clan to Windsor in the same lifetime. I don't think it works that way.

We asked Derek about it after the ritual and he could only shake his head.

"I don't know," he said. "I just don't know anymore."

We asked him why.

"Things are so complicated anymore since your great-grandfather and his sister joined the bloodlines of the Crown with those of the Order by marrying into the Tyrell family. The intricacies of entanglement are so profound now that even Robin can't sort them out totally. The Tyrell line and the Windsor line flow together in so many people it's hard to say which side of the sword anyone is on. It's not even just the Windsor line, either. The line of the kings goes back long before this dynasty. There are Stuarts as well. My mother was one, or do you not wish to know that story?"

Of course we did, and indicated as much.

"Generations back, as the records of the Archives bear witness, there was a man named George Edmund Stuart. He was the Sacred King at Ypres in what was then Belgium, during World War I. He was a soldier, shot behind his own lines by one of the Order. The war ended soon thereafter. His great-great-great granddaughter was my mother. George Stuart's mother, a descendant of the old Stuart dynasty, had made a Greenwood Marriage with the eldest son of Queen Victoria, who became King Edward VII."

"Royal on both sides," Kieran remarked.

"Yes. And my father was a Watson of the Tyrell line."

"Kevin Watson," I said.

"Yes. But not the one you think. Not Kevin Michael. Kevin David Watson, later Kevin David FitzWalter, later Kevin David Windsor-FitzWalter."

"The Duke of Cornwall."

Of course, Neil., another Greenwood Marriage. Babies born at Imbolc are conceived at Beltaine.

"You are correct. Kevin Michael Watson was the High Priest on the Tor that Beltaine. His HPs was my mother, and though he knew very well he was not my father he married her. Actually, he probably did so because he did know who the father was, although that night on the Tor he only knew there were two strangers in the circle who celebrated the rites with them. One of them was chosen by the High Priestess, the other by Kevin's cousin Constance, Robin's mother. As far as our mothers were concerned, each of the strangers was the Lord of the Trees, incarnate for that night to father their sons, as they had both seen in a vision."

And I think we know who the second man was.

Why shouldn't it have been, Kieran? If George Edmund Stuart was a Greenwood child and served as Sacred King, who's to say how many royal bastards have been born for that reason and died without notice.

Robin's a bit too long in the tooth for that job now. He's supposed to be in his prime, "at the height of his bloom", I believe is the phrase.

His progeny, perhaps.

Perhaps. But we're being rude. We should be talking.

He'll think it's a long thoughtful pause; besides, these are things better left as thoughts and not spoken aloud.

"And your cousin Robin is really our great-uncle."

He peered at me strangely over his spectacles, his blue eyes piercing me, trying to see into my soul. He nodded slowly.

"Yes. And your cousin. He bears the blood of Kings and Killers of Kings, even as you do, as I do, as our children do and yours will, and as your other cousins and their children do. The important thing is we do not know who is chosen or why, or for which role, or even in which generation it will come. It happens when it happens, and to whom the Gods see fit to call it into. It's in the open now once more, no longer hidden in the darkness and made to look like a tragic accident. Because of this I figure the King, when he appears, will be of the main branch of the family, probably as Stephen was, the actual King. The rest of us are just the reserves."

"And the man who slays him?"

The old man looked my brother straight in the eye, but I felt as if he looked through me also. I was drawn into Kieran's mind whether I willed it or not, and at a time I thought I was solidly anchored in my own train of thought. We stared at him through Kieran's eyes, heard him through Kieran's ears.

"Traditionally of the Tyrell line, no matter what branch. I've never heard of it being one of the other three Companions."

"Companions?" we said through Kieran's mouth.

"The other three men who are with them when the time comes."

When the time comes.

I do not know which of us originated the thought, but it resounded in the one mind we seemed to share between us, reverberated in our soul, familiar in its sound. So very, very familiar.

"Before that, however," he continued, "there is a time when things begin to fall into place. Each is aware of his role as he Awakens to memories of how it was in the past for him, and they find each other, become a very tight ring of companionship for whatever time they have. Then the fifth man shows up bearing some omen, knowing all that has transpired in the past. They are complete, and within a short time the King's blood is spilled and the Land healed until the next time."

"You've left out the best part," we heard a voice saying, a voice which came from the body which housed us both.

"What?" asked Derek.

"The glory of it all. The sheer glorious beauty of it. We would not have changed a moment of it for an Empire, nor asked for a second more of that lifetime."

The old man trembled as he looked at Kieran, as he looked at us, moving closer. Beyond his face we saw my body in the chair next to him, stiff and unmoving, eyes open wide. It was all I could do to resist returning to it, but my will was stronger than its pull, and my brother needed me, needed my strength and energy to help him hold the presence which now spoke through us, through him.

"Oh child, you have no idea."

Kieran? Is it the Duke of Cornwall?

I don't know. He called him child.

"Father?"

"Do you call the Lord of the Trees or the man your mother married?"

"The one who lay with my mother upon the Tor."

"Then fetch your cousin and tell him we have much to say."

The plural "we" or the royal "we", I wonder.

How many of us can you get in here, Kieran?

How many ghosts can fit on the head of a pin?

Derek was as pale as a ghost himself when he stood to obey, but obey he did, and we remained motionless while we awaited his return.

Is that you Stephen, or is it Kevin?

Yes.

Quiet, Neil, I'm talking to the other one.

You're not talking at all. You're thinking.

Fine. I just want to know who it is in here with us.

What makes you think there's anyone else?

I know the feel of you. You were with me at Stonehenge.

I've always been with you. We both have. With both of you.

It's both of you, then, both Stephen and Kevin?

There was silence, then darkness, then light, then the most incredible feeling of blissful detachment, then of the totality I had felt back at the henge. Kieran and I were together, the way we had been before we had been cut apart. We clung together somewhere beyond space and time, falling, falling happily through blue skies...

I was back within my own body and Kieran in his. Daylight was a cruel assault upon our senses as it streamed through the open window.

Kieran? Have you been awake all this time?

No. I was with you, remember?

Remember? Yes, I did. All that and more.

And so did he. Memories that were too vivid to have been dreams. Memories of lives and deaths and loves and tears and laughter, of hellos and goodbyes and the unexpected knowledge that we were heirs to it in ways we could never have imagined.

With newly made tears meandering down my cheeks I struggled to rise from the chair in which I'd spent the night. If I'd been stiff after my pseudodeath at the henge, I was in worse shape that morning; those who are inclined to go wandering about without their bodies should be warned of the condition they might find them in upon their return. It didn't matter; I wanted to touch the hand of my brother, to feel his existence in the flesh once more.

Robin looked up from the recording device at the sound my motion made. One disc had been filled from the look of it, and the second was about half to the grey point, the shiny black half awaiting further dictation.

Kieran took my hand and smiled.

Anmchara.

"Well. You're back. It is Kieran and Neil now, isn't it?"

We nodded.

"You two are so much alike, even in voice. It's going to be difficult for me to edit this in terms of which parts came from which of you."

"Excuse me?"

"You don't remember?"

He looked at me incredulously; we both shook our heads. We had lived the visions, not heard the words.

"It was Stephen, setting the record straight as he would have it known for history. The Duke's journal is wonderful material, but there's a lot in there the Dame Protector knew was too open, too much for the public to know, so it has been sealed to all below the Order's rank of Knight Postulant, and to the public entirely. Parts of it have been revealed by the family, but this, this is a perfect account of how things really went."

"What about the voices you mentioned?"

"Well, at one time your voice began to wear out, so he used Neil for a few hours. He says the two of you frequently do that yourselves and that was what gave him the idea."

"What about Kevin of Cornwall?" I asked.

"What about him?"

"Didn't he say anything?"

"No. Was he here as well?"

Should we tell him?

If you can't trust your Uncle who can you trust?

"He said 'they' were with us."

"No," I corrected him, he said 'we'. It could have been the royal we, not the plural."

Derek, silent so long as his cousin added to the knowledge of the Archives, leaned forward in his chair and pressed the palms of his hands together, tapping the fingertips together slowly as he strove to understand the full meaning of all he had heard. His voice was soft and thoughtful as he weighed first one fact, then another.

"I doubt a man of his age in the age in which he lived would use so archaic an expression to a member of his family. Still, if Kevin were here and there were two of you, why didn't he speak through one of you?"

Kieran slumped back into his chair.

"Because it no longer makes a difference, as it makes not a whit of difference as to which of these twins is which, or which of us lives now in which of them."

The voice came from Kieran's mouth, but from within my mind also, and I knew the truth of it. The King and the Land and the person whose role it was to deliver the King back to the Land were One, a Trinity as holy as any devised by any religion, and they were One as Kieran and I were One. We were a part of it all, glimpsing our own future as we had glimpsed the past, yet the visions we had seen this time had come to us in the same manner as the first visions I had seen when Neil's sword had unintentionally found it mark. We both had seen it all from both sides, both the King's and the Duke's, both as slayer and slain.

Perhaps it truly did not matter.

It matters to me.

He had never left my mind.

Relax, Kieran. It's a long way away at any rate. Father is alive and well and a relatively young man still. We have years yet, and either way I'm sure it will all end the same way it did the last time. We'll go together. From now on we'll always go together.

Promise?

I held my breath. Could I make that promise? I didn't know if it would be that way this time or not. We'd Awakened out of turn, the thrust of steel into my body, the sight of my blood the trigger to conjure up memories of a similar incident long ago. From there to Stonehenge to reinforce the process, and then to Glastonbury to make certain it didn't fade. What awaited us I had no idea.

If it is the will of the Gods, so mote it be. As close as we are I'm not sure that the death of one of us wouldn't take the other anyway. I hope it is so, Anmchara.

"You're very telepathic, aren't you," asked Robin.

"Yes," I answered.

"I understand they were too, both from the Journal and this."

"Yes. It became absolute at the end. I suppose it just stayed with us."

"Which one are you?"

"Neil."

"Yes, of course, now. But were you my father or Derek's?"

"I know. I know what it feels like to have your father die before you were born; both of you have suffered that."

"Then you are my father."

"I don't know. I really don't know. I don't know if what I know is what Stephen knows because he is Stephen, or what Kevin knows because in the end there was no part of one which was not also a part of the other. We are both Stephen and Kevin, just as we are both still Kieran and Neil, because we chose to answer to one name or the other, because it was convenient to those who had a need to identify us separately. We speak because you can't hear us the way we hear each other, and sometimes just because it feels right to use words instead of thoughts."

They reacted differently. Derek removed his spectacles, rubbed his eyes, removed a cloth from the breast pocket of his suit jacket and polished the lenses with it. Robin stood up, crossed his hands behind his back, and walked to the window.

I don't think they were expecting any of this.

Were we?

No. But it's good to know. It explains a lot of things.

Do you think they believe us?

Yes. I think we said things they recognised, but I think they are afraid of the implications of what we are now, what we have become.

Derek was the first to break the silence. I could tell by the quaver in his voice that this night, however long it had been, had produced a profound effect upon him.

"I would like the two of you to consider staying with us for awhile. We have much to learn from you, and, I hope, much you can learn from us."

"The education the Order gave Kevin David Watson was splendid. We have retained some of it."

We're staying?

If you wish. At least they'll let us explore what's been unleashed here. And help us grow with it. Yes. By all means. Let us stay.

"And we look forward to regaining the rest."

Derek and Robin smiled and looked at each other, almost as we did.

"Good," said Robin. "Due to special circumstances I am prepared to bend a few rules. You are free to read anything in the Archives, classified or not. You are also free to correct any errors or omissions you may see, but please do it on another piece of paper, not on the originals. We are old fashioned; we prefer paper originals which can be transferred to micro or electronic later. Backups are important in all media."

Derek offered to make the necessary arrangements with our family, and I wondered whether or not it would be a good idea to go home first before our long stay in Glastonbury commenced, but Kieran thought we should begin at once, the picture of Gwenna's face in his mind changing from the sweet little sister we would miss greatly to the ominous child-crone we had seen upon more than one occasion.

Glastonbury. So much of our past, it filled our present and determined our future.

Glastonbury. It had been a beginning once before. Only the Gods knew where it would end.

Chapter Five

Our stay at Tyrell House finished off our adolescent years and saw us well into our twenties. Of course we did not spend all our time there, but used it as our base of operations and study. There were trips for educational purposes, such as visiting some long-forgotten battlefields in search of artefacts, or for political expediency, as in our annual autumnal visits to Scotland to visit our cousin Queen Alexandra and to relax at our ancestral home, Stonehurst.

Alexandra's exact relationship to us was distant, though she was indeed a cousin, a descendant of King Charles III through his second son, Henry. Neither Kieran and I have ever been good at recalling back more than a few generations of anyone outside the immediate family, so I cannot say with any surety which one of his twins the line came through, but suffice it to say that when the time was right for an independent Scotland to move back to the Monarchy they chose to pick from their midst Andrew, Duke of Edinburgh, who as it so happened, lived in Edinburgh. I think it was partly because of his title as much as his personality. However, the fact that his French wife was a direct descendent of the old Stuart family still living in Paris, didn't hurt his popularity any, especially when they adopted Stuart as the official family name. His son David had been a popular King as well, and now David's daughter ruled the country in much the same way Queen Victoria had ruled the Empire, and was loved in the same way. Her second son Malcolm was about our age and frequently joined us at Stonehurst to relax.

Malcolm was an astounding fellow, over two metres tall, weighing about eighteen stone and built like a champion wrestler, with ginger hair and a ginger beard and a laugh which could shake the glass in a window. He hated guns, but loved bow hunting and had brought down some trophy bucks with an old fashioned longbow. He was equally conversant in Irish or Scottish Gaelic, English, Welsh, Breton, or French, and claimed to read both Latin and Greek, but not to speak them fluently. If such was to be an indication of the future of Scotland it could do much worse.

His wedding to Genevefa of Breizh was nothing short of spectacular, for they staged it in full medieval splendour, replete with horses, armour, and us as his groomsmen. He wore Royal Stewart tartan, we wore Balmoral, and the bride wore the traditional Breton garb of the 12th century with a veil of Nottingham lace given to her by our mother. Fashion echoed the occasion for nearly two years, but no one looked as fetching beneath all the finery than did tiny Genevefa, her perfect little face with its huge dark eyes looking for all the world like some rare porcelain doll.

Together they were quite a pair; she in pattens barely came up to mid-chest height on him, yet there was the unmistakable aura about them that this was truly a match of love, not politics. Malcolm was twenty-six. We were a year younger and realised that we would soon be expected to begin the search for our own mates; the dynasty needed the security of a generation to follow us.

It was two months after the wedding that we realised how important it all was. Derek called us into his office, his spectacles in one hand and a cleaning rag in the other. After years of working with him we realised this signal. He was upset, he didn't want to meet us eye-to-eye, and with his specs off he could not see us, ergo he did not have to look at us as he spoke.

"There has arisen a concern for the succession," he began, pacing back and forth slowly as he spoke, all the time polishing the lenses. "Parliament has put the question aside for years, as it seemed to be years away, but your father approaches sixty and the Monarchy must be secure."

I don't like the sound of this, Neil.

Nor do I.

"Is Father in ill health?" I inquired.

He tried the spectacles on and looked at me, his eyebrows drawn together. Only in that attitude did I recognise in the frail white-haired man before me the strong teacher who had brought us into his home eight long and well-lived years before.

"No, no. Nothing like that. This is, I pray to the Gods, a concern for the distant future, long after Robin and I have left this world."

That's a relief.

I still don't like the sound of it.

"There has been discussion in Parliament about the complexity of having both of you reign jointly. There is no precedent, unless you wish to recall the Triumvirate in Rome, but that was not a Monarchy, and it was highly unsuccessful politically in the long run. Pompey and Antonius were ultimately overthrown."

Ahhhh, the Romans.

The good old bad old days.

We nodded seriously.

"The fear they have is two-fold. First, they are afraid that through no intention of your own a civil war might erupt, certain factions favouring one of you, and certain others supporting the other. I have tried to persuade them that the two of you would not allow this to happen, but I don't think they are quite convinced."

"What rot!"

It was my sentiment as well, as was usually the case. We seldom disagreed on anything.

"The other consternation is the future of the succession. You will most probably both marry and have children. What becomes the order of succession with them?"

My brother was quicker than I to speak, although we had framed the answer simultaneously.

"Same as always. The firstborn. Whichever of us has the first son, that child becomes next in line."

"Even over the other of you? If you are both King, he would have to wait until you are both dead. And what happens if that son should die?"

"The crown passes to the next eldest."

"The next eldest brother? Or does the succession pass to a cousin if the next eldest male is the cousin?"

"To the cousin. It makes no difference. Genetically we are identical."

He took off the specs again and once again began polishing the lenses methodically, as he always did when he was thinking, as if symbolically cleaning the spectacles would help him see things more clearly in his mind.

"But your wives will not be the same genetically, unless you marry identical twins, and with the incidence of twins occurring in pregnancies of twins married to twins we might only be scratching the surface of complexity. Besides, the chance of you finding acceptable twin wives is an enormous set of odds in itself. The main point is that with different mothers you will have different political alliances, and if there is the slightest mote of a chance of politics or civil war being sparked around the two of you while you are alive, think of what it would be around your children after you are gone."

The threat was there, and it was real, even if we didn't want to face it.

"Perhaps we should both marry the same woman," Kieran joked.

Why not? Our tastes are always the same.

"Or perhaps one of us should remain single."

He replaced his specs and looked from one of us to the other.

"Which one of you would consent to that? No, it's not a good idea."

"What about this: the first one to marry and produce an heir, male or female, establishes the entire line of heirs."

Derek shook his head at my suggestion.

"No. Especially not if the heir is female and the other one of you produces a male heir. There would be a civil war for sure. If only you two hadn't been born the way you were. Even normal twins are born minutes apart; there is a definite firstborn. But no, you, gentlemen, had to be joined in a way that the doctors had to lift you simultaneously from your mother's womb. Why?"

"Because of our refusal to be parted in death."

They both looked at me for a long time in silence.

That was the reason, wasn't it?

Yes, Anmchara. But it was the Duke who made the decision.

And the King who accepted it. We both knew what we were doing.

But not the effect it would have hereafter.

Regrets?

No. But it certainly has made this life interesting.

Kieran broke the silence.

"How immediate is the political problem?"

"Oh, they'll probably talk it to death in the Commons. The Lords will take forever to make up their minds about it. Whatever is decided, it will be argued back and forth for some time to come."

"Then we have time to come up with some options of our own."

"We could draw straws or flip a coin for the crown," I joked.

"Or play chess, or cut cards," Kieran joined in.

"Or you could finish off what you started when we were fencing."

I don't know what possessed me to say that, and I urgently and ardently wished the words had not come from my mouth, but they had, and the room and everyone in it seemed frozen in that instant as I knew I had spoken some rare and undeniable truth.

One of us must die.

The other must kill him and wear the crown.

It was for the good of the Land.

Chapter Six

*T*he thought flashed through us instantaneously. We were once again in the same old cycle, only this time it seemed there was no need to Awaken as we had before, for we had never truly slept in between, merely been disoriented by the world and bodies into which we had been reborn. The visions had not been traumatic as they had been in our other lives; when other children had dreamt of flying or falling, we had remembered both and accepted them as happy memories without the fear of impact or pain or death. That glorious instant which had fused our spirits had also left its mark upon our form, for the flesh which called us back had been but a reflexion of what it had been destined to hold.

Occasionally we had seen glimpses of the time between the blue sky, the wordless brilliance which had engulfed us, the darkness which followed, and the sterile white light of hospital and the surgeon's laser knife. There was a place which was not a place in a time which was not a time, and we were complete and happy there until life sought to separate us with walls of flesh once more, but our combined will was stronger than even that, and the barriers left us a chink through which we could manifest our oneness.

I can't do it, Neil.

Do you think I can?

43

You're stronger than I am. You'd make a better King.

Anmchara, it is the King who will die. Therefore you will take me.

No. I cannot. Besides, the one who lives will become King. I could not rule without you at my side.

We cannot do this thing together again. Look what it has done.

One of us must live this time.

Perhaps only a day or so, to prevent this effect.

No, Anmchara, for a lifetime, to rule the Land.

It was more than either of us could bear, yet it was a thing we knew must be borne with grace and dignity; there was no indication it must be borne immediately.

"One of us must die," I said flatly, surprised at the calmness of my own voice."

Derek was painfully slow in answering.

"I can see no other way. I'm sorry. The thing is, however, the timing of it. If one of you should die too early and then something happen to the other before he is crowned or before there is an heir, we're left in worse condition than if you both live."

"This isn't going to work, Derek. Not your way. As head of the Order I'm surprised at you."

Kieran?

Hear me through, Neil.

"We are who we are, what we are and we know only a part of the scheme. We do not know what the Gods intend here. In fact, we only know that between us we have your Sacred King and his Slayer, but even between Neil and myself we are not certain who is who. Our memories are identical, from both sides of the sword, even to the point that when he was injured in our fencing I, too, bled. We both felt the wound as the sword's point opened the flesh, and the hilt of the sword as the blade slid in. I am not even certain we returned to the same bodies we started off with after the incident. It might have been me in that body over there and him getting pushed out of this one."

You really think so?

Anything is possible. We've already proven that much by being here under these conditions.

By this time Derek's spectacles were being pushed up on his nose, another indication of his trying to understand.

"We've more or less mucked things up by what we did last time, or at least the way in which it was done, and although we do now plead our ignorance in knowing what our actions would bring, we cannot escape responsibility by claiming it was an act of love. What seemed to be selfless then now seems quite selfish if it threatens the kingdom with the possibility of civil war. This time we must make certain it is done right, and for it to be done right, several conditions must occur.

"For one thing, we must be certain which of us is which. I don't think sacrificing Kevin of Cornwall would have satisfied the Land in the way that the blood of the King did. I think we both need to do the Visionquest and take the Consecration Oath, and the sword point, for that matter, although it seems Neil already has his scar. That might flush things out."

As emotional as I still felt him to be he was handling things smoothly, logically, and I let him feel my approval.

"For another thing, the Companions have not appeared. I'm certain we'll both know them in an instant when they do show up, but so far they haven't. The only time we can recall them all showing up simultaneously was in Roman Britain when we were called to them instead of the other way around, but they were Druids and they had the ability to tune to us before we arrived. For all the years we have remembered in between they have not been more adept than the Order can make them as Knights, and in the case of Jack Beaudry there was not even a formal education until after his Awakening."

Good one, Kieran. I'd missed that point.

Shhhh. You're spoiling my concentration. It's our survival I'm discussing here.

Sorry. Don't let me stop your forward inertia.

"As both Robin and you have pointed out, in the journals we have read it seems that there is invariably a kind of feedback between those who have Awakened which occurs as the others begin to Awaken. So far we have felt none of this. This would suggest to me that we have a good long time before we need to discuss this much further. When and if the time comes, we, not Parliament, will be the first to know, and we will accept the will of the Gods unequivocally in this matter. Until then, please, let us just celebrate what life we have together without this hanging over our heads at every moment."

The old man had tears in his eyes as did I. I was actually surprised at my brother's eloquence, for at no time did I feel he was drawing upon me for words or ideas. Other than my mental interruptions in his train of thought the telepathy between us had been shut down.

"Derek," I said gently, "we did not live to see you or Robin or our other sons be born, or grow, or turn into the people you became. I don't know if either of us will this time. At least we know what happened to you now, and we are proud of both of you. We did not realise in our childhood that our grandfather was more to us than that, or our great-uncle. They were old men and we were children, and we loved them for who we were told they were to us, not the sons we had never known.

"We will do what we must, when we must, but for now, please, let us have something of this life until then. I promise, if it does come to the same end once again we will bury our personal feelings in the matter and willingly accept our roles, whatever they may be, as we always have."

Well put.

We will, Kieran. There is no other way for us, no matter what we may want.

I know. You're right.

Do you fear it?

Not the dying. I've always welcomed that part.

As have I.

The living is what I fear, not just living this life without you, if that is my lot, but the loneliness of the next life, waiting to find you again.

You mean looking into the eyes of every blue-eyed stranger and wondering if you're in there? I remember that one all too well, even though it was always years before I knew what I was looking for.

Exactly. That's the real sacrifice, the real pain. Not the dying.

"All right," the old man sighed. You've made your case. I suppose if it is the will of the Gods we will have civil war. They've not prevented it in the past, not with the blood of Charles I or Stephen FitzStephen, or even Edward V, just as there's no way to be sure the death of one of you will prevent it."

We saw them flash before our eyes in an instant, the headsman's axe and the long brown hair trailing behind the severed head as the cloth cap slipped from it in its tumble to the ground, the amazement and sickening disorientation as our eyes met at last and the final spark of consciousness fled; the scene in the forest as one of us stood next to the other while the arrow sped into the heart of the green-clad King standing at the oak tree in eager anticipation of fulfilment, the burgundy-clad friend who closed his eyes and picked four acorns from the ground; the boy in the Tower of London who stood proudly and smiled as he felt the cold steel part his flesh; the man catching the child's blood in a flask to pour it on the ground outside, and the familiar look of the other child's eyes as he awoke and was smothered with his pillow to prevent his sounding an alarm...

I could feel Kieran holding on to me mentally...

Neil?

I'm here.

Are you feeling...

Yes, Anmchara. Let them pass through you.

In the peripheral vision of the physical world I could see him begin to lose his balance as my other senses felt him begin to swoon. I reached out to him with my thoughts as my hand grabbed his wrist and began to pull him to my side. The touch itself must have been enough, for he steadied himself and I felt the dizziness pass as the other attendant emotions swept through us both with all the heat, light and euphoria of the first time. We held our breaths as the waves of it broke over us, too afraid of losing the moment to move. It was better in the reliving than at the time it happened, for we felt none of the guilt or grief now, only the link with Eternity.

It seemed a long time before we dared to breathe again, or I could find my voice, yet those moments must have been between the worlds, for Derek had not moved, had not blinked, had seemed to sense no time passing while we lived, killed and died thrice in his presence.

"Yet those deaths served the Land itself, all of them. We remember them vividly. People, however, are harder to satisfy," I said with conviction, still wondering at the familiarity of the eyes of the smothered child.

Chapter Seven

*A*nd that was that for a time, for a long time, or so it seemed. We had buried the needs of the future for the needs of the present, knowing that what would come to us would come in its own time, just as it had always done, and would always continue to do. The times were merry, for the most part, although some were quite profound.

Our Visionquest was one of the profound times.

It had not been a necessity, of course. We were too obviously Awake for it to be, and we were, after all, the immediate heirs to the throne, but we were also Tyrells by blood, and one of us was supposed to be one by action as well.

We fasted, as was the tradition, to make our bodies lighter upon us as we sought out the non-physical realms. The tradition did not take into account that we already had one foot in the Other World and the other on a banana peel. We chose to search for our visions in different cells, separated by a wall about four metres in thickness, just to see if anything would come out differently between us.

It didn't. The moment we left our bodies we found each other and embraced in the manner only those unencumbered by flesh can do, delighted at the company of each other. All the vision showed us was each other, or so we thought at first. Then things began to change and we found ourselves forced back into our cells, looking at the candle glowing before us, casting its tiny dancing yellow light onto the bare stone walls of the chamber. We followed the light into its source and the visions began.

She was beautiful. Her black curls framed her delicate face with their small, soft tendrils, like feathery shadows against the paleness of her skin and the deep violet-blue of her eyes. Her lips were like Diana's bow, finely arched and sweetly full. In one perfect hand she held out to me an apple, in the other, a pomegranate. I took neither, but chose her lips instead, circling her small waist with my arms and kissing her gently at first, but ever more urgently as I felt the passion arise within me. She dropped both the apple and the pomegranate upon the ground and began to return my ardour with her own, pressing her body against mine and guiding my hands to her full white breasts and beneath her soft green gown to the secret places of her desire.

I drew her to the ground and joined my flesh with hers, delighting in her every sigh, her every moan as we moved together in the most ancient rhythms of pleasure, her rose-scented hair tumbling around my face as her eager body urged me toward fulfilment. The rush of it was as sweet as death, and the release almost as absolute, for we lay still as the dead afterwards as red and white rose petals fell all about us. I looked across her to see the apple and the pomegranate upon the ground, a bite taken from each.

Then the whole thing faded and I was back in my cell, the candle sputtering and dimming before me, and the embarrassing, uncomfortable realisation that I was in need of changing my undergarments.

Derek and Robin both questioned my brother and me separately before we had a chance to speak together. Of course we could have shared our thoughts at any time, but in this matter we had agreed to remain silent from each other until we had been debriefed. There seemed no reason to "cheat" at something like this; it was a matter of sacred honour as well as the fact that we really wanted to keep this part a totally personal thing. The fact that we had met in spirit before the visions had begun did not change any of it, and we didn't believe such a matter was anyone's business but ours alone.

Nonetheless, the visions we reported were identical. It was Lady Sovereignty who had lain with us, and accepted us both in the time honoured manner She accepts Her chosen Kings. Nothing had changed, except the attitude of Derek and Robin: we were both destined to rule. Despite this, and just to be certain in case of any eventuality, we both decided to go forth with the Vigil and the Consecration of Knighthood.

The Vigil was set up for Samhain, with the Consecration at November's dawn. For creatures such as Kieran and I who had passed so easily through the Veil at our death and rebirth it seemed the perfect choice of times, for the Veil between the Worlds would be transparent at such a time, if not altogether missing. We would be at our spiritual peak, ready to embrace and be embraced by whatever the Gods saw fit to bestow upon us.

The Vigil itself was euphoric, for we were not to be separated as we had been before, but knelt in watch over two swords upon the High Altar of the main Temple , one of us on either side of the altar. The swords themselves were not the usual ones used in this ritual, but the two most ancient relics of the Order: the Sword of William Rufus and the Sword of King Stephen. The latter had belonged to our great-grandfather Stephen II, but before that it had belonged to Stephen I, and it had turned out, also his natural son, Stephen FitzStephen, presented to him by his father at his knighting as the token he was to take his father's place as Sacred King. Each was the Sword of the King, yet since our great-grandfather's Coronations his was the one used in those ceremonies. It seemed both would be used next time.

We knelt before the High Altar until we became as stiff as the marble which made it, filling ourselves with the aura of all that had been written in blood upon the steel before us. No, neither sword had taken the life of the King who had owned it, but each had been carried thereafter by one upon whose hands the blood of the King had been shed.

I saw them then, the visions which had always been left out of what we had seen before, the passing of the sword from King to Knight before the ritual of Sacrifice, from Rufus to Walter Tyrell at the hunting lodge, from Stephen FitzStephen to his burgundy-clad *anmchara* at the front door of his grey stone manor house, from Stephen Windsor to Kevin of Cornwall before the fireplace where once it had hung at Stonehurst. In the last case it had been brought back by the fourth Companion from its safe-keeping here in Glastonbury for just such a purpose, and had been returned to its place above the fireplace for a time until the same man could convey it once more to Tyrell House.

There was a litany spoken with the passing of the sword, one known by those Awakened, but not committed to writing. I could hear it ringing in my ears.

"The signs are given. The time has come when to the appointed place I must travel to fulfil the promise of my birth. As the seed is sown, so must the grain be reaped for the nourishment of all."

"Why must you go unto this place?"

"To give up my life that the Land might be healed."

"Why must you go unto this place?"

"To give up my life that the Land might be healed."

"Why must you go unto this place?"

"To give up my life that the Land might be healed."

"Thrice asked, thrice answered. And by what right do you claim the honour to be the Blessed Sacrifice?"

"I am the son of Kings, and bearer of the blood which heals. This vessel must be shattered that the bounty within might return to the Land to nourish it and its people."

"And do you do this of your own free will?"

"Of my own free will I offer you my sword in assurance that I do."

"So Mote It Be, then, Sire.

"So Mote It Be, and may the Gods grant us Their Grace to do this well."

Neil? Was that you?

No. You heard it too?

Heard it, saw it, lived it. It was us.

Yes. Many times over.

Something we had forgotten?

No, something I think we remember at the end, when it's needed.

How did it make you feel?

Immortal.

I don't follow you.

Don't worry, you will. Or I'll follow you. Either way it will all work itself out in the end.

Neil? I mean why would the prelude to one of us killing the other make you feel immortal?

Because we are. We've retained it all this time. We didn't have to grow up all our lives and find out only at the very end who we were.

We're still picking up details, like that one we just found.

Found us is more like it. No, that will continue for as long as we do, but we've got the main connexion already. We never lost it this time.

And you know how worried that makes the Order.

I know, Kieran. But I'm not at all certain we haven't come back like this for a purpose. Otherwise the Gods wouldn't have let us.

You don't know that. It might be some kind of a test or something.

That's a purpose in itself. No, I think perhaps we're evolving. It does happen, you know.

Sorry, Neil. I can't quite see other primates having the concept of Sacred King..

Perhaps not, but I've seen gorillas mourn their dead with almost a religious ritual. The Fossey Institute has done great research into the concept of ritual in primates. Humans are just a little more abstract, a little more evolved.

And we're just a bit further up the trail?

Why not? We're in closer touch with the next world.

"Neil," he whispered suddenly out loud "do you think we're going mad?"

It was a thought I had never even entertained; in that there was after all a subtle difference between us.

Hush, Kieran. We're not supposed to say anything tonight.

All right. But I can think it to you. Do you think we're going mad?

As in "madness in great ones must not unwatched go"?

Precisely.

No, Anmchara. We are but mad north-northwest. When the wind is southerly we know a hawk from a handsaw.

I felt the worry in him, the concern, and then I all but heard it evaporate into the mental equivalent of a giggle.

You always did love Hamlet.

We both did.

Still do. Only this time no baiting Claudius.

Do you think he's back again?

We both paused to wonder about it. We were back. Frank, Stephen's uncle and the Claudius in question had died nearly six months before we had. We had shared lives before with him, before the psychic manipulation of a twenty-first century intelligence agency had shattered something in his soul and driven him to acts of high treason, murder, mayhem, regicide and attempted murder which had played havoc with England's spiritual destiny for generations. What were the chances he had found his way back to life at the same time we had once more, and in the same place?

I don't know, Neil. I just hope we'll recognise him and his intent sooner if he has returned.

We were silent even in each other's heads for a long time after that, awaiting the dawn and the ordeal which would bring with it our Consecration as Knights of the Order. It was not a new thing to our memories, for as Kevin of Cornwall we had experienced it with resolve and courage, embracing the sword as if it had been a lover, taking it more deeply into our body than had been intended, and offering our own blood and life for the service of the Order, the King, and the Land. His memories belonged to both of us, imprinted upon our souls as had been those of our great-grandfather so vividly that experiencing them again first-hand seemed almost redundant, yet there still somehow seemed the need to proclaim ourselves anew in our generation and reaffirm the vows which bound us throughout Eternity. There would be little blood shed, and with Stephen's ability to suspend pain, little suffering.

The whole thing was like sex; just because we had experienced it all before didn't mean we didn't want to repeat the experience.

In the last long hour before the dawn She came to us again, not as the beauteous Lady of Sovereignty, but as the Hag, shrouded in black tatters, a long sharp knife dripping with blood in one hand and a skull in the other, yet I knew Her in this form and loved Her still.

She offered me both with Her bony hands, but I took neither. Again I went for Her lips, thin, parched and cracking, and my arms encircled her skeletal waist. She dropped both skull and dagger and guided my hands to Her shrivelled breasts and beneath Her tattered robe to the cold and barren places of Her withered body.

I drew Her brittle body gently to the ground and joined my flesh to Her cold flesh, trying with all the life within me to warm Her and give back to Her the youth and beauty I remembered from our previous encounter. I shut out all but Her eyes, the same violet-blue as the time before, and willed my vitality into Her. My life, my breath, all that I was I yielded to Her as I sank into the abyss of those eyes and poured myself into Her, willing that She should sever the ties between my spirit and my mortal body if it pleasured Her to do so.

There was light. There was darkness. There was peace. There was nothing.

There was the sensation of Kieran's presence once again, as the tendrils of his thoughts reached out to find me.

Neil?

We touched without touching, spoke without speaking.

I'm here, Kieran.

Did you see Her change?

No. I thought I was dying. It was quite pleasant. What happened?

We died, but She sent us back. It was pleasant, but strange to die in Her arms instead of yours. But She was so beautiful at the end. So beautiful. Then She transformed again into a raven and was gone.

I had never seen the Morrigan in Her crone aspect before, only as the beautiful Lady of Wisdom and the Queen of Battle. Her beauty was always so profound that it stilled the fears of Her warriors and led them as willingly to their deaths as the King went to his. The Great Queen, as Her name translated from the Gaelic, was as much an aspect of Lady Sovereignty as was Britannia, and a part of our heritage through our great-grandfather's maternal line, the O'Conors, to whom She has always been a Patroness. I was only saddened by the fact that when the transformation from crone to maiden had occurred I had already lost consciousness from the ordeal and missed it.

Another subtle difference between us, Neil? A bit quick on the trigger?

I almost laughed aloud, but contained myself.

How do you feel now?

Drained. Dazzled. How about you?

Here. Let me show you what you missed.

The images began to form before my eyes and the feelings followed them as he projected his experience to me, the same as my own for the most part, except the ending. He had been slower, less intense with Her than I had, less eager to give himself to the oblivion he courted. As his youth and life flowed slowly into Her the old body fleshed out, became full-breasted and supple, the wrinkles vanished, the sallow skin took on a pale brilliance, the tattered black robe became a feathered cloak, and in Her passion She gave my brother the ecstasy of a death so sweet I could but cry as I shared it with him, locked in Her arms, fully conscious of his life passing through Her love into the brilliant peace of what waited beyond. I had lost that consciousness, yet that special bond we shared gave me the part of the vision I had missed.

Then She brought him back, as if from a dream, standing over his still form until he could focus his eyes once more upon Her dark radiance, whereupon She transformed into a raven and fled back to Her own realm.

As my second-hand vision faded the first rays of dawn struck the world above us and we were joined by Derek and Robin who helped us rise from the positions we had held in the flesh for so many hours. In all our courting of the Lady we had remained frozen in the flesh upon our knees, unmoving in the mortal world of time and space, yet the visions had been as real to us as the pain which accompanied our attempts to stand.

We were joined by others, Knights of the Order and Priestesses of Chalice Coven who were to see to our Consecration. As much as Kieran and I had willed to do this part simultaneously it could not be so; there was only one notch on the floor in which to place the pommel of the sword of the Knight Postulant, and there was no way tradition would welcome the creation of another. This was an individual matter, and needed to be gone into spiritually as an individual. Our unique status was not unique enough to change years of precedent. The best we could do was to share it in our usual way.

Robin determined we should go in alphabetical order, which put me second. The waiting was terrible, but I held on to Kevin's memories and calmed myself with the knowledge that this was token death only, not even as real as what our vision had brought us. It mattered little where I stood as Kieran was led forth to do his duty, for as before I joined his mind and held my consciousness there to experience it with him. Together we were Kevin of Cornwall who had been through it all before. Together we were Stephen of England who could hold the pain in a white-hot ball before his eyes and feel none of it.

The sword handed to him was the Rufus sword, older by a generation than its counterpart, but identical in length, shape, quality of metal, and huge cabochon garnet set in the pommel. A velvet square had been placed upon the notch to avoid scraping the garnet as it bore the pressure of Kieran's weight upon it.

I'm here, Kieran.

I feel you, Anmchara. Let's do this thing. I hope I can join you after.

I watched with him through his eyes as he walked freely and steadily to the place of Consecration, feeling the tip of the sword with his left palm.

It's not as sharp as I would have liked. Kevin's was like a razor.

Kevin's was nearly a thousand years newer. Twenty-first century steel can take a keener edge than Norman steel.

It's going to hurt like hell.

Pain isn't the focus. I'll steady you. Besides, you only have to break the skin and bleed enough to let a few drops fall to the floor.

He knelt upon the velvet cushion, bare-chested as was I, and I felt the creaking of his knees as he went down to the position we had so recently held for an entire night. We could see only the white robe of the Priestess who was chosen to steady the sword for him, for our eye level had been lowered by the kneeling, but we resigned ourselves to our duty as the words were spoken over us, placed the pommel of the sword in the proper groove and stared at the bloodstained floor between us and the hilt of the sword. How many times had our blood flowed there?

We inhaled deeply in preparation as we leaned Kieran's chest forward slightly and placed the sword's point against his skin.

Would you rather just join me in the other body when it happens?

No. I must be aware of this. Remember what you missed by yielding your consciousness too soon.

As you wish. Let's do it.

As we exhaled we leaned forward with our full weight, felt the pressure of the cold sword turn to something which burned a path through skin and flesh, and tried to hold the pain a few inches away from our body as the blood began to trickle down the steel blade to take its place with that of our predecessors. It would have been perfect except for one distraction.

The Priestess knelt before us, her delicate face filled with a mixture of serenity and compassion, the curls of her long black hair framing her pale skin like dark, soft tendrils, bringing out the unspoken depths of her violet-blue eyes.

Chapter Eight

*W*hat happened next was sheer confusion. Her smile was more in those eyes than upon her lips, a smile which contained as many promises as the secrets it held. It was an entrancing smile, one which drew in the mind of the beholder, and we beheld it together through Kieran's eyes. There was nothing else in the world but this woman, not the sword which pierced our body, not the blood which spilled upon the floor, not the pain which tried to warn us that what we were doing had gone beyond token and approached actuality.

The smile remained, banishing all else from our thoughts, even as the room began to spin and I felt the disorientation of seeing her from two perspectives: Kieran's and my own as the link between us snapped, as I felt my own body encasing me once again, as a searing pain of my own strained for acknowledgement, as I fell upon my own sword and crumpled to the ground.

The ritual stopped. I heard my mother scream from the observers' bench and felt hands upon my shoulders gently raise me from the floor, withdraw the sword from my body and staunch the blood flow with the salve which had been prepared for later use.

Neil?

I'm all right, Kieran. How about you?

I'm fine.

"No, please. Bring him here beside me. He has earned this as well."

Sorry to mess up your show.

No, really. We should do this part together.

My blood fell in the wrong place.

There's no difference between our blood. Even the DNA would test the same.

Father and Robin tried to help me walk over to where Kieran knelt, but I insisted on doing it myself, with all the swagger and bravado of one who has seriously messed up and needs to redeem his image.

Kieran's wound had been dressed in the interim, and only the matter of the accolade awaited him. I was proud to kneel with him, but did not feel I had the right to the accolade myself. You can imagine how surprised I was when I felt the blade touch my shoulders at the same time Kieran was touched, as Derek and Robin both conferred the title upon us. Still, there was something wrong. The DNA might have been the same, but I needed my own blood to commingle with what had been spilled there. When the sword was returned to me I returned its point to the place it had found just a hair's breadth below my old fencing scar and pressed hard enough to reopen the fresh wound. It was not pain but white fire which shot through me, blinding me with it's brilliance as my blood joined that of my brother and our ancestors.

This time I stood on my own, withdrew the blade on my own, and on my own I wiped it clean again with the linen cloth provided for such usage. What had been done a short while ago by accident had been affirmed by conscious determination, and to me it made all the difference. A Knight of the Order needed to operate by will, not chance.

I now believe the whole room saw me do this and stood in silence watching with tacit approval. I only know that she saw me, and the smile in her eyes went to her lips, lips I had tasted in a vision not many weeks before.

Kieran saw, felt, acknowledged, reading my motivation in my mind before there had been a reason to ask it.

"Do you feel better now?" he asked aloud as the Priestess dressed my wound once more.

"Physically, no. Spiritually, emotionally," I answered looking at her as she bit her lower lip in concentration, "yes, in a big way. I couldn't let it be only one of us there with our ancestors, even though I had left my mark in my own place."

He smiled as I winced. The glamour had worn off and it hurt like hell for both of us.

Now what?

First we have to be introduced to her.

Why so formal? She's already seen us bare-chested and bloody.

How appetising.

Perhaps it is to her. We can't know her thoughts as we do each other's.

I don't know if that's a blessing or a curse.

Both. Perhaps it's a good thing she doesn't know how we feel about her.

What if she does?

What do we do? Toss a coin?

No. Court her. Both of us. We have three chances. She'll choose me, she'll choose you, or she'll choose neither of us.

"Well," she began, "I'd say you two have had a bit of a busy morning. I'm sure Their Majesties will want to congratulate you as soon as you've washed up and dressed in something a bit less bloody. If you wish to change now, your clothing has been laid out for you in the second antechamber. I presume you know the way to the gent's washroom by now."

We nodded.

"Well, then, everyone will be upstairs waiting for you. Congratulations. It was a different version of the ritual, to be sure, but most impressive. I'm glad you both came through it so well. The last Knight we consecrated had to be taken to hospital. He passed out at the sight of his own blood and we couldn't revive him. Turned out he had low blood pressure or something."

Her laughter was precious to me, to us, like the sound of silver bells jingling in a May breeze. She curtseyed to us as she turned to leave.

"Wait, I heard Kieran say, "don't go. There's something you must know."

Gods, Kieran. You're not going to just blurt it out are you?

She turned back.

"What?"

He took her hand.

"Officiating High Priestess outranks everyone else in the room, especially newly made Knights, which is our role here today, not Princes. The title outranks Prince and Princess, even King, because the King is but a servant to the Lady, which is what the HPs is in token. Even though the Queen is the HPs of the Land, if you are the one wearing the Moon Crown and she is not, you outrank her. Although a ritual may require you to kneel, never curtsey to anyone while you wear that crown."

He gave her hand a little squeeze and dropped it gently. She removed the crown and curtseyed again to both of us, her eyes lingering on mine for as long as they did on his.

"And now that I have been taught my place I relinquish it. For the rest of the day I am merely Eleanor Rhys-Davies, servant of the Gods, Their Majesties and Your Highnesses."

So much for the introduction. Now what?

"Will you be joining us upstairs?" I asked.

There was a hint of the tease in her eyes and her smile as she looked back and forth between the two of us before she answered.

"If that is your wish, although it can only be for a short time."

"Why?"

"I had rather thought of going to bed."

She was immediately embarrassed by her statement and the look of interest it had brought to our faces as we, too, thought about the idea and found it most pleasant.

"Oh, no...I didn't mean that the way it sounded. It's just that I've been up since about this time yesterday, presided at the Samhain ritual upon the Tor last night and spent the night there, then came straight here to do this with you. I'm not going to be much company for you if I should fall asleep in my cream sherry, now am I?"

"We could take turns trying to awaken you with a kiss," Kieran suggested.

"Or fall asleep beside you. We've had a long night as well, remember?"

In the subdued flame-light of the Temple it was impossible to tell for certain, but it seemed that pale skin of hers blushed slightly, more in anticipation of something hinted at beneath the surface of polite conversation than in embarrassment from her previous remark which had touched just that feeling we all had shared. There was an attraction there on all sides, one which grew with every glance, every breath, every heartbeat. She could sense it from both of us, as we could sense it in her. What we had felt, seen, heard, smelled and tasted in our Visionquest seemed to us to stand in the flesh before us, trembling slightly as her eyes touched first one of us and then the other. The tension between us was absolute and absolutely thrilling, as delicious in its own sweet way as its release would be, for there was no doubt in my mind that the vision had been foreplay to such an outcome.

"Of course I do, and you two have both lost a lot of blood. You should probably get quite a bit of sleep yourselves to help the healing process."

My brother was relentless.

"Will you tuck us in, then?"

Her eyes danced with amusement.

"Both of you?" she asked in mock surprise.

"Absolutely. We do everything together."

"Everything?"

She's thinking about it, Neil. She's really thinking about it. Perhaps there's a fourth option. Perhaps she'll choose us both.

"Yes," I said quite seriously, my mind indulging in fantasies I'd never dared to have before.

It wasn't true, of course. We had always seemed to keep our sex lives somewhat private, although we had occasionally slept with the same women consecutively, it had never been a ménage a trois. We did have the same tastes in women, and it was sometimes interesting to us to see if they could tell us apart in bed. Until today it had seemed that only the scar on my chest had provided the clue as to which of us was in a lady's bed, though from our last vision it seemed there was a small difference in intensity and duration. I knew I could pace myself better with a woman than a Goddess, so with that determination and Kieran's new wound we should be dead even.

She looked to Kieran for confirmation.

"Yes," he repeated, the same tone of seriousness in his voice.

"Oh my."

"Kieran? Neil? Are you two going to get dressed and join us upstairs?"

The voice came from the visitor's bench across the Temple and behind the railing. It was Gwenna, looking very grown up indeed with her golden hair piled high atop her head and a long dark grey knit dress which hugged her nineteen year old body as if it had been painted there.

"You go on up," Kieran called to her. "We'll be there shortly."

A strange smile crossed her face. She had chosen to come to watch us bleed. Why? The first time had been traumatic for her, when Neil had skewered me with his rapier. Why did she put herself through it all again, and doubly this time? Was she testing her own recovery from the first shock? I wanted to chide Father for bringing her to such a ritual, but I knew he would insist it was within her rights, and after all, she was of legal age to make such decisions herself.

Still, there had been something in that look...

"You must know something about us, Eleanor," I heard my brother say. "Even when we are not together we are. He watched my entire ritual not from where his body stood or sat or knelt, or whatever he was doing. He watched from within me, from my eyes, felt it all through my body. He was consecrated with me. What he did on his own was his idea of bringing the body in line with what had already happened to the spirit."

"Transmigration while still alive."

"Yes. I guess you could call it that."

Kieran, something's wrong with Gwenna.

Wrong? What do you mean? Is she ill? Is she in danger?

No. Maybe in danger, but I don't think it's from the outside.

Can it wait, then?

Not while you move in on my girl..

Your girl?

All right, then; our girl.

That's better.

This is important.

Hold on a second.

"And that's another thing. We're telepathic. He can be very distracting when he decides to think at me when I'm talking to someone."

Kieran, be careful who you tell our secrets to, and be very careful who else is around to hear you.

You know Eleanor wouldn't betray us.

No, but there are those who might. Besides, I'm a little hurt you didn't consult with me first before telling her.

I'm sorry. I didn't think you'd mind. So what was so important?

Gwenna.

Yes. About Gwenna.

She had that odd look on her face again today. The older she becomes, the more pronounced it gets.

So what is the immediate urgency about it?

Kieran, it's just that I've remembered where I've seen that look before and why I don't trust our little sister.

Tell me.

That's the same look Frank had when he tried to kill me the last two times.

Kill you?

Me, you, us, Richard, Stephen, whoever. The memory is the same for both of us. There's no point in splitting hairs as to which of us it was. Remember looking into his face just before the knife slit Richard's throat. Remember the face Stephen saw down the length of the sword at his throat as he lay on the floor of Nottingham Castle.

God's Hooves, Neil. Gwenna?

Yes.

Then close your mind even to me, Anmchara.

Why?

Remember that Frank was also a telepath.

Chapter Nine

Kieran was correct, of course, but the question which gnawed at my mind was whether or not our Uncle Frank could have carried the ability with him into this life. It had been his penchant for tracking us by tuning into us whenever we communicated with each other nonverbally which had nearly cost us our lives upon more than one occasion, yet that ability had come to him, we had believed, from the same psychic warfare training and manipulation by intelligence forces which had driven him mad in the first place. We had assumed it had been a thing which had happened in that one life alone and under conditions of torture. Would it carry forward into another life? Had he been so traumatised spiritually that it had followed him back here in the person of our sister? Perhaps the trauma we had associated with her at the time of my accidental wounding had been the recognition of something much further in the past, an Awakening of sorts, for she had seldom been our golden darling since that incident.

We don't know Gwenna has that ability.

We don't know she hasn't.

She has never shown any signs of it around us.

That we know of.

Granted. That we know of. It's only the look I've noticed.

Be careful.

Why? It was during intense links that he found us, not just casual thought. As a matter of fact, when we started out all we could transmit and receive was intense and emotional. We never were capable of conversation such as this. This is unique to us as we are now, because we're twins and because we are still linked from before. I think we are safe enough.

I hope so. I would hate to have to switch this off. I'm not certain I could.

We could always test her and see.

No. No baiting Claudius this time, remember?

Sorry.

Still, it's frightening to think verbalisation might be safer than telepathy.

"Excuse me," said Eleanor, setting the moon crown once more upon her head. "but it's not really polite to carry on such exclusive conversations. As acting HPs I really feel I have the right to chide you in this."

We looked at each other and then her. The crown was on to be sure, but it was upside-down, the crescent frowning downward from her forehead instead of smiling upward. We both began chuckling.

"Am I missing something?" she inquired.

"Do you always wear it that way when you're displeased?" Kieran teased "I mean it really looks like a silver scowl there on your head."

She felt at it for a second, grinned sheepishly, and removed it.

"I told you I was exhausted," she giggled.

"Sorry for our rudeness. Kieran and I can communicate much more rapidly if we don't have to actually speak."

"I see. You must have had a lot to say."

"Yes, but I think it's been covered. Will you promise to wait for us here while we go and change?"

"No, but I will meet you upstairs. I have to change myself."

"Into what?"

Kieran!

Sorry. It was too good to resist.

We began to giggle with the mindlessness of those who have gone without sleep for too long. Then we were transfixed by the realisation that the last time we had seen that face it had belonged to someone who had been able to transform Herself or us into anything She had wanted. How kind of Her to choose for us our destiny by taking on the form of the woman we were so rapidly coming to love.

"Go on then, Eleanor. We'll see you upstairs."

I stood in the shower stall next to Kieran's until the hot water around me ran cold, feeling the hard needles of water cleansing and invigorating the tired flesh which housed me. Sometimes it seemed alien to me, too bulky, too slow for the way my mind raced within it, yet as bodies go it was lean, athletic, and I supposed pleasant to look upon. The salve and spray-on bandage had made the wound beneath my scar impervious to the water, but the pressure of it full-force was more than I could bear and had to content myself with keeping my backside to the showerhead and letting the water flow down my shoulder to clean away the dried blood which had adhered to my chest hair. They were with me again as they had always been, the red of the blood, the white of my skin, the black of my hair, the trinity of colours which made up the tapestry of our religion and our lives.

The image occurred to me of a black and white chess board upon which a number of pieces stood, each with the face of someone I had known in one life or another. Herne the Hunter, the antlered God of the Greenwood and The Morrigan sat at opposite ends of the board moving the pieces. Burgundy knight checkmates green king. Both are removed from the board and replaced with a burgundy king on a green horse and a green king on a burgundy horse. Other players are removed and replaced with faces just as familiar. The Lord and the Lady laugh.

It's just a game you know, Kieran. All that matters is that we play.

I showed him the image and he laughed too.

I suppose you're right. There's really nothing to worry about. The worst that can happen is we die, and it's not even as if that's permanent.

No, the worst is that we could die before our appointed time. What would happen to the Land then?

Richard died. Stephen came back to finish the job. Edward was a child. There are ways. The Lady provides Her own sacrifice.

Then what of the Order? Why must we guard the King with our lives if none of it matters?

Because you were right; it is a game, and those are the rules.

For some reason that answer satisfied me more than anything Derek or Robin could have said. What player in a game is allowed to question the rules? He just follows them. We, apparently were not even really the players, merely the pieces in a game in which kings and knights were no more than pawns, yet for some reason I found the thought not at all degrading but comforting.

As we dressed ourselves in loose shirts to avoid putting pressure on our wounds we had a trinity of thoughts: the Lady we served by serving the Land and King, the lady we had both resolved to win, and our little sister Gwenna, no longer a child, who could dazzle men with her golden beauty and freeze their souls with the look in her grey-blue eyes.

"Enough of this," Kieran said emphatically. "We have someone waiting for us upstairs, remember?"

How could anyone forget?

It seemed she could, for there was no sign of her when we arrived amid the toasting crowd upstairs. Mother and Father embraced us gently, but our eyes searched all the while for Eleanor Rhys-Davies among the well-wishers. Uncle Julian, Father's youngest brother, looked splendid in his formal Balmoral attire, and we were quite surprised to see another flash of tartan enter the room, preceded by a bellowing laugh.

"Malcolm!"

I don't know which of us shouted it out first; it seemed to be one voice coming from two mouths. If we had been disappointed in the absence of our ladyfriend we were equally delighted in seeing our cousin.

"Were you there?" asked Kieran. "From where we were there was no way to know if the gallery was full or empty."

"Oh I was there. You proved yourselves most gallantly, both of you, even if it was a wee bit different than my own interpretation of the ritual."

He winked at us and ran his right hand through the thick, long ginger mop of hair.

"And here I wasn't even aware you'd been a part of the Order," I said.

"Ah, well, just as there seems to be a Tyrell in the Windsor woodpile on your side of the family, there's a FitzHugh in ours. Come on, lad, you didn't really think the scar I bear came from wrestling a wolf, did you? That was just a tale I invented to explain it away to those who had no business knowing the truth. Of course I could have said I was just cleaning my claymore and it went off, but I believe you have already used that line about your rapier."

It was impossible not to love him. He was more like a brother than a cousin of so distant a degree, and his ability to liven up any conversation was absolute, for the twinkle in his eye seemed attached directly to his tongue.

"So where's Genevefa?" I asked.

"At home, making us a family. We're expecting twins, but don't worry, they're fraternal, a boy and a girl. You're still the only identicals in the family."

I think I would have preferred them to be identical, just so we could find out how much of what Kieran and I shared was due to that and how much was because of the way in which we had died, although I suspected the only true test would be on separated conjoined twins, those who had spent the full time of their prenatal existence joined physically.

"So, where is your lovely sister?" he asked.

"Isn't she here?"

"No. I saw her during the ritual but she wasn't here when I came upstairs. I was supposed to deliver a locket to her from my mother. She'd apparently left it at Glamis when she visited there last spring. At any rate, she seems to have slipped out somewhere."

"Well, that makes two that got away, then. Our HPs, Eleanor, was supposed to meet us for a cream sherry, I believe she said. She seems to have gotten off somewhere too."

God's hooves, Neil, you don't suppose they're together.

Now that's a disquieting thought.

"Well perhaps they got off somewhere together," suggested Malcolm.

"No," I said, "probably just a coincidence."

I wanted it to be just that, a coincidence, wanted it desperately, not quite sure why it was so important that it be so. Gwenna could not have made the connexion between Kieran and Eleanor and myself so quickly, because at this point there was no such connexion, except in our minds. If she could read them she'd see that, unless she could also see our visions.

That's an even more disquieting thought.

What is?

That she could eavesdrop on our visions. I think you're giving her more power in your own mind than she has.

"So how long has Gwenna been in training as a Priestess?"

"A little over a year," I answered absently.

"Oh, I see. We start them a year later in Scotland, waiting until the eighteenth birthday to begin."

"Yes, I remember some discussion of the term 'eighteenth year' and whether to interpret it as the year in which a person turns eighteen or the year in which the person is already eighteen. That seems to be the major difference between Scottish and English tradition."

You don't suppose she's learned something as a Priestess which has amplified her abilities, do you?

Nonsense. She's only in basics at the moment. Don't try to make her Morgan Le Fey or something like that.

"That and pronunciation and spelling of certain words. You tend to use Irish Gaelic pronunciations and spellings, while we, naturally, use the Scottish."

It was Morgause, not Morgana who tried to do in her brother.

Thank you. It depends on whose version you read. Besides, she had only one half-brother. Gwenna has two, and full brothers at that.

"There you are," she grinned as she came around the corner.

She was elegant in the simple green gown she wore, elegant in herself, in her carriage, elegant enough to be a queen. I could feel the impression she made on Kieran, for the shade of green she wore matched the more lavish gown the Lady had worn in our vision.

"How long does it take two men to shower and dress, anyway?"

Longer than it takes them to undress.

Be nice, Kieran.

I intend to be. She's perfect, Neil.

I know.

"You're doing it again, aren't you?"

"What?" I asked innocently.

"Thinking."

"Of course we were. Just thinking how beautiful you really are, even without the moon crown."

Don't even think it, Kieran.

I don't have to. I can imagine it.

"Eleanor Rhys-Davies, have you met our cousin Malcolm?"

"Not until now. Honoured, Your Highness."

"The honour is mine. Sorry I arrived late, or I'm certain we would have been introduced in time for me to warn you about these two."

"Don't worry, they've already warned me themselves. I don't scare off so easily."

She looked pointedly back and forth between the two of us; whether she was merely flirting or openly inviting us to pursue her further it did not matter. Kieran and I were hooked, as surely as the salmon we delighted in taking from the rivers of Scotland, for it was there they spawned and here the same natural urge had been planted within us.

Spawn and die. Spawn and die.

What?

Nothing. Just a phrase that went through my head. It seemed appropriate, though I haven't the slightest notion of why.

I really had no idea of from where the words had come to my mind; it seemed as if I had heard them somewhere, spoken softly or whispered in a voice not unlike my own, yet I could not remember where or when. Did it matter? Probably not. Eleanor was what counted now. The past was behind us.

"Is it warm in here, or is it me?" she asked taking a sip from the wine glass in her hand.

"A little of both, I should imagine," Kieran answered.

"Malcolm!"

Gwenna entered the room like a panther poised to spring. Though outwardly she was self controlled, within her the energy of her youth was coiled tightly, begging to be set free. She seemed in a better mood than we had previously observed as she threw her slender arms around his neck and kissed him on the cheek. He responded with the kind of affection one might expect from an elder brother, a hug and a quick peck on the forehead, then pulled something from his sporran.

"My locket," she gushed. Wherever did you find it?"

She seems unusually pleased with life today.

The lady doth protest too much. This is not like her.

"You left it on the dressing table when you stayed at Glamis. One of the servants found it, actually, gave it to Mother, and she sent it back to you through me with her best regards."

"How is your mother?"

"She'll live to be a hundred, bless her, maybe longer if she relaxes a bit more. The responsibility of ruling a nation takes up an awful lot of time. I'm glad it falls to Robert, who is in excellent health, thank the Gods, and not me. I don't think I would want it. Gennie's expecting in May, a boy and a girl."

I think Kieran missed the look she flashed us. It was a smile, sort of triumphant, with a touch of something more malignant surrounding it.

"Another set of twins. Well perhaps the girl will keep her brother from doing anything as foolish as these two have been known to do. How's Alex?"

"Fine, although I expected it to be Duncan you inquired about."

It seems to me she actually blushed a bit. Did our sister have a secret attachment to the youngest Prince of Scotland?

"Of course Duncan did say to send his love, and that he's hoping you'll get to Edinburgh this spring as you hinted you might."

"Tell him I wouldn't miss it. He's promised me the Grand Tour."

"Yes, and he said to tell you he found that place you had spoken to him about and he would be glad to take you there, whatever that means."

Her look of victory was complete.

"Thank you, Malcolm. You don't know what that means to me."

"What place?" I asked.

"Oh, just a place I had remembered hearing about, somewhere sort of intimate that our ancestors used to frequent. Sorry I have to leave the party now, dears. You were magnificent. Take good care of them, Eleanor. Just try to keep them from doing too much, Neil especially. He likes to bleed too much, and you wouldn't want that pretty frock spoiled, now would you?"

She left the room with a grand curtsey to Mother and Father, sweeping past us all like a whirlwind, leaving at least four of us a bit confused as to what we had really seen or heard.

"Duncan's going to have his hands full with her," laughed Malcolm."

"Do you think it's serious?" I asked.

"Could be. He's a bit young and hot-headed. Still, Robert was married at twenty, and it's been a good marriage. What about Gwenna?"

"Hard to tell. It's the first any of us have known there was even an attraction. Still, a marriage union between England and Scotland would be a welcome thing to a lot of people. Do you suppose your mother would make them Duke and Duchess of Edinburgh? The title has been vacant since your uncle died without issue. After all, Duncan does live in Edinburgh."

"I suppose, if Alex and I agree to it. Robert is Tanist, I'm Prince of the Isles and by marriage Duke of Breizh, Alex is to receive some title when he weds, and Duncan will get one also."

I should have paid more attention to Eleanor and less to Gwenna and Malcolm, for when I looked back to her Kieran had managed to gain her undivided attention, and had his arm about her waist.

Not fair.

All's fair, et cetera.

Fine. If that's the way you want to play it. Don't expect me to leave you alone. You're going to share her with me one way or another.

That's not fair, Neil. I want to be alone with her first.

I thought all was fair. After all, I shared your pain. I think I deserve to share your pleasure. I won't be obtrusive. I'll just sit there in your head and experience it all first-hand with you instead of getting the images from you afterwards.

He ran his hand up and down her back as he thought it over.

She should be consulted. She should know in advance.

You've never been concerned about that before, either way. You've never asked me to tell someone you were going along for the ride.

This one's different.

I know. I just wanted to make sure you realised it after the way your mind has been working.

I want to marry her.

So do I.

"What is it now?" she asked.

"We're fighting over you," I grinned.

She put her arm around my waist and pulled me close. The touch of her even through my silk shirt was like electricity crawling from where her hand lay to my spine and all along it, delicious tinglings and the hunger for her growing within me as she slowly rubbed her fingers over my shirt.

"Why? I thought you two did everything together."

Chapter Ten

*W*e excused ourselves from the celebration, as did she, begging exhaustion from the day and long night before and the ordeal of the morning. Parting with her was difficult for us, but we knew our limits; the adrenaline which had kept us going to that point was fading away, and there was not enough caffeine in the world to replace it. We finally bid her adieu amid much flirtation and innuendo and with the promise to see her later that night.

With this in mind we lay down to what we hoped would be a healing sleep, undisturbed by the world and untroubled by dreams. What we got was something else indeed.

Something was in the air; it was Samhain and the Veil between the Worlds had been stripped clean away. We were the playthings of the Gods and danced merrily to Their unheard tunes, three of us dancing the merriest of all.

Beltaine was the time for fertilisation of the body and of the earth. It was six months away, on the opposite side of the sun, the last phase of the year's waxing into the light. In the short days of November it waned into the darkness, waiting to die, the Veil down to ease the beginning of its passage. This was the time for the fertilisation of the spirit, for the seeds of the soul to be planted in Eternity.

This was the time in which we entered the world of slumber.

We had not been asleep for long when the dreams began, familiar dreams, dreams that we had shared before, both as dreams and in the flesh, for together we had travelled these roads throughout time; only the names and faces and backgrounds of history changed. We were King and Knight, slain and slayer in the forest where the blood of the King nourished the great oak against which he stood to receive the arrow, in the stone circle where the gladius did its work, at the wooden stake where the garrotte released him from his body, in the graveyard where his aide took him hurriedly with two bullets, on the lawn of the manor house where the rapier pierced his heart, falling from the summer sky to the henge below, locked in an embrace that had dared even the Gods to separate us.

This replay of our lives was more detailed, more vivid than usual, for a space of time which had gone before accompanied them, and although we could still not recall which of us had done what, the face of one of the other Companions was beginning to focus, shifting back and forth in time, overlaying upon itself each face worn from the time he had dressed in blue in the forest to the blue canopy of his parachute which had opened above us as we fell, until we saw him as we knew him already in this life. The eyes had not changed much from that time, nor had his height, but the ginger hair was definitely new. Malcolm, our cousin, had Awakened, and all at once, not with the usual episodic stages we had remembered from our past, but then as I have said, it was Samhain and the Veil was in shreds, waiting for the Lady to weave it back together again.

We searched out each other even in our dreaming state, much as we had in our mother's womb, anxious for the presence of one another against the isolation of the confinement of the flesh, yearning in that dream state to return to the oneness we had been before rebirth into this world had torn us apart.

It was in this frame of mind more than any other we began our relationship with Eleanor, for Kieran had indeed been right. This one was different.

How different we had no idea at the time.

All we knew was that Eleanor had been given to us in our most devout meditations as a vision, as a sign, as a way in which to realign ourselves perhaps, or as a physical link by which to reunite.

A ritual existed to unite the Holly King and the Oak King with the Lady, a rite which had not been performed to our knowledge in the modern world. It had been used in the crowning of King and Tanist at a time in our history in which the Tanist was always the ritual slayer of the King, and thereafter succeeded him to the throne, whereupon a new Tanist was chosen and the ritual was repeated. It had somehow found itself into the Archives, and Kieran and I had always made a mental note to find the right time and the right Priestess with which to perform it.

What time could be more auspicious than the night of the day in which we had been consecrated as Priests and Knights, and who better than the Priestess who had conferred the titles upon us? The rite was a pact, a sealing of ourselves to Lady Sovereignty and to the Land in a way most ancient. As we had been sealed to Her that morning as Knight to honour the Tyrell blood within us by shedding it, so must we balance that act to honour the Windsor blood by sealing ourselves to Her as Sacred King.

In the course of a ritual the Great Rite is performed, uniting the forces of male and female for that divine energy which the union brings. It is often done in token, the cup filled with wine or some other liquid being the female symbol, the knife or sword being the male. So the cup and the liquid are consecrated, by the plunging of the blade into the cup. In our consecration we were the cup, our blood being consecrated, our willing bodies taking the blade held or steadied by the Priestess, a token of a token, although one token was flesh. The rite we planned was not in token, but in actuality. Both male and female forces would be in the flesh, and we would release such energies as might please the Morrigan and the Dagda who also mated upon this night to ensure the perpetuation of the world.

We picked Eleanor up about a half hour later than we had expected to, having lost track of time looking for the ritual in the Archives but we made up for it with bouquets of white and red roses, and she forgave us with little hesitation. The pale blue gown she wore suggested to us a portrait of our great-great aunt Anastasia, done up for the Second Coronation of her brother. The portrait hung in the upstairs bedroom of Stonehurst where both of them had been born. There was definitely a strong resemblance there in the colouring, the smile, and especially the eyes, eyes which widened when I remarked upon the resemblance.

"Interesting," she said. "I've always felt an attraction to the Duchess of Cornwall. Her life has been one of my models. Odd the resemblance you see. We are related, but only by marriage."

"How so?" Kieran inquired.

"Let's see. Your great grandmother was her sister-in law and my great-great-great aunt, or something like that. Queen Emma had four brothers and the eldest, Thomas Tyrell Jones, was one of my ancestors. He inherited his mother's bookstore and home and gave it to his daughter Elizabeth. She married Laurence Rhys-Davies II and they begat Laurence III, who begat Evan, who begat me."

I was intrigued. She was a Tyrell after all, and our cousin, though separated by a degree more distant than had been our ancestors Elizabeth II and her consort Phillip Mountbatten, a point Kieran was as quick to catch as I.

"No," she laughed. "Even Henry VIII could not have made a case for consanguinity between us."

"Why should he have wished to?" asked Kieran, perhaps a little too intensely.

"Oh, perhaps to shock the populace," she grinned, mischief in her eyes.

"They don't shock as easily as they used to," I observed.

"We could always try," she suggested.

I looked at Kieran over the top of the glossy black Halley-Manz as he helped her in. She slid across the seat to the centre as he walked around to the right side to get in. I climbed in on her other side and Kieran drove us off slowly.

"We need to talk," I began. "Something has occurred to us which concerns you and we need to discuss it before we go much further."

I could feel her stiffen beside me, as if she anticipated something painful about to happen.

She thinks we're going to reject her.

Worse than that. She thinks we're going to give her some kind of high and mighty pronouncement about princes and commoners.

There's nothing common about her.

I know, but the fear is there.

"How long have you been a Priestess?" I asked.

The tension eased a bit as the question put to her had nothing to do with what she had expected to hear.

"Fully ordained, consecrated and initiated?"

"Yes," I replied.

"Five years ago last Imbolc. I aspected Brighid at the festival two hours later at Wookey Hole."

"That was you?"

I was incredulous. We had been there with the rest of the crowd along the banks of the underground lake, our wooden torches doused and afraid to move in the absolute darkness of the cave. Then from our far right a spark had been struck, a candle lighted, and she had appeared, a vision in white with long red hair, standing in the bow of a small boat as it had been rowed toward us. The Priest at the water's edge had lighted his torch from that candle and had helped the Priestess from the boat to dry land. Our torches had been lighted, one at a time, until the cave had been illuminated to a brilliance which reflected in the water and cast strange long shadows upon the far walls.

The ancient Celts who had used those caves as their temple and home would have been delighted with the scene. The Priestess had blessed the crowd as the Goddess Brighid and given an Oracle for the year to come. I didn't recall the words, but the figure of the Priestess and the spectacle of that predawn ritual will stay with me always.

"But your hair was red," I protested.

"For four years my hair was red," she laughed. "I thought it extremely Celtic of me. I dyed it back to its natural colour about two years ago when I realised that being of Welsh descent, black was just as good a colour for Celtic hair, and it was my own naturally."

Perhaps I shall never understand women.

At any rate, the memory was enough to distract me momentarily from the direction in which I had intended it to go. Fortunately Kieran had been less overwhelmed by the whole thing and was able to pick up where I had left off.

"Eleanor, when you were in training to work for the Order did they give you access to the Archives?"

"As far as the stacks which contain the rituals. We always had access to the religious end of it, though some of the historical and political material was restricted, mostly things having to do with people who are still alive. The Order seems to distinguish between Mysteries and Secrets."

I could not suppress a chuckle at the way in which she had said it, especially since it was so painfully true. Still, the Order was relatively secret; although its existence was known its exact membership and function was never discussed even in times when the means of and reason for my great-grandfather's death had been readily accepted by the public and his death and that of the Duke of Cornwall looked upon as the highest form of patriotism.

"You didn't happen to find a copy of the old Tanist ritual did you?"

"I translated it into modern English for my thesis on polarity. Why?"

Neither Kieran and I had time to speak before she answered her own question.

"Oh. Oh I see. Well it certainly seems appropriate, considering the circumstances. And you want me to act as HPs?"

"If you're willing," Kieran replied softly.

Do you think she'll agree?

Yes.

The silent interval seemed much longer than it actually took, the tension building between the two of us as she thought the offer over.

"I'm extremely honoured, of course, but..."

I thought you were sure she'd agree to it. It has to be her to make it work.

"I hadn't quite counted on it to be that complicated. Of course, if that's what you really want, I'd be happy to go along with it. I just hope it is what you really want, because you don't have to go to all that trouble if you don't. I'd rather not profane something like that just because the two of you fancy a three-way romp or something. I'm not Victorian, you know. I have my own fantasies, and yes, you two are very attractive to me. Oh Gods, I feel like such a tart telling you all this, but in all conscience I would feel worse if you were planning to use this ritual just to seduce someone who is already willing."

We could not be angry at her concern, for considering our previous behaviour it might have been warranted. She was honest, she was real, and she was embarrassed to the bone for admitting what she had to us. She tilted her face down and leaned upon her hands so we could not see her expression. I ran my hand through her hair gently and assured her that although the idea of a triad was more or less what we had originally planned, this ritual was even more important to us, and why.

When she lifted her head she was all Priestess, radiant with the energy she had drawn upon.

"Yes. I understand. It must be done quickly, while the Veil is parted, or not at all. If we wait until Beltaine the effects will be more personal and less profound. What you are seeking is not for yourselves, although there are those who would see it otherwise."

"Tonight," I suggested.

"Tonight," she confirmed. "But where?"

"The Temple of the Order," suggested my brother.

"No," I countered. "A more ancient site for such an ancient working. Wookey Hole Caves. We have fur rugs at home to lay over the sand. We need to go back there anyway to pick up the other paraphernalia we'll need, and something with which to make a fire down there. We don't need the electric lights. We'll do it all by fire, just as our distant ancestors must have done."

"Fine by me. I doubt we'll even notice the cold once the circle is cast. Don't forget, you need two swords. One circle is cast deosil, the other widdershins, and you must do them simultaneously."

"Is that what that part meant? I understood all of it but those directions."

"That's another reason it had to be her, Neil."

"Another? What were the rest?"

"We both saw you as the Goddess or vice-versa on our Visionquest, for one, and for the other..."

"We've both fallen in love with you."

She took one of our hands in each of hers and squeezed softly for a silent moment.

"And I think I have with both of you. I have only one question. Which one of you is planning to be King and which one Tanist?"

It was a question which had to be answered somehow, though both of us had been avoiding it for obvious reasons. Kieran and I didn't have to look at the other to feel the confusion between us at trying to sort out the roles we must eventually play.

Neil?

"We haven't gotten that far, why?"

"Because the Gods will hold you to it. One of you will have to kill the other in the end if you go through with this ritual."

Go on, Neil. She'll have to know sometime.

"We've known that for years, Eleanor, and planned for it. We've done it all so many times before that neither of us has any fear of it, only of being separated from each other and those we love."

"Eleanor, love, there are a few things they didn't tell you as a Priestess."

By the time we had finished relating our story we were home and had been parked for about half an hour. She wanted to know everything we remembered in minute detail, trying to pin us down on certain things to determine which of us had done what to whom in an effort to sort us out. It didn't work. We had come through the Veil in both directions united, and the memories had slipped through whole on both sides. We had come to the conclusion that it did not really matter in the end who lived and who died. We had spent long periods of time inhabiting each other's minds and bodies, long enough that we figured if one body died we could both still survive in the other, and if that didn't work, we'd find each other again in the next life, as we always seemed to do.

"What if we rework the ritual slightly, so the King and Tanist are both represented, but neither role is specified? They both become King, after all. The Tanist succeeds the King he kills."

"Just as it will be with us, *Anmchara*."

I usually reserved that term of endearment for our thought-talk, and was surprised to hear myself say it aloud.

"*Anmchara?*" she asked, pronouncing the word almost perfectly.

"An old Irish word for soul-friend. We saw it in a book once and it stuck with us. Later we saw it translated as 'spiritual adviser', but we've always stuck to the literal translation."

"*Anmchara*. It fits. I like it."

"I think you're the only one who knows that story too. At any rate, is there not a way we can make this a bit open-ended? When the time comes one of us will die. That much is certain. At this point we don't know who it will be. We are both Awake, both consecrated Knights of the Order, so it could be either. Now we must even it up by consecrating us both to Her as Sacred Kings."

She had a habit of gnawing upon her lower lip as she thought, probably an old habit from her days of study. It made her more childlike, more vulnerable, and I wanted to reach out and protect her from anything that might ever harm her or bring her grief.

"Your father is still alive. The title could pass to him. He's the Twice-Crowned King, after all."

"But he is not the one who has gone through this lifetime after lifetime, as we have. The Sacred King has not always been the one with the crown upon his head, despite what the Seminary teaches. The Order has known that for years. The blood must be there, but it is not always legitimately begotten. During the years when Christianity was the State Religion it seldom worked that way. Ask Derek about his ancestor, George Edmund Stuart, who died in Ypres to bring us eventual victory. Better yet, ask us. That was the only time I can remember having been shot to death. We both were."

"And one of our Companions has Awakened already. We need to be ready, just in case, and let the Gods work out who lives and who dies later."

"How?"

"Rapier and dagger. We've done it before."

I saw the images in Kieran's mind of the torch-lit lawn before the mansion as we circled each other, steel flashing both the moonlight and the reflection of the flames, and for an instant I almost retreated wholly into the scene and all its exuberance. Yes, it would be good to do that one again. I saw Malcolm's face distinctly in the crowd, his blue waistcoat and coat striking next to the russet coat of the man who stood next to him on one side and the man in silver and grey on the other. I could not see their faces, but I knew I would one day.

"As you almost succeeded doing once again already, or so I've heard the tale told," she said in a voice which suddenly seemed far away.

Kieran, off, slightly in the distance, there's a black carriage on the drive behind them. Do you see it?

It has always been there.

Can you take the scene forward in your mind with me to after the death?

You mean experience it again, here and now, with her here?

Yes. It's important.

Yes, but it will be stronger together. We should tell her what we're doing.

No time. We'll lose it.

Take my hand.

I reached across her lap to my brother and felt the warmth of his fingers gripping mine, squeezing slowly, and then relaxing. The link grew stronger, became absolute as we watched and experienced it once again, the smile, the nod, the thrust, the instant of fusion and sweet ecstasy of release from the one body, the sadness and delight of the moment as the blood flowed into the ground and the slayer ran toward the waiting coach, the witnesses blocked by the three Companions in the crowd. The door to the coach opened and the woman inside was

"Eleanor," we gasped in unison as we snapped back to the twin bodies which our current incarnation had provided us.

Chapter Eleven

"What? Are you two all right?"

It took a moment for us to focus, to see the look of worry upon her face. We had no idea of what we might have looked like while a part of us journeyed into the past, or how long it had seemed to her to have taken. We only knew there was a piece of the puzzle there for us to retrieve, and we had not dared to risk losing it when it had been within our grasp.

"Yes, love," I said when I could, "we're fine. How are you?"

"All right now, but you had me panicking. You both stopped breathing for over a minute, and I was afraid to feel for your pulse in case there wasn't any. Do you do that often?"

"I don't know. We're not around to know what happens when it's happening."

"Where were you?"

Tell her all of it, Neil.

Do you think that's wise?

I think it's imperative. She has been connected with us for a long time.

I wish we could link with her and let her experience it herself.

Perhaps in time. For now just tell her.

She sat there motionless as I explained to her what she could not have understood had she not already known so much of the background of our lives, how the rapier duel we'd staged already in this life had triggered the onset of the memories we had only glimpsed in fragments as children, and how precious was the memory we had just relived, almost as precious as the memories of the time immediately preceding this life, and how we had just caught a glimpse of her aiding the King's slayer as he fled the crowd.

When I had finished there were tears in her eyes and a smile came to her lips.

"Then it was all true, not just some fantasy, some silly dream I have carried around in my head. Let me tell you the rest. I wore a black gown that evening. I knew what was going to happen. I usually wore pale blue, and my hair in ringlets with pearls in it. You both wore black pants and white ruffled shirts. I have carried this vision around with me since I was a child, never knowing why."

It all rang true. The three of us had been together before. The immediate revival of those past feelings should have been our first inkling of what lay beyond.

"There's more, you know. You were just as inseparable then as you are now, even in death. I lost both of you that night. One of you killed the other, and the survivor was killed not two hours later. I don't know what happened then."

"I do. We've been allowed to read Kevin of Cornwall's journal. You fled to Scotland, pregnant by one of us and sought refuge with the Order."

"Whose child was it? I mean whose then."

"We didn't know for sure. You were right about us being inseparable. It seems the three of us were very happy together."

"So my dear, it seems your fantasies are more like memories."

She took it better than we expected. It actually seemed to relieve her mind and make her relax more, enough that we were both easy about leaving her alone in the vehicle while we gathered the equipment necessary for the ritual. When we returned she was busy reworking the ritual in her mind and somewhat excited about what she'd come up with.

"The important thing is intent," she began as we started out for the caves. "The ritual is the same no matter how it is translated. There is no magic formula or esoteric vowel sounds in it which produce the desired effect; the transformation is much more primal than speech. What if we do the entire thing in silence, even the casting of the circle and the calling of the quarters. Keep the vision within ourselves. We know what we're seeking, correct?"

"Unification with the Lady," said Kieran.

"Exactly. You've both mated with Her in your vision, both been accepted as King. Now you need to bring it into this world on a physical level. Carry the vision of your magical selves with you as you do this, as I will hold myself open to Her. Let Her choose who is the Oak King and who is the Holly King as She receives you, and perhaps She will give you the image. If not, it is Her will, and at least it won't be hanging over your heads for the rest of your lives."

She didn't seem to understand that part of it and we both tried to explain again that it didn't really matter anymore. We had already found the connexion we had missed in all other lives and would be content hereafter to accept either role. There was no longer pain or guilt on either side, and although we feared the emptiness of the loss, it was all we feared, and we knew it, like everything else, was only transitory until next we met. Now we had even more reason for joy: we had her, and would have for all time.

Strange how concepts change when death ceases to be an absolute. Everything becomes tolerable because it passes. Patience grows, because eternity is such a vast frame against which incident is hardly visible. There is no threat because there is no fear. Even pain can be endured, because it is finite and we are not. The notion of morality changes from season to season. Love is the only constant, the one thing which binds us so tightly to each other, the reason for our death and our rebirth.

"If I could only remember it all the way you do," she sighed. "I know you're right of course."

"Perhaps this will help," Kieran suggested. "Perhaps the Lady will let you share the memories as we have them until your own come back."

"Oh I can remember bits and pieces, but not like you, not death as you've described it. I guess I've always died in my sleep. I don't even know if I've always been a woman."

"Not necessarily. We remember one of us being a woman at least once. It certainly complicated matters. She was definitely a woman, with all her hormones in the right place, but she had the memories of a man. Can you imagine the frustration when she found herself Awake for no apparent reason in what appeared to be the wrong time, the wrong place, and the wrong body? She should have been the King of England, not an artiste in Los Angeles, as it was called at the time. Unfortunately, or maybe not, a young man she knew read some of the visions she'd written down, and he realised they were all true. He was also Awake, but a computer programmer, not a Knight of the Order."

"At least you found each other."

"Yes. But it was somewhat bittersweet for us both, remembering what had been and waiting for what would be, both of us powerless in that life to do more than chalk up omens of coming events and fly over here at every opportunity to look for the past."

Still I wouldn't have traded it for anything, Kieran.

No, Anmchara. The good parts were wonderful. The bad parts we survived, as we always do.

We had arrived at the caves. The parking lot was as empty as the moon was full. In the stillness of the night we could hear the rush of the Axe River which flowed just beyond us, through the caves and powered an adjoining mill. Frogs called to each other as we passed them, laden with firewood, furs and other goods. Past the metal railings we walked, through the area designed for tourists to queue up while awaiting the guided tour. The key to the old wooden door had been tucked unceremoniously into a tin nailed above it, left by whatever group had used the grotto for their Samhain rites the night before. The folks who ran the tours during the day had not bothered to pick it up, but Eleanor assured us they seldom did, and the lock could be readily picked; she'd had to do it the night before her Imbolc ritual when they had gone for rehearsal and found the key missing.

We ignited one of the torches and walked in, down the pathway wet with condensation, down into the heart of the cave system. We passed the stone formations of the Witch and her Dog, frozen there for all time, as the Welsh legend told, by the sword of King Arthur, on past the first pool, to the great chamber where our distant ancestors had once lived beneath the Mendip Hills and worshipped the Old Ones in similar fashion as we continued to do, offering them their best at the time of sacrifice, as we intended to do.

We lit the second torch and the cave seemed ablaze with light, the ghosts of the past dancing in their flames, welcoming us to that holy place in that holy season, and we were filled with the awe of the temple built by the Gods themselves. There is something profound in the journey into the womb of Mother Earth, more profound than entering any manmade temple, no matter how beautiful the masonry, how cunningly wrought the artistic design, how devout the service within. The age alone was on a scale even we who had known millennia could not comprehend. Each stalactite which dripped from the ceiling like an enchanted icicle was older by far than our most ancient memories, each fold and crevice in the curtained walls of stone had been placed there before man had walked upon this island.

Along the manmade trail we walked to the third chamber, where the underground waters had become a small lake from which the walls of the cave rose and opened shell-like into a canopy above it. In silence we built the little fire upon the shore in ancient ritual, flint against steel, as we had been taught when we first began to learn the male mysteries. The straw and sawdust caught the first sparks and sent them into the kindling as we knelt around and fed it, warming ourselves against the perpetual chill of the place. In silence we spread the furs before the fire, not synthetic fibres, but the real furs of animals. The ritual was primal and required the mindset of those who were both slayer and slain, hunter and hunted, bound gloriously to each other and the Great Mother who bore them both and who would receive them again in death to bear them yet again. The Lord of the Dance of Life was the Lord of the Dance of Death, both Lover of the Lady, and after His death, reborn as Her son.

The Green Man and the Grey Man, the Oak King and the Holly King, were but two sides of the same coin.

As were we.

We disrobed as the ritual demanded, oblivious to the chill, and donned the antler crowns as Eleanor once more put on the crescent crown of her office and matter-of-factly tossed her own clothing onto the pile with ours. We raised our swords in salute to her as she stood upon the fur, her body golden and magnificent in the firelight, looking every inch the Goddess she would represent in the rite. We began at opposite ends of the sand, he cutting his circle deosil or clockwise in towards and around her, and I cutting mine widdershins or anticlockwise. The circles overlapped each other with her in the vesica their intersection made, in the same way the circles intersected on the cover of Chalice Well, but instead of the arrow crossing the vesica to indicate the fertilising male energy in token, we were there to provide it in fact.

As we turned to the quarters and called in the Gods tacitly we felt the energy within the place respond and build until it filled the cave and us within the sacred geometry we had drawn, building that bridge between the worlds of Gods and men and blurring the lines between us. We were no longer Kieran and Neil who leapt again and again between the worlds, shattering our identities and rebuilding them anew, but King Stag, both of us, eager to serve Her in our season and die in Her embrace.

She knelt in that place between us and reached out to us wordlessly, and we answered her summons with our love, holding her, kissing her, electrified by her touch and wanting nothing more than to lose ourselves entirely in her. The Lady filled her spirit even as we sought to fill her body, and beckoned us onward with the heat of Her breath in our ears and the wetness of Her kisses as She opened to us and welcomed us inside.

It was like a dream, one we wanted to go on forever. I embraced them both as they rocked together and yet my mind was within Kieran as the unearthly pleasure engulfed him, engulfed us, as King Stag ran wild and free in the Forests of the Lady, as he offered Her his life and poured it out into Her in one final ecstatic surge, its sweet release drowning us all for a time. A moment later Her mouth was on mine and I felt the spark of Kieran's mind touch mine again, reaching out to me as the Lady led me through the same pastures of delight. I felt the traces of my brother's presence within her with joy, for there was no part of him which was not a part of me also.

Kieran embraced my soul as I embraced Her body. I carried him with me as I explored the Mystery of Her depths, slowly and completely, my heart worshipping the beauty which engulfed me, moving with me, with us, to the oldest rhythms of all. I felt Her ache as I felt my own, and drew even closer to fill it, wanting to give her everything I was, eager to explode into that brilliance and the dark oblivion which followed. She was the river of life in which I swam, struggling upward like the salmon, driven on and on to that one perfect spawning pool in which his life must be released, even as it created new life.

I felt Her tremble, quiver against my final thrust, and I saw and felt once again the sword pierce my heart and the hand which wielded it, not in pain but in the overwhelming passion of release far sweeter than orgasm. As the memories flooded my senses, our senses, the flesh answered the spirit and the vessel of the Lady consumed us in her own delicious response.

Somewhere straddling the River Boyne the Dagda, ancient All-Father of the Irish filled the Great Queen even as I filled Her Priestess. Life and death entwined, spiralling together in tantric unison, pulsating together in harmonies no mortal could comprehend.

Beyond the dazzling explosion of light, beyond the darkness of oblivion there was a place that was not a place in a time that was not a time, a place in which three living humans existed without need of the earthly trappings they had come to depend upon. We were, without form or motion, only knowing that we were, and that we were together, the pattern of our lives inexorably intertwined, braided together throughout the ages and for all time to come.

You are Mine.

The voiceless words fanned the three tiny sparks we were, not extinguishing but intensifying them.

We were Hers, as we had always been, as we always would be, with all the joy and pain it brought, with all the responsibility and privilege, with each life we entered, engendered and exited, in the instant of creation and destruction, in the fullness of light and the emptiness of darkness. We were Hers, bound to that boundless love and seeking no freedom from it, for in the same manner She was ours, to thrust us forth from Her dark womb when it was our time to live, and to receive us there once more when that time was over and we heard the call to come home and rest ourselves from the world. She was the Land and all which lived, all which died knowing Her or not. It did not matter; She knew them and only awaited them to throw off the burdens of forgetfulness, to claim their right of Her and shoulder their responsibilities, yet forgetfulness was more often easier to bear.

We were Hers in full consciousness, waking or sleeping, and the joy of the reaffirmation of those unspoken words was the acceptance we had sought.

How long were we there? Only She knew, for we did not exist there temporally. When we returned to the cave we felt fire still blazing beside us. With eyes still closed we lay in the drowsy afterglow, stroking each other tenderly, the bodies once again entirely human, tired but more than satisfied and glad of the warmth and companionship of each other. I pulled Eleanor toward me gently and kissed her thoroughly, enjoying the smell of her, the taste of her, the feeling of her, no longer as King Stag mating with the Lady, but as a man enjoys the goodness of a woman. My hands went to her full breasts and my mouth followed, making a wet trail which led between them. Across the fur Kieran lay, one hand drifting across her inner thigh, the other upon the small of her back.

"We've done this all before," she sighed. "I've never been able to tell you apart, or love one of you more than the other."

Her fingers traced ovals around our recent wounds.

"Did these hurt terribly?"

"When they were made, yes," Kieran answered. "Now, no. We didn't even feel them just now."

"Good."

She turned to Kieran and kissed him as she'd kissed me, and I knew what she'd said about us having all been together like this before was true. The desire for her was still strong within us both, and although the circles still surrounded us the rite was for our benefit, not that of the Gods. We set the ritual crowns aside, staying within our own bodies as we shared her, our pleasure and hers the same as any mortals might enjoy.

I suppose there was a little of the voyeur in me, for I felt not a shred of jealousy as I watched my brother take her, only the echo of their own joy as she moaned beneath him.

"Neil," she whispered. "Don't leave us."

"I won't, love," I assured her.

I was fascinated by the sight and sound of them, realising just how identical Kieran and I were; if he watched us it would look the same. She held out her hand to me and I took it.

"You are beautiful," I said. "I love you both."

She reached out her other hand and touched me on the thigh.

"Closer. Come closer. You don't have to be alone. I want you both, just as I always have. Don't you remember?"

She stroked me lightly with her fingers until I could stand it no more, nor even understand why I had resisted in the first place. She turned her head slightly and guided me to her mouth.

Kieran?

Join us.

Chapter Twelve

*I*n the dark of the year we had found the flame which would both warm and light up our lives for as long as we wore this flesh, and Eleanor was her name, Eleanor who had been our darling before this life and would doubtlessly be again. She joined within herself the eternal and the now and when we were with her we had no sense of time, for when we were with her we were a complete world unto ourselves, happy, loving, and with no thought of anything else. It was more than physical love, although that was exquisite beyond belief, whether it was two of us or three. It was the magical energy we created together as if the addition of her female force magnified and blended with the male energies we generated to produce something much greater than the sum of its parts. To us she would always be the representative of the Lady we served, and every moment spent with her was a blessing.

As the nights grew longer and colder we found more time to slip away to her and to bask in her bright warmth, a mirror of the Lady's promise that Spring and Summer would come again to a world in need of the sun.

When the Spring did come, it was with mixed feelings we greeted it, having received the news of Genevefa's miscarriage and tragic death just hours before the traditional oak planting at Windsor, an annual event begun in 2067 by Sir Jack Beaudry to commemorate the anniversary of the crowning at Westminster Abbey of Stephen II. Kieran and I were touched by it, remembering the oaks planted in Sherwood Forest to commemorate Jack's Consecration as a Knight of the Order. This year we planted ivy also, in Genevefa's memory.

Malcolm came to us the following week, haggard and thin, having cared little for food or sleep since Genevefa had been rushed to hospital. The explanation the doctors had given him had been no comfort, and only his allegiance to us had kept him from following her into the grave. He was a torn man, a part of him grieving to the bone for his lost family, the other part Awakened, knowing the endurance of the soul and remembering his life with her had been of little importance, one or two stitches of the tapestry we all wove on the loom of the Gods. If he looked carefully he might pick those stitches up once more on the other side and bring them back through again.

We embraced him as our brother as well as our cousin and drew him into the link the three of us had not shared since just before we had jumped from the aircraft to the trilithons below, letting him feel the joy between us as it had been then, relaxing the pain which bound his heart and mind in tight coils of despair. At the end we felt him sigh, exhausted emotionally, letting out all he had held back until he was free of the weight he had allowed himself to bear.

"Lads," he whispered to us as he sank into the chesterfield, "you have no idea what you've just done for me. I wish you'd been at the funeral."

"I wish you'd have let us known in time to have been there," I replied.

He wiped his eyes and looked at us incredulously.

"What do you mean? I rang you right after she died and was told you were on holiday in Ireland."

"Nonsense," I said, angry at someone whose identity I did not yet know for making such an outrageous lie. "We've never been fifty miles from Glastonbury since before our Consecration, and certainly not even that far in the last month. Who told you such a thing?"

"Gwenna."

That little...

Easy, Neil.

"Why would she lie to me?"

"I think she was playing 'keep away', trying to keep you away from us and vice-versa. She's the one who told us about Genevefa just before the Equinox ritual."

"That was four days later. She'd known all that time?"

96

He was angry; he was bewildered.

"Why? Why would she do such a thing?"

It's still just a theory, Neil.

It's getting more believable each day. Keep us separate and we haven't the strength to accomplish much.

Just remind him we have no proof.

"We're not certain. We don't even know if she's doing these things consciously, if it's her doing these things herself, or if someone else is controlling her actions."

"Such as?

"Frank."

His eyes widened in surprise and he rose halfway from his seat on the chesterfield.

"You think he's back?"

We both nodded.

"Here?"

"Possibly. At least in England," I said. "Perhaps even living at Windsor."

"You don't mean Gwenna herself."

"Unfortunately we do," said Kieran.

"We have no absolute proof, just little things only we would notice."

"Such as episodes of odd behaviour, and the way she looks at us with Frank's eyes. I'll never forget those eyes, no matter how many times I go through death and life."

He looked at Kieran for a long silent moment as he sat back down, then turned his eyes on me.

"And you agree?"

"Neither of us will ever forget those eyes," I said.

He thought a moment before he spoke again, tugging at his beard as he did so, contorting his face into a strange caricature of himself.

"And this is the woman Duncan plans to marry."

"What?"

The question came from both of us simultaneously.

"She didn't tell you? They're planning to wed this fall."

"It seems there is a lot she's not telling people," said Kieran. "Well, at least we know she's not to be trusted, whether Frank has returned to us or she's some new threat on her own."

Somehow the idea of our little sister marrying Malcolm's youngest brother did not bring us the joy it would have under different circumstances. Something was in the air all right, but its fragrance was less than sweet. Duncan had always seemed to us the worst of Malcolm's family, an opportunist at best, a coddled brat at worst, who had his nose in the air and a chip on his shoulder at the fact that he had three brothers ahead of him in line for the throne of Scotland. The fact that our sister would marry such a person would have been somewhat of a disappointment in itself, despite the glorious alliance it would make between our nations. The suspicions of what lay within our sister coupled with the idea of them joining forces gave rise to all kinds of nasty fantasies. Malcolm didn't need a direct mind link with us to realise what they were.

"If she had anything to do with Genevefa I'll kill her myself."

The idea had briefly crossed my mind. Eliminating two more heirs to the Scottish throne before they were born would have been Frank's style, but then Frank had been an old professional in his early sixties, an intelligence agent, a mercenary perhaps, possibly even a hired assassin; Gwenna was a Novice Priestess at best and less than a third his age. There was no way she could have the power to pull off anything like that through magic, and she'd been at Windsor when Genevefa had become ill. I told Malcolm of my thoughts in the matter and watched his face relax, although his posture told me he was still ready to carry out the threat he'd made.

"Relax," said Kieran as he rubbed Malcolm's back. "Remember how you felt a few moments ago. Wrap yourself in that feeling and let it flow through you."

The fact that he believed it was possible has me worried. Perhaps we should look into this a little deeper.

Shhhh. Not while I'm touching him. This isn't the same kind of mind link as our thought talk, but I'm afraid he might be able to picture what's in my mind. Let me calm him first. We'll discuss this alone later.

I joined my brother in trying to pull the anger and the hurt from him once more. When he was stabilised we took him down another level and let him sleep on the chesterfield until morning, the first real sleep he'd had in over two weeks.

We were the ones who couldn't sleep, and we didn't feel like burdening Eleanor with our worries, so we did the next worst thing; we decided to do a bit of Sherlocking over the nets. It might have gone better if we hadn't have had such a difficult time trying to decide who was Watson, which after awhile became extremely funny to us as we had still to decide which of us had been Kevin David Watson, let alone John Watson. It deteriorated into a specious discussion as to whether or not Dr John Watson was of the Tyrell line, and if so, had he been in some small way associated with the Order, and totally decomposed into notes for a further adventure of Watson and Holmes in which the good Doctor had to off his long-time friend, a descendant of an illegitimate line of George III, because he carried the sacred blood of Kings and neither Victoria nor any of her children were quite what the Land had in mind for a sacrifice.

You should have seen what we did to Macbeth later that night; Duncan and Lady Duncan (Gwenna) became the villains of the tale. The problem was it all fit too well, and we didn't wish to alarm Malcolm.

As literary artistes we were horrid; at detectives much better, for we continued running the nets until daybreak. We were close to falling asleep when the data returned: Gwenna Windsor had booked passage to Inverness on the sleeper coach from Euston Station four days before Genevefa's illness, had rented a vehicle at the station and had returned it here the day before. She had not been as smart as Frank, though. She had used her own name, even had the transactions debited to her account instead of paying for it in cash.

Little sister had a lot to learn before she could play many-times-great-uncle's games.

Of course we could have been wrong. There was nothing except her being in Scotland to remotely suggest her involvement in a death which, though caused by a rare condition and even more rare complications causing two miscarriages and subsequent haemorrhaging, had been ruled natural.

Why was it we were so eager to paint Gwenna as a villain? Was it because there had to be one in our lives? Because we could not accept the loss of Malcolm's family either? Or was it because we had truly recognised that malefic force within her, peering from behind her angel face with the cold eyes of Sir Francis Eddings-Roth?

"If we find her guilty in this we will know for certain," Kieran said.

"And if we find her innocent?"

"It still doesn't mean we're not right about her on the other matters."

The knock at the door went through us like a bolt of lightning. We had been so intense about our project we had not considered the possibility of another human stirring this early. Kieran answered it while I tidied up around the computer and stuffed any notes we'd made into the inner pocket of my jacket.

It was Derek, looking very upset. His eyes were red-rimmed, and he clutched a handkerchief tightly.

"You've not been to bed."

"No. Sorry. We got involved with Malcolm and lost track of the night."

"Is he still in here with you?"

"He fell asleep on the chesterfield."

"Well, perhaps he needs a bit more sleep then. I'm sure the news will keep until he can bear it better."

The edge on his voice was jagged, as if sheer will-power alone kept him from bursting into tears on the spot.

"What news, Derek? What's happened?"

"I don't know how to break it to him. So much has already happened, his wife and the babies she was to bear him, and now his brother."

The feeling started at the pit of my stomach, a churning, sick feeling which made my knees tremble as it shot up my spine and made the small hairs at the base of my neck stand on end.

"Which brother?" I asked. "And how?"

"Alexander. He and Duncan were rowing your sister around to the front of Dunskaith, that old ruined castle on the Isle of Skye, and the coracle they were in somehow ripped on a sharp rock or some such, took on water and sank. Don't worry about Gwenna though, she and Duncan are all right. They made it up the rocks to safety, but poor Alexander slipped and hit his head on the wet rocks. They managed to drag him up after them, but the blow to his head had done its worst."

Gwenna again. What was she doing on Skye?

And Duncan. An unholy alliance, to be sure.

"Queen Alexandra wants Malcolm to return home as soon as possible. You can speak to him better than I."

Chapter Thirteen

*P*erhaps sleep had been the key to his control, for he handled the news far better than we would have expected. Not a tear was shed, not a curse uttered; he merely closed his eyes for a moment, drew in his breath slowly and deeply and let it out again in the same manner.

"Are you all right?" Kieran asked.

"Yes. I was just saying goodbye. I have not forgotten the peace he has found, nor will I forget him. I loved Alex, probably more than either of the other two. He was a dreamer, a scholar, a fine poet and a fine man. Much finer than any of the rest of us. There was nothing mean or cruel about him. He brought joy to us all. He will be missed."

For a moment he looked as if he would lose his composure, but it remained, strong and steady as his faith in the Gods and his memories of lives and deaths past and of what lay beyond this world.

"Mother is going to need help with this one though. You will come home with me, won't you? I'll need your help to bring her through it."

We assured him we would and began packing, suggesting to him that perhaps we could all spend some time at Stonehurst as soon as obligations had been taken care of. His eyes lit up immediately with the first real sign of life we'd seen from him since he'd been at Glastonbury. Stonehurst held strong and dear memories for all three of us, ones we wouldn't mind reliving for a few days at least.

The funeral was monumental and cold as the snow piled up around the grave site. Representatives from nineteen nations were present in that frozen Spring to honour the memory of the Scottish Prince and give comfort to his grieving mother, many of whom had barely returned home from the funeral of her daughter-in-law. Alexandra, looking more each day like Queen Victoria in her long black wool gown and hat, received each of them with stoic dignity and grace as inwardly her heart crumbled at the second loss in so short a time.

True to his ancestors and his own poetic heart, Alexander had insisted his burial be at Culloden, beneath the Scottish flag which flew over the end of the battlefield the Jacobite troops had occupied in 1746. It seemed fitting to him that there should be a flagbearer there for all eternity. It was ironic for us as heirs to the English throne to stand there in that place, looking past the Scottish flag to the English flag which had flown over the other end of the battlefield for centuries, realising how many had died that day on both sides for such a bleak piece of land. Still, it was the land which took them back, not caring what colours were on the rag of cloth they waved. When Scottish independence came again, as it did from both the United Kingdom and the European Commonwealth, it was won with a pen, not a sword.

We had been Stuart as we had been Windsor. Our blood had served both sides in turn, and despite the separation of the nations it was the Land beneath them both we served.

Neil?

What?

We've died here.

I know. I feel it too, as if I should remember more...but I cannot..

It's a different feeling, and I don't know why.

Or how.

It's a good feeling.

I have a question, but I'm not sure it will ever be answered.

What?

Were we on the same side?

What?

Were we on the same side?

Why?

I just wondered if it was one time one of us didn't kill the other. Perhaps we died together fighting side by side. At least I'd like to think so.

I put my hand on his shoulder.

So would I, Anmchara. I don't think we could ever kill each other in anger, even if we weren't Awake at the time.

The service was long and we were all nearly frozen when it ended. We rode back to Inverness with Malcolm, our teeth chattering behind our stiff upper lips, which unlike his had no moustaches to keep them warm. Not a kilometre down the road Malcolm pulled a silver flask from the pocket of his overcoat and offered it to us.

Our first thought was to recoil, having met with unfortunate circumstances due to a similar flask some generations back, which prompted a chuckle from Malcolm.

"Now I thought you knew me better than that, lads, although I will admit the container does look a wee bit like the one you described to me. I swear to you what's inside is pure uisquebagh, with nary a drop of anything to dilute it."

I thanked him and took a sip from the proffered flask, expecting the smoky bite of a single malt Scotch, but found instead a smooth, light Irish. A look of pleasant surprise upon my face must have betrayed me because a glint of triumph twinkled in Malcolm's eyes.

"I thought you'd appreciate it," he grinned. "You've changed my evil ways, all right, corrupted me with your own. Mum would kill me, a Prince of Scotland drinking Irish Whiskey."

Neil?

It's Bushmills all right.

My brother's hand was quick in relieving me of the flask. As he took his turn I could feel the golden warmth spread throughout my body, and toes which had before been numbed with the cold began to wriggle in their boots with feeling once again. Kieran passed the flask to Malcolm and smiled contentedly.

"What we need is a proper wake for Alex," he suggested.

"Alex would have liked that," Malcolm said after a long draw on the flask. "Let's wait until we get to Stonehurst, though, and do it up right. Just us and Eleanor. Just the ones who understand."

"Fine idea." I said. "But I wasn't certain how you'd feel about having Eleanor there now that Genevefa's gone."

"It is because Genevefa is gone that I think Eleanor must be there. Otherwise we'll just become a threesome of lonely old sots. She has the grace to keep us honest in our waking him, to make sure it's not just a matter of getting splattered and feeling sorry for ourselves. Not that I don't already. Gods, I'm glad we have a driver. Here, have another before I drink this all myself."

Kieran took the flask, then passed it on to me.

"You know," he continued, "I think Alex would have understood us and all of this. He was very sensitive spiritually. I think in another day, in another time he would have become a monk if he'd had the choice."

"Perhaps in another day and time he was," Kieran suggested.

"Perhaps."

"How do you think your mother is holding up?" I asked.

Malcolm shrugged and did that pulling thing with his beard, this time running it backwards up his face with both palms as he thought.

"As Mother, or as the Queen?"

"Both."

"It's hard to say. Alex was everyone's favourite. It's going to be difficult for her as a mother. As Queen, however, she'll be all right. She has the sympathy of the world with her right now, and that will surely help her in the upcoming inter-European economic talks. God's teeth, do you really think Gwenna and Duncan did this to him?"

We'd all been skirting around the issue since we heard the news, afraid to place blame where it so obviously seemed to be because of the possible repercussions in both kingdoms. Hinting about Gwenna's seemingly impossible connexion with Genevefa's death was one thing; no one outside of the three of us would have any chance of taking it seriously. This, on the other hand, was a definite possibility and accusations in the matter would bring scandal to both families and nations whether or not they were ever proven to be true.

Murder and High Treason, which the murder of an heir to the throne certainly must be, had been reinstated as capital crimes over a century before, and the traditional method of execution for royalty was still beheading. Lurid scenes of the block at the Tower of London came to mind, the headsman's axe or sword lopping off the heads of Mary Stuart and two Tudor Queens, and various Enemies of the Crown under Kings in both Mediaeval and Renaissance times. Lady Jane Grey had been about our sister's age, her husband about the age of Duncan when they had been executed. Our own remembrance of Charles I still dizzied and disconcerted us.

Beheading was not, as some imagined, a humane and quick way to die. Give me a sword through the heart any time, but leave my head upon my shoulders. Consciousness does not disperse as quickly as supposed, and there is a disoriented confusion, a nauseating dizziness confounded by the fact that there is no stomach attached from which to retch. Sensation does not depart from the limbs as in other deaths in an orderly fashion, being drawn back uniformly from the extremities to the centre and set free in one clean burst of conscious spirit through the heart or head, but is cut off from the consciousness before it can be gathered in, which is why so many ghosts are the victims of decapitation. Those who cannot transcend this phase remain earthbound, seeking the rest of themselves before they can go on.

Yet perhaps it was what this malignant spirit needed. We had tried to cut Frank off from us by making certain not a drop of his blood nor fragment of his flesh ever polluted English soil, yet his spirit was free to return. Had it been left earthbound in the first place he could have done no worse than frightening the occasional tourist.

Still, we had no proof of anything. We had not even had a chance to speak with them yet, as they were still in hospital in Sleat from hypothermia. Their initial testimony to the local constabulary had been taken as fact and no inquest had been ordered. The fact that they had possessed motive, access and opportunity for murder never crossed the minds of anyone. Homicide was bad manners, something in which royalty did not indulge.

Yet it was the question of belief Malcolm had begged. Did we really think, did we believe Gwenna and Duncan had killed Alex, could have been responsible for his death, either directly or indirectly?

"Yes," I said, not wanting to meet the questioning or pain in his eyes.

"Yes," concurred my brother, touching my mind with his.

But why are we so certain and how are we going to prove it?

Why? Because it has a familiar stench to it, subtle yet direct, like the almost painless sensation of a very keen knife slicing Richard from ear to ear as the strychnine convulsions became unbearable. How are we going to prove it? I don't know.

"Then I'm afraid that makes it unanimous. We have to stop them."

"We have to do this by the book this time," I warned. "Remember what happened last time. Don't let them know we have any suspicions, just do a bit of quiet sleuthing and turn anything we find over to the proper authorities. They've been afraid to investigate because royalty is involved. If royalty brings them the evidence they need that will let them off the hook."

"Meantime?"

"I think we're all safe for awhile. Another incident on the heels of these last two would draw too much attention."

I drained the last of the flask and screwed the top back on. No, I didn't think we'd be easily taken in again. The memories of our past entanglements with the spirit who had once been Francis Eddings-Roth were all too clear. Had there been less trust in a close friend and more an instinct of survival and the courage to question whether or not it was truly time for the King to die our lives might have been strangely different. We had not been Awake then; the spirit who had become Kevin of Cornwall had only been three years old when Frank had lured Richard from the house in which his pregnant wife lay into the stormy night to his death, telling him it had been his duty to die then for the Land. When Richard hadn't agreed he'd poisoned him, giving him the choice of a slow painful death by the strychnine he had consumed from the flask or the blessed speed of the knife at his throat. Choosing the knife, as Frank had guessed he would, was somehow equated with giving his consent to the act, and in Frank's twisted mind had sanctified the act and had left him without guilt, though he had managed to kill the other three men who had been with them and to dispose of the bodies.

Richard, however, had not merely gone away, but been reborn a few hours later as his own son, Stephen, later to Awaken with Kevin and die with him. Had Richard been allowed to live into his fifties before he had Awakened, the relationship between Kevin and him, though close, might have been a bit more tempered by age and we might not have died together and come back as we were, neither of us quite certain of our identity.

It didn't bother us often, but for some reason, possibly the amount of uisquebagh in my system, it gnawed at me that day. The sense of I and Thou between us was absent, and for the first time I regretted it, regretted the definite "I did so-and-so" or "Remember when you did such-and-such and then I did something else". I think it was the lack of definition in our lives which bothered me, and the fact that in the next life we'd still be sorting this one out.

"Malcolm?"

"Yes?"

"Can you tell us apart?"

"It takes time, but yes. There are subtle differences in your posture, for one, in your mannerisms. He tends to play with his fingernails, whereas you are more apt to scratch your head."

I pulled my hand back from my hair self-consciously.

"He also lets you talk more than he does, sort of prods you on to talk for both of you."

He's got us there.

"Can you tell which of us belongs on which end of the sword at the end?"

"At the end?"

"Oh come on, Malcolm. There are three of us Awake here now. When the number reaches five either Kieran or I will die. We don't have to pretend it's not going to happen. We're quite prepared for it, and between us it doesn't matter which, but we figure it might be important to the Land."

"No, I hadn't forgotten. I just don't like to dwell on it. No, I can't really say which of you was which before. It's as if you've taken a glass of whiskey in one hand and a glass of water in the other, poured them into a pitcher, and are now trying to separate them by pouring them back into the two glasses. There's so much of each of you in the other that I cannot see how it would make a difference."

"That's what I was afraid of."

"Can Eleanor not tell you apart?"

"No. But then she couldn't once before, either, at least not in the dark," Kieran smiled.

Malcolm turned a shade of red which clashed horribly with his hair and beard.

"Oh I see. It's that way is it? Well I'll not tell a soul."

"Just as you didn't before when we staged that duel."

His mind went back through the ages until he had the picture as clearly as did we.

"She was there then?"

"In the carriage."

"I remember. Therese. And she remembers all this?"

"She does, and more. She's counted several, including World War I. She was sister to one of us, wife to the other."

"And last time? Was she the Duchess of Cornwall?"

Kieran nodded.

"She was Stacy, who knew exactly what was going on and urged us forward. She rang us up to say goodbye before we left Stonehurst."

"Then gentlemen, I have a confession to make. From about a year after her son was born until the day that life ended for me I was her lover."

If he had burst into flames before us we could have been no more surprised. Our memories of him as Owen Watson were very distinct, and part of them included a very pronounced relationship with a young man named Jack Beaudry, another of our Companions.

"But you and Jack…"

"Jack was a beautiful young man and I loved him very dearly. I don't think I could ever love another man as much as I loved him. He died in an airline crash on his way back from Rome. He'd gone to research a paper on architecture for a University level class. It had been a weekend trip, so I let him go with about six others the tutor thought were special students. I had no idea it would be the last I would see him."

He seemed as shaken in the telling of the story as he was over the recent loss of his wife and brother, perhaps more so.

"Well," said Kieran "He'll be along again any time now. At least you have that to look forward to."

He gave an odd little smile and daubed at his wet eyes.

"So much has happened since to both of us. It will be a strange reunion, that's for sure, but I am looking forward to it. You know it wasn't Jack's body that was so important to me, it was the person inside, and I'm fairly sure that person hasn't changed all that much. After his death I spent a lot of time with Stacy. We'd always gotten along, and we were both very lonely. One night we both had a bit too much to drink and comforted each other right into bed. I was surprised how much I enjoyed it. I guess I've been surprised ever since. I wonder if she remembers that part."

So did we.

All in all Stonehurst seemed to be shaping up into an interesting holiday.

Chapter Fourteen

Stonehurst was the same bleak grey stone Stately Home it had been in our great-grandfather's day, set against the same storm-painted sky. The stables had gone unused for two generations and were badly in need of repair, but other than that the differences were minute; the trees, all but the old oak, had grown substantially. It still carried its trunk-scorching, limb-blasting lighting scar as a badge of honour, commemorating the day the Lady first made Her pact with Stephen. The portrait of Kate O'Conor, for she had been as yet unwed when the picture had been painted, still hung above the fireplace and the mountings where the Sword of the King had once hung. In its place crossed rapiers were now fixed, the two with which our adolescent duel had been fought.

It was our property now, given to us by Father when he decided he no longer had the inclination to take his holidays outside England. Travelling was something he did as part of his kingship; when he sought relaxation he seldom went further than Bath, unless it was to visit us at Tyrell House. It was a place familiar and especially beloved by us, filled with memories of both joy and sorrow, one continuity which had stretched through three generations of our memories. Richard, Stephen and we had always loved the ruggedness of the place; it made a statement about the force of human will working upon nature but somehow blending with it, and the downstairs library was still the equal of any outside a museum or the Archives of the Order, real books of paper and leather and ink, not electromagnetic images or microfiche.

The only thing the place lacked was the warmth and wisdom of Mrs Stewart, the housekeeper who had been with the place for generations. In her stead this life brought us Molly Ross, a fortyish woman of great organisational skills and domestic talents, but with all the personal warmth and grace of an ostrich. Indeed, she resembled that bird in many ways; she was long of neck and leg, walked with a peculiar up-and-down gait, and peered out over her black-rimmed spectacles with intensity. Mother had apparently hired her sight unseen from her references and saw no reason to let her go because of her personality quirks, for after all the place was vacant most of the year and the woman was a treasure when it came to its upkeep with dramatically reduced expenses.

We did what we felt best about the situation; we kept her on but sent her off on holiday whenever we used the place.

Eleanor had arrived before us and managed to fill the place with the scent of freshly baked bread, one of the most perfect scents known to mankind. That and the fire in the study did much to warm up the natural coldness of the place, as did her smile. By the time we had put our bags away there was a grand tea laid out for us, and we all found it welcome.

We watched the fire as we indulged in delicate sandwiches made with that still-warm bread, biscuits and various sweets and took within us the soothing warmth of the tea, one of the more civilising influences of British culture for centuries, and we talked.

She seemed not at all surprised nor embarrassed by Malcolm's memories of her. It had been a good relationship for them both, yet one based upon friendship more than the grand passion of the heart which is why they never married each other. With each of them the grand passion had died with their mate, and neither wished to bond that way again, yet both were young and in need of companionship. The memories were still warm between them, especially so since Genevefa's death had put Malcolm in the same situation as he had been then.

For the first time he broke down as he embraced her, all the pain, all the grief of both human experiences undermining his resolve and that part of him which knew from experience how impermanent death really was. She cradled him in her arms as a mother would cradle a weeping child and soothed away his sadness until he stopped sobbing and relaxed.

"It's all right," she cooed as she stroked his ginger hair. "Tears make the eyes brighter. You have to let go now, let her go on. Don't hold her here. Remember the old saying that if you love someone you must set him or her free? If that person loves you, he or she will come back to you. She can't come back to you unless you let her go. The same for your brother, though I think the tears are for your wife."

"For her and the unborn children."

"They were never born, so they never died. They just stayed on the other side. You're a Priest. When you were consecrated as a Knight you were also consecrated as a Priest. You know all of this. The Lady has Her own reasons for these things. When you took your oath to Her and the King you gave up your right to question Her."

He nodded and sniffed back his unshed tears.

"You're right of course. I know better. Of all people, I know better."

"By the way," she asked, "how is it that Queen Alexandra allowed you to take an oath of fealty to another crown?"

His attention diverted, he plunged headlong into the answer with no further show of sorrow.

"It was within the family's right to do so, and none of the others were interested. With Robert there to succeed her I was expendable, and it's not as if Scotland and England have a chance of going to war in the near future, or I hope the far future either. We're for the most part the same blood anyway."

"But what if something happens to Robert?" asked Kieran. "He and Margaret have no children yet, though they've been married what, ten years?"

"Eleven. No, I understand completely. They've talked about various fertility options, even tried a few of the drugs, but to date all they've had was the one stillborn child six years ago. It seems to be a curse upon our family, Genevefa's miscarriages and Margaret's stillborn and now lack of fertility."

"There's a clinic in Edinburgh, if it's still there. If it hadn't been for that clinic Stephen and Stacy would not have been born. If the problem is Margaret, then you could technically get an egg donor; as long as it's Robert's sperm the child would continue the line."

"Yes, it's still there. They know about it, but Margaret refuses to go there. She wants a child of her own body. You know how women can be."

The remark seemed to distress Eleanor who abruptly began picking up the dishes and carting them off to the kitchen. It had been a casual remark, not intentionally implying anything, but she seemed to take it as a personal insult, an action not like the Eleanor we were used to. Kieran excused himself to follow her and find out if she were all right.

"Is it something I said?" asked Malcolm.

"Perhaps, but nothing you said should have produced that reaction. Kieran has a way with her. He'll find out."

"I would hate to think..."

"Don't worry. I think the basic point has been made, Malcolm, that if anything happens to your brother Robert and your mother then the King of Scotland would be the vassal of the English crown. That should not be."

"No. It should not. It would start up too many hostilities. We're fine as allies, on a level as peers, but most Scots would resent being vassals to England again. Of course it would mean you could effectively make Stonehurst the seat of government if you wanted to."

"I doubt either of us would want to pollute it with politics. You did use that word in the plural, didn't you?"

"What"

"'You'."

"Of course."

"For a minute there I thought you'd had a breakthrough as to our roles."

His laugh was of one syllable.

"No such luck. I serve you both either way. One dies, the other becomes king. I suppose right now I am technically in the service of your father, though we know he's not the one."

"Still, what would you do if Fate brought the crown to you? How would you reconcile yourself to the oath made to the Lady and us with the oath made to your own nation?"

"They are the same oath. Although technically I am bound to your crown, It is in spirit I am bound only to the one of you who dies, and am released from that vow as soon as the act takes place. My binding otherwise is to the Lady, and as the one who wears the crown of Scotland is bound by that crown to the Land , so he is bound to Her. I am Awake, but I know I am not the King, merely the Knight. I shall not wear the crown of any nation while you live. More important would be the question of what happens to you if my little brother decides to eliminate me next."

Neil, I've found out what the problem is.

What then?

It isn't what Malcolm said, exactly. It's the topic.

What?

The whole topic of fertility.

Why.

You'd better be sitting, Anmchara.

Why?

It seems we're pregnant.

The feeling was one of vertigo. The whole room spun around me as the pit of my stomach began to swarm with small winged creatures. I had not heard him right, surely.

What?

Preggers, Anmchara. We're going to be the father of a little princess before the year is out.

"What's the matter, Neil?"

I had not realised the look that must have crossed my face, confusion, delight, worry, elation, love, fear, surprise, all there at once. The complication alone to not only our lives but the lives of all who touched on ours was overwhelming. There would have to be a royal wedding, and soon, but which of us should be the official groom? It had been a lot easier in the years before the Monarchy had been restored. Richard had been handfasted to one sister and legally wed to the other. Now handfasting was considered a legal marriage if not declared null at the end of a year and a day, and definitely binding if there were children produced in that time.

In either case the child was our heir. If I should marry her and be slain as King she would succeed me. If Kieran were to be the one who died I would inherit and she would follow me at my death, unless there was a male child born.

Should I tell Malcolm?

The problem was that the wedding of an immediate heir to the throne was a big thing which took months to prepare. We needed a wedding very soon.

We're on our way back to you now. Wait for us.

"Nothing. Just a touch of dizziness. Probably too much sugar in the tea and biscuits and all. I'll be fine."

Of course the fact that Gwenna had already announced her engagement to Duncan's family and was expected to announce it officially to ours and the public as soon as was deemed decent after Alexander's funeral was a reason to have a quiet secret wedding of our own; we did not wish to trip over the toes of our beloved sister, for weddings were traditionally set up for the glory of the bride.

My mind raced. We could do it right there at Stonehurst that night. Stephen had married Emma by his own hand in the very room in which I stood. Either of us could marry Eleanor by the same right, and with Malcolm as witness too, but which one of us would she marry?

Which one?

It was obvious she'd been crying too when she rounded the corner with Kieran. The trails made by her tears had streaked her makeup slightly, and her smile was a bit insecure. She clung to Kieran's waist as he clung to hers.

"Sorry. I didn't mean to make a scene. I just sort of broke down with all that talk of pregnancy, not knowing how to tell you."

"What?" asked Malcolm.

"Oh. It seems the love of our life is going to have our baby."

Malcolm showed the same surprise that I must have shown, quickly realising the problems this scenario had created for all concerned as well as the benefits.

"Well," he said when he was able to speak, "which one of you is going to make an honest woman of her? Or shall I?"

The idea had never entered our heads. We did not know for a moment whether or not it was in jest for a full moment.

"Is this a proposal?" asked Eleanor.

"Well, if neither of them is gallant enough to propose, I certainly won't let you down. It's not as if we were complete strangers, my dear."

She smiled.

Kieran and I fell to our knees before her, simultaneously asking her if she would marry us.

"Yes", she answered, without indicating which of us she had accepted.

"It would really be easier if you married me, my dear. If you marry the King and end up sleeping with his brother you could be beheaded for High Treason."

It was an old law, one which had seen the end of Anne Boleyn, and could be invoked by anyone, including Gwenna.

"If I should marry the brother of the King and become the mistress of the King, what then?"

"Then they would both be very lucky brothers."

"And if I should marry them both and they both become King?"

"It cannot happen," said Kieran. "We've been through all this with Derek and Robin. Parliament will ultimately ask one of us to step aside, for the good of the nation. The succession is already a problem. How much more of a problem would it become in the next generation?"

"Even if your children had the same mother?" she asked.

It was a question we'd both played with since before we'd met our Eleanor.

"It won't work," I said as gently as I could. "We understand, but the people of England wouldn't. We may be a Pagan majority, but except for the Beltaine festival when anything goes, most of the folks out there are still conservative when it comes to home, family, children, and above all, sex. They would understand a King who has a Queen and a Mistress on the side; that's been the nature of things from the beginning. They would not understand one woman and two men in any capacity."

"So one of you takes the crown and the other takes me."

It was a simple, logical statement, made more simply and logically than any woman under such an emotional burden could have been expected to make. She said it flatly and without the emotion we knew lay just beneath the control. Such a woman had the makings of a true Queen.

Neither of us could answer her directly, for we knew too well the answer and knew the decision we made that night would be binding on us for as long as we both lived in the bodies of Kieran and Neil.

Which one of us, Neil?

I was wounded by you once already, nearly killed. Perhaps that was the sign that I am the one to die.

Perhaps.

Could you do it, Kieran? Could you kill me?

If it is what I must do, I will have to find a way.

We must at least attempt to settle this tonight. If I become sole King my being with her as your wife will not jeopardise either of you. You will succeed me, and our child will succeed you. That would be better for the child, not having the pressure of ruling under the hand of a Prince Regent, which you would undoubtedly be anyway. Too much room for political intrigue with a child on the throne. Think of what our little sister might pull then.

You're right of course.

Do you think this is easy for me, Kieran?

You don't have to kill your twin.

Consider Eleanor and the child payment for that in full.

He withdrew from my mind with a sigh and turned to Eleanor, taking both her hands in his.

"Lady, will you do me the honour of becoming my wife tonight and allowing me to claim fatherhood of our child?"

She looked at him and then at me.

"You've chosen the crown?"

"It was not from lack of love for you. I just believe I am the one destined to die. I was the first to remember Stephen's life, and I took the wound at my brother's hand which almost killed me years ago. It may have been the sign we've been looking for. I will never love you less, nor will this change anything between the three of us, but our child must be protected as you must be, and it will be a lot easier if Kieran makes you his Queen upon my death than if I do so while I live."

She kissed me as if she thought I would die when she stopped, a kiss which mixed sorrow with happiness yet promised even more. Her lips were sweet and warm and I felt my body begin to tremble at the thought of the delights they had created. No, I would give her up in name only, and though our nights together would have to be discreet, they would probably be even more appreciated because of the subterfuge.

"I accept, Kieran," she said. "Or is it Neil?"

Chapter Fifteen

*T*he ritual was simple, as simple as it had been when Stephen had taken Emma as his wife before the same fireplace on a Samhain Eve so many years ago, although upon that occasion the Gods alone bore them witness and Emma had been possessed by Lady Sovereignty Herself in the guise of Britannia. On this night both I and Malcolm witnessed the rite as Kieran drew his rapier from the pair crossed upon the mantelpiece and upon it swore his oath to Eleanor, who answered it with her own. Malcolm, however, had the only objective view, for I joined with Kieran within his body and his mind, watching through his eyes and hearing through his ears as the vows were taken, looking into the eyes of the woman I loved as deeply as did he. The words came from his heart and mine also, for my oath, though unspoken upon my own lips was to her, and every inch as binding upon my soul as was his verbal pledge binding upon his.

We were one at that moment, as we had always been, yet that very moment was to begin our separation. Malcolm and I congratulated them, then he retired to one of the guest rooms, and I went to the upstairs room which had been my great-grandfather's, leaving them to consummate the marriage in private by the fire.

Why are you leaving us?

I could not ignore his voice within my head.

Privacy, Anmchara.

There is no need.

Yes, Kieran, there is. Tonight of all nights. She is your wife before the Gods and before the Law. It will never again be exactly the way it was.

No, Neil. She was our wife, our Lady from that first night in the cave. She was ours together centuries before that. We three were happy. We can still be.

Later, perhaps. But tonight she is your wife, to be alone with, with no one watching, no one caring if you spend the night or when you leave her side. Get used to being alone with her. The world will see you as married. What we can manage later is between us, but it must seem to the world, at least for now, that you are the only one in her life. There must be no scandal about the child.

Will you at least link with my mind?

No. Not tonight. Give her my love, for it is that love which insists it must be this way, for both of your sakes and that of the child. May it be wonderful for you.

We love you.

I know.

Try as I might to shut out their lovemaking Kieran kept throwing images at me. The touch of her, the taste of her, the delights I knew so well, all flooded my senses. I felt her soft breasts cradled in hands I knew were empty, and wet hot kisses upon my lonely lips.

Stop it, Kieran. Please. It's only more painful for me this way.

I'm sorry. I reach out to you from habit.

Please don't.

Tomorrow?

Perhaps.

I'll tell her.

No, please don't.

Why?

I have to learn to live alone. I have to learn to be a King.

There were no further attempts to contact me that night, at least none of which I knew. After some difficulty I finally wooed sleep to my bed and let it cover me with its dark blanket of oblivion. Unfortunately dreams pierced the darkness and I found my sleeping self reliving the first night Richard and Kate had loved before that same fireplace, propped on plush velvet pillows, glasses of champagne in their hands.

The heat of her, the sensuous stroking of her gentle hands, the scent of her sweet upon everything she touched, her white teeth nipping me playfully, punctuating the long wet trails her pink tongue made upon my skin, my bonny Kate, my sweet Kate, Kate of the thousand kisses, Kate of Kate Hall, Kate the Bountiful in whose torrent of flaming tresses I buried myself and quivered and quaked with each delicious undulation deep within her. My Kate, my love, my sister-in-law and handfasted Lady, my aunt, my mother, my great-great grandmother...

And then the dream became a familiar nightmare.

They came for me upon a Samhain Eve, Sir Francis Eddings-Roth and his three minions, took me from her side and drove me through the rainy night to the site of the nuclear power plant, trying with all the persuasive powers dear Frank could muster to convince me I must willingly give up my life for the Land right then, right there, at the site of a disaster I could not see, hear, feel, taste or smell. I protested that it did not feel right to me, and although I was more than willing to accept the will of the Gods I did not believe the time or place warranted it just yet.

His voice was as smooth as oil as he bade me drink from the silver flask to steady my nerves, to take the chill of the storm from my bones, and I accepted the drink. So real it was to me, the pain which followed, the convulsing in my stomach and limbs from the treacherous fluid I had ingested that even in the dream I welcomed the choice of the quick knife at my throat to end it with a quick rush of warmth spurting to the ground.

My life fled, a spark of light hovering in the darkness, remaining long enough to touch a companion spark emerging from the hapless form of another of Frank's victims, the youngest of the men who had been in the car with us. In that brief instant there was recognition, attunement, and the knowledge that our meeting was not the first, nor would it be the last time. Then he passed through the torn Veil to remain awhile and I returned to Stonehurst, to the body of my own son, Stephen, and meshed within that flesh as the birth process began.

From there the scenes went back in time, though not necessarily in order. We stood within a ring of stones, dressed in the garb of Rome but with Celtic torcs around our necks, myself and he who is now my brother, with three white-robed druids. One of us had a gladius in his hand and plunged it into the other. The only pain was the breaking of the slayer's heart as the one he loved above all others died slowly in his arms.

The King stood against the old oak in the forest, receiving the arrow in his chest with immeasurable joy as his dearest companion stood quietly at his side, cursing himself in shame for not having the self-confidence to pull the bow as had been his given task in that life, yet secretly relieved by the passing of the responsibility, and perhaps more haunted in the end because he had shirked his duty to both the Gods and the King and his great friend was dead anyway.

In ancient Britain the Sacred King sat upon the ground, his back to a wooden pole, as the garrotte was looped around his neck and tightened behind him. His friend sat before him, holding his hands tightly. They smiled, their eyes fixed on each other's until the end, and a part of the King remained with his friend from that day until he joined him in death.

The two engaged in a staged duel on the lawn of a mansion. Three friends were in the crowd to aid the escape of the slayer. After several intense passes one man smiled slightly, gave a tiny nod of his head to his opponent, and did not parry the carefully aimed thrust. His death in the arms of the other swordsman was quick and satisfying, and the slayer made good his escape.

Each was as real as it had been at the time, filled with all the sights and sounds, the feelings, tastes and smells of the original experience, yet in each of the dreams or visions of the years before Richard there were two things which disturbed me. As in previous times the experience remained two-fold. I was still both slayer and slain, feeling the bliss of death and the agony of killing or watching my King die, knowing the loneliness of life without him. My decision to take on the role of King in this part and to give Eleanor to my brother as consolation for having to do the deed had changed nothing. There was still no assurance as to which of us was which.

The second thing was disturbing both pleasantly and unpleasantly, pleasantly because it meant we would soon regain an old friend, unpleasant because it meant all this would have to be worked out sooner. Of the three besides Kieran and myself one now wore Malcolm's face, one kept his face hidden, and the face of the third was beginning to come into view. Another of our Companions was beginning to Awaken.

The dreams ended abruptly as the low moaning in the background, of which I had been dimly aware, rose to a shrill whine which pierced both sleeping and waking consciousness. Unearthly it was, and unbearable, as it seemed to come from nowhere and everywhere at once, turning into a sound somewhere between a shriek and a sob. The dull thump of heavy bare feet down the hall could only have been Malcolm, whose fist a moment later rapped insistently upon my door.

"Are you all right in there?"

Kieran? Do you hear it too? Are you awake? Are you two all right?

"Yes, I'm fine. I'll be out in a second."

Yes and yes. What on earth is it?

I scrambled from the ancient four-poster and threw the down comforter around my naked body as I walked to the door, opened it, and headed with Malcolm and the candle he held down the stairs.

"They're fine, Malcolm."

Not on earth, Anmchara. That's a Banshee if I've ever heard one.

Blessed Mother Morrigan who's dead now?

Someone close to us, I'll wager.

"What is it, Neil?"

"The O'Conor Banshee. I remember hearing it here when Grandfather William died."

"Who?"

I was still partially in the past and had to change gears quickly. "Prince William. Stephen's father. Our great-great-grandfather. Sorry. I've been having old dreams."

"You too?" he asked as we rounded the corner and hit the last three steps.

Eleanor took one look at us and broke the tension with the laughter she found impossible to stifle.

"Look at you. Look at all of us."

We were all four wrapped up like Red Indians in quilts, comforters and blankets, and each of us was as naked as the day he or she had been born beneath it all. No one had bothered to unpack a robe or any night clothes. We, the next generation of Royalty of England and Scotland, looked rather silly to be sure.

The noise picked up again, banishing the smiles from our faces.

"A Banshee, is it?" asked Kieran. "Oh Gods, I'm afraid to switch on the news."

"They won't know for hours," I countered. The death is about to happen within the next few minutes, is happening as we speak, or has just occurred. The media won't be informed until after it's official."

"Sweet Gods, but I am getting tired of funerals," observed Malcolm. "Do you have any feeling for who it is?"

"Maybe Robin or Derek," I said. "They are both up there in years."

"Yes. Most likely. In which case I say farewell with love and commendations for a job well done in this world. Peace and joy until next we meet."

"So mote it be," added Eleanor.

Somehow, though, I think we all knew it wasn't that simple.

"It wouldn't be Gwenna," I continued. "She's in hospital on Skye, but only slightly under the weather from having been in the cold water for too long. Nothing that could kill her."

Neil you don't think...

No, but I fear it greatly, especially after the turn things took for us last night.

Did you have the dreams too?

You mean you actually found time on your wedding night to sleep?

No. I had them waking, with Eleanor holding on to me for dear life each time I killed, each time I died.

"Do we ring up Windsor, or wait for them to contact us?"

"Give them half an hour, then ring them up. If someone's died in his or her sleep it won't be noticed for hours."

The waiting was torture, but necessary. A sleeping clerk might take the call as a prank and dismiss it. After the sun had shown its face would be time enough to clear the air. It was not as if there were anything we could do to prevent the event from happening; once the Banshee had sung there was no way to stop the Coach of the Dead from collecting its passenger. The mythology was just that, mythology, but its truth was just as real. The Banshee, or more correctly, Bean-Sidhe, Lady of the Shining Ones, was the Lady of Death Herself, the Great Queen, the Morrigan, and Her will was absolute.

The communications lines at Stonehurst had always been fairly primitive, in keeping with the idea that this was the place to get away from the rest of the world. Only audio telephones were present, and for the four of us and our manner of attire this was, perhaps, a good thing. I checked the grandfather clock on the far wall; it was almost six. Plenty of time for folks to be up and about there, preparing for the day's events.

I scanned in the number and waited for what seemed an inordinately long time for the ringing to change to a human voice, at least ten sets of double rings. The voice confirmed my fears by its tone alone, shaken, filled with the stress of both fear and sorrow. It was Father's valet, Victor Aynsley.

"This is Neil. Is everyone all right there, Victor?"

I could feel Kieran link with me, unwilling to wait for answers.

"Oh Your Majesty, I don't know how to tell you."

The title he gave me said it all. Victor would have never have called me Majesty if Father lived.

"Tell me slowly and clearly. Exactly what happened."

I could barely hear him through the pounding in my ears as my heart thumped the adrenaline throughout my system. It was worse than I had feared, not just Father, but Mother as well.

No one was quite certain how it had happened. A small group of Argentine terrorists who called themselves Las Malvinistas had somehow gotten onto the castle grounds and found their way to our parents' bedchamber. Once there they bound and gagged both Father and Mother and shot them both in the head, leaving a list of demands for the surrender of the Falkland Islands, or as the Argentines called them, the Malvinas.

Fortunately, security was harder to pass on the way out than on the way in and the four of them were apprehended, although three of them managed to kill themselves in the process. The Yard had the sole survivor of the attack in custody. Other representatives of the Yard were on their way with a special security team to collect us and bring us back home where we could be guarded around the clock until the safety of the nation was once again assured. They would bring Gwenna back from Edinburgh at the same time.

I thanked him for his information and his prayers and told him to take a week's holiday if the police would let him get away, then set the receiver back down with a trembling hand.

I explained it to the others as best I could, with Kieran filling in the bits I'd left out. Oddly, none of us could cry, perhaps from outrage, perhaps from the weight we felt descending upon our own shoulders. For Malcolm it was more likely that he had no tears left.

"Edinburgh," he said at last. "I thought your sister was still in hospital on Skye."

"So did we. Evidently she and Duncan are back in Edinburgh, working on wedding plans."

"Hate to spoil them, my dears," I said, "but between a State funeral and the Coronations she'll either have to settle for a private ceremony or wait more than a year, and Gwenna's not the sort to wait for anything."

"At least we know she wasn't responsible for this one. They have one of the killers."

Kieran's observation was obvious enough. The killers had been Argentine terrorists. Gwenna and Duncan were safe in each other's arms in Edinburgh. How could there be a connexion?

Perhaps I am more suspicious than my brother by nature, or perhaps it was because I had learned from my love of the mystery genre, especially from Dame Agatha Christie, that the person least possible to be the murderer usually is. Still, the dispute between England and Argentina over those little islands had remained unsettled and unsettling for hundreds of years, launching great battles between us several times. It might well have been just as it seemed.

The best we could do for the moment was wait to see what Argentina's reaction would be, and contemplate reinstating the time-honoured practice of hanging, drawing and quartering to deal with the man in custody if he lived to be convicted in a court of law.

Chapter Sixteen

Kieran and I were no longer allowed to travel together for the sake of national security, and separation from him at such a time was more difficult than I could have imagined. Still, it gave us the opportunity to see how far-reaching was the sphere of our thought-talk, an experiment we'd never had cause to try before. I started out before him with Malcolm, on a journey by motorcar and train, and he and Eleanor flew a few hours later. How they managed Gwenna I don't remember, but she and Duncan arrived some time after we did.

Strange, but I don't recall ever really being out of touch with Kieran. Every time I checked in with him he was right there inside my head as he'd always been. There was no distance between us on that level, and I believed then as I still believe that we will never be more than a heartbeat, more than a breath apart on any level.

The journey seemed to take forever, our emotional states being what they were, a mixture of stunned grief at what had happened and anxious anticipation of what was to come. There was really no one with whom we could have communicated except each other, not even Malcolm or Eleanor, who could have understood the nuances of our feelings at that time. Those who remember both death and life see both from a different angle. True, both Malcolm and Eleanor shared that ability with us, but not as twins, sharing perceptions in a way only twins can.

I hope they didn't make one of them watch while they killed the other.

The image had haunted me from the first moment I had heard of their deaths, bound, gagged, and shot to death in their own bed. I could die, Kieran could die. That was easy enough to accept, as we had accepted it so often. It was simple for us; there was no fear in it, and seldom any pain, at least for the one who died as King. But although our parents carried the Blood, it lay dormant within them; they were unaware except by their faith that they would one day return.

I don't think they were really interested in torture, Neil. Just simple political assassination.

I'm just remembering how it feels to watch the one you love die violently. The emotion can be more torture than anything physical.

I saw before me the face of the King as the garrotte tightened, his lips trying to smile as his eyes did, but quivering in their attempt as the larynx was crushed; I looked into the bright eyes of the man before me and relaxed as the sinew bit into my neck. I held the King's hands and felt their strength fade; I released my hold on life and fell into the sea-blue of his eyes.

It's better than having to make it happen.

I remember.

I held him, my left arm around his back and shoulder while my right arm made the arc upward with the gladius; I leaned into the blade as the cold steel ripped through the warmth of my chest cavity. I cradled him in my arms, bleeding and gasping for air with punctured lungs, praying the Gods would take him quickly; I felt the warmth of his arms around me and surrendered my final breath to his lips.

So do I.

The images were bittersweet, filled with torment and peace, resistance and resignation, and above all, with love. This was our way of dealing with death, a way we could comprehend, familiar to the point that we found its contemplation soothing, reassuring, a welcome reminder that no separation is forever.

For awhile I gave myself over to the memories entirely, feeling my brother's consciousness close at hand as together we slipped into the past to share moments we both held dear. I could hear the drone of the aircraft's engines as he heard them, punctuated by the staccato of the train's wheels against the track beneath me, and above it all was the ring of blade upon blade as the swords flashed upon my mind.

Do you think we really might use the rapiers again? I feel as if we've already rehearsed that one well enough to pull it off with style and grace.

It does have a nice dramatic flair, I must admit.

Yes, and we both get some pleasure from it, the sound of steel on steel, the rush of adrenaline, the intensity of it all...

The total immediacy of the moment...

Being totally Awake and alive in the instant where life and death converge...

There was a sweeping exhilaration in thinking about it this time, a mad euphoria, a delicious mania which swept over me in contemplating my own demise under such conditions. I recalled again, not the instance of our boyhood fencing match which had ended in bloody confusion, but the one in distant past where the Land had been so well served. Our eyes met, blue on blue. I took the blade straight through my heart and felt the bliss of perfect love pouring out from me into the world as I left it; I felt the electric tingle shoot up the sword and up my arm as I completed the thrust which set the King's soul free.

Do you feel it too, Kieran?

You mean this?

It seemed to swell as we fed each other's manic ecstasy until the feedback from it became almost tangible and we saw ourselves again as Stephen and Kevin embracing and falling together through the sky.

Why do we resist it, Kieran, either of us in either role, when we have such memories?

Habit, mostly. They memories were not always pleasant after the fact for the one left behind.

But this time you have Eleanor and the child, and you will have a kingdom to run. It will be worth living for, you'll see. And I will never be far from you, I promise.

And in the end we will find each other once again, as we always have, as we always will. You're right of course. Rapiers, by all means. I must finish what I started all those years ago, when we all thought it was but an unfortunate accident.

There's no such thing with us, is there?

No, Anmchara. We are the playthings of the Gods.

And would never wish it to be otherwise.

There was a warm glow of satisfaction, of inner peace and contentment within us both. We had settled upon the end of what we were just beginning, knew the final outcome, and looked forward to it. Whatever happened along the way would be inconsequential to our pact with each other and the Land. No matter how rocky the road before us we could endure it, for the end chapter of this volume of our lives had already been written, and all roads we travelled from that moment forward would lead us to its happy conclusion. If the issue of life and death could be settled so easily, how difficult could anything else be?

The scenery flowed by the window, pasture after hill after quaint cottage after ancient grove, one scene blending into each other like the work of some mad modern painter who had added to his interpretation of three dimensions the dimension of speed. The clattering of the wheels upon the tracks was not regular enough to lull me to the sleep my body craved, for there were other sounds which intruded, the sounds of the train's own echo bouncing from structures we passed, the wind which howled with us as we headed south to England and to the home we'd not lived in for nearly nine years.

Malcolm had dozed off, his head bobbing slightly against the glass as we hit irregularities in the terrain. At least he had the dignity not to snore.

The funeral is going to be an ordeal.

Only one of us needs to worry about that.

No, not ours. Mother's and Father's.

Yes, probably. And the Coronations, but nothing we can't deal with together. Parliament will be surprised to hear we've worked out the succession between us.

If they will go along with it.

Why shouldn't they?

I don't know. I've had a problem with them since Oliver Cromwell did his bit.

All a necessary part of the plan, if you recall. How else do you justify killing the King in a Christian society?

Put together a band of Argentine terrorists.

Sorry, they missed. They got the wrong King.

It's so easy for us. I still feel badly about them. You don't think they suffered any, do you?

No, Neil. Not if the first reports were correct. A bullet through the head is rather quick. They might be a bit disoriented, but at least they're together. We can bear this a good deal better than one of them could have without the other.

Odd thing. We haven't spent much time with them in the last few years, but it was wonderful to know they were always there. I shall miss them.

As shall I.

He was silent in my mind for a long time after that, leaving me to ponder alone why we could be so manic when the subject of our own deaths came to mind yet almost maudlin at the thought of the death of anyone else. Perhaps it was because we were a permanent fixture with each other in our serial immortality, and others, no matter how much we loved them, merely slipped in and out of our lives. They were of great importance to us now, but in two or three lifetimes more they would be but a pale memory.

And then there was Eleanor, who somehow seemed to turn up with relative frequency. Therese, Stacy, Eleanor...how many more times, how many more places? A face beneath an Edwardian hat and coiffure appeared briefly before my inner eyes, dainty features, light brown hair and blue eyes, nose perhaps a bit too sharply pointed for classical beauty, and pearls which dropped from garnet clusters dangling from her earlobes. She stood in a crowd at a train station, Euston, perhaps, or Victoria, awaiting the arrival of someone, a brother perhaps? A husband? Both?

My reverie was shattered by the tooth-wrenching squeal of brakes as the train slowed to a stop. From the car in which I sat I could not see the sign which bore the name of the town, nor could I reason why an express train carrying the new King of England would stop on the way back to the preparations for his parents' funerals.

"What's going on?" asked Malcolm as he suddenly joined the world of the conscious.

"We seem to be stopping."

"Ridiculous. Why? Oh Gods, I hope it's not more terrorists. This is no time for you and Kieran to be apart."

He rose in his seat as the uniformed constable entered our coach and headed our way.

"No need to trouble yourself sir," said the young man.

He was about our age, perhaps a few years younger, new to the job if the fabric glaze still on the uniform and dazzling shine of the brass was any indication, and more than a little flustered at his current assignment.

"I'm sorry, your Majesty. We've, uhh, we've had to make a stop to bring Chief Inspector Dodd aboard. I know we should have been asking your Majesty's permission before we did so, sir... Sire... sir."

He fumbled for his words like a third form boy reciting before the class for the first time.

"Easy there. Don't get yourself all flustered, constable. And sir is just fine. I'm not old enough to be your sire."

He smiled ever so slightly, his round, freckled face reddening all the way to the ears which stood out a bit too far from beneath his sandy hair.

"No sir. I mean yes sir."

"What's your name, constable?"

"Edward Jenkins, sir."

"Well, Edward Jenkins, thank you for telling me why we were stopping. My friend, here, and I were a bit nervous about more terrorist attacks."

"Oh, no, sir. Not on this train. You're well protected here."

"Thank you for such a splendid job. You may go now, and send Chief Inspector Dodd to us when he gets situated."

"Yes sir. Thank you, sir."

He bowed slightly as he turned to leave, turned back once more and bowed again before exiting the car.

"Reminds me a bit of Jack the first time I met him," I chuckled.

Malcolm smiled wistfully.

"Yes. Quite the same personality, easily embarrassed and all. I wonder where he is now, who he is, and how he's taking the, how shall I say it, recall to active duty?"

"I'm sure he's taking it well enough. I don't sense any distress coming from him, do you?"

"No. I guess he's fine. I just worry. So much has changed."

"Between you?"

"Yes. He was a good mate. I wonder if he remembers and how he feels about..."

"About your past relationship? Let me tell you a little story. Once, during the Roman occupation of Britain, Kieran and I were lovers. Our names were Lucius and Marcellinus, although we're still debating which of us was which of them. We met you and Jack and a third Druid at a stone circle and Marcellinus killed his lover with a gladius. The blow wasn't clean, though, and Lucius died slowly, bleeding his life away in his lover's arms. Marcellinus took the last breath of his King into his own mouth, along with some of the blood, which he swallowed in his grief. A few days later, driven by guilt he couldn't bear and quite drunk on cheap Roman wine, he put a noose around his neck, tied the other end of the rope to the top branch of a yew tree, and jumped."

I watched Malcolm's face as he remembered the incident.

"I don't think we ever knew you were lovers."

"Few did. The important thing is that the King accepted it for what it was, love, and thought no more about it. The man who had been Marcellinus, however, refused in subsequent lives to remember the parts of it that had been beautiful. He pushed aside the whole incident as sordid and felt guilt every time any of it popped out in a vision. For a long time it turned into homophobia; he couldn't deal with the idea of two men loving each other, except at a respectable distance. This played havoc with him each time the two of us came back together, for the love between us has always been intense; it builds as the years go by because we never lose it, never forget it. To complicate things further, the Knight, the Tyrell, the one who killed the King felt incredible guilt for having botched his job, for having caused his King pain and not taken him out swiftly. This made him pass his duty on to another when he was supposed to shoot him with an arrow many years later in the forest. He was afraid he'd only wound him and leave him suffering."

"And it was the man in grey who shot him."

"Right. And set Frank up to kill him the second time. The first, with the garrotte had been a matter of necessity. Having the Knight where the King could focus on him was important at that time for the safe passage of his soul, or at least we believed so back then. It's been done without him present at all and the King has returned."

"Richard."

"Yes. At any rate, all this guilt piled up on him until by the last time we were back Kevin of Cornwall couldn't face any of it. He was in denial that they had ever been lovers and very homophobic, remembering only the gladius, the guilt, and supposing the relationship between them had been brothers."

Malcolm fussed with his beard as he always did when his mind was engaged in deep thought.

"And then I showed up, his own cousin, and with Jack as my lover. It's amazing he didn't shun us both entirely."

"No, I think that was what brought him out of it. He saw someone he knew, respected, and loved as a member of his own family and realised you were no ogre, nor was Jack, and how deeply you cared for each other. It was the beginning of his healing, but not all of it. Stephen made him face the truth about their past, showed it to him from the other side, made him feel there had been no pain, only love, and forced Kevin to see the blood on his own face. What he had been carrying around all that time was the guilt of having swallowed the blood of the Sacred King, in short, of stealing from the Land and the Gods. It had been a spontaneous reaction with no thought of sacrilege, but until that moment that single reflex of swallowing the liquid in his mouth had been a blot upon his soul."

"And it's no problem any more?"

"None. We're free, both of us. Love is what counts, not what shape it comes in. That little bit of blood didn't matter. What he didn't remember, what the grief had kept him from feeling, was that he did have a part of Lucius within him already, a part which would stay with him until death released them both."

"And Jack?"

"I have a feeling there will always be love between you, no matter how it is expressed, and no matter how it is expressed it will be just as real as it was last time. Don't worry about it. Just accept it however it manifests this time."

Well put, Anmchara.

Hic et ubique? How long have you been eavesdropping?

Long enough. Eleanor just wanted me to tell you she misses you, and she just dreamed about an incident at a train station, late 1800's or early 1900's, waiting for us.

Lovely. Tell her I confirm that. I saw her there a few minutes ago. How are you two doing?

About the same. We should land in about ten minutes.

We're running late. Had to stop to pick up some Chief Inspector.

Malcolm's face turned from mine to watch the scenery roll by, yet by his reflection in the glass I could see most of what was going on in his mind. He weighed my story and my other words against his own current and past needs and loves, the recent loss of Genevefa, the Awakening to a consciousness in which she was but a small bright ember, her warmth still within him but fading into shadowed memories. His long-term comprehension had taken precedent, the vivid recollections of those whose lives had entwined with his again and again over the centuries, whom he loved, lost, mourned and found again each time as the interlace repeated its pattern anew. Each meeting reinforced the pattern, reinforced the relationships, made them as indestructible as the human soul, though in each instance there was room for learning, room for growth, just as in one whose recall of the past is fragmented at best, or at worst non-existent.

"You two grew up knowing all this, didn't you?" he asked after long moments in which the click of the wheels against the tracks was all that broke the silence.

"Partially. We knew we were a part of each other, and a part of something bigger. We had bits and pieces. It didn't really start until we somehow re-enacted part of the rapier duel we had fought in...when was that? Eighteenth Century?"

"Sounds about right."

"We started having visions then and connected with Stephen and Kevin later at Stonehenge at the Summer Solstice ritual. From there on in the path has been rather well marked for us."

"You've had years, then. I've had a few months at best and it's still confusing to me at times. The last few times are fairly clear, and one or two in the distant past, but I only get fragments myself of some of the really distant ones. I wonder what...do I dare still call him Jack?"

"That's about all you can call him for now."

"I wonder what Jack is going through."

I was about to suggest it was probably the same thing he'd gone through about four months before when the forward door to the coach opened and a tall thin gentleman in his mid-forties entered our presence. His hair was dark and greying at the temples, and his moustache was quite a mixture of salt and pepper. He was in plain clothes, suit, overcoat, shoes and hat all in shades of brown, with a tie in a shade of russet which could hardly be considered conservative. His eyes were blue and familiar as he walked up to us with a mixture of concern and mirth and nodded confidently, searching our faces and eyes for a sign of recognition.

"Chief Inspector Everett Dodd, your Majesty, your Highness. Well, it looks as if I'm the only one not born to the purple this round, gentlemen, but by the Sword and the Rose and the scar I bear it's good to see you both again, although I'd rather have had a better occasion call us together."

Malcolm just stared at him for a moment, searching beneath the greying hair and the wrinkles in his face, into the eyes and deeper still. Tears he had spared for so long did not spare him but spilled from the corners of his eyes as he rose and clasped the older man to him.

"Jack. I know it's not Jack anymore, just as I'm no longer Owen, but by all the Gods and Our Lady's Grace it's good to call you that just once more."

"Keep calling me that if it suits you. It's my second name anyway. But I suppose I'd better get used to calling you Your Highness."

"Malcolm is fine."

"As is Neil."

Kieran, you're not going to believe this.

You've found Jack.

How did you know?

Still eavesdropping. Flying is so dull when you're planning to remain inside the aircraft. Give him my love.

Chapter Seventeen

On the fifteenth day of April, in the year 2155 of the Common Era, beneath clouds of blackest black and deepest grey, Geoffrey and Katherine, King and Queen of England, were laid to rest with their ancestors at Windsor Palace. The Gods saw fit to hold back the rain on that bleak day until after the single coffin which held them both had been covered with earth. They had lain together in the same bed for every night of their marriage, at last dying there. It seemed heartless to deprive them of each other's company for all eternity by sealing their remains in separate boxes; even Gwenna could not bear the idea. The coffin had been especially built for them, and their bodies arranged so their hands joined together as they had been so often in life.

We knew it was only the mortal shells we buried, knew the freedom of their spirits, still we did this in a tribute to the love they had always shown to each other, to us, and to their nation. They had been much beloved by their subjects and would be mourned for a long time. With that in mind we took it upon ourselves not to settle in at Windsor, but to arrange for the grounds to be open to the public while we went on to the Tower of London, still the best fortified castle in Europe and the place Stephen II had intended to use as his palace had destiny not caught up with him before its restoration had been completed. Gwenna and Duncan opted not to join us at the Tower but instead took the penthouse at Sinclair House in Kensington until the official investigation could be concluded.

The apologies from the Argentine government had been received before we had arrived at Windsor. They denied any complicity in the terrorist activities, vehemently disavowing knowledge the group even existed, and though they would, indeed, prefer to have the Malvinas recognised as their territory, they would rather see them forever called the Falklands and acknowledged England's last colony than to have Argentina's honour impugned in this matter.

This left a list of demands, three dead terrorists with no identification, and one living prisoner claiming to be Alejandro Locasta, an Argentine national who insisted on prisoner of war status. Argentina disagreed with his claim, however, showing him to be neither born nor nationalised in that country according to any of their records, and denied a state of war existed between our nations. We were free to do with him as we wished to the extent the Amnesty International Accords would allow.

Kieran expressed a desire to deal with him as Guy Fawkes had been dealt with, so we could read auguries in the man's bloody entrails, but as much as the idea of a good hanging, drawing and quartering appealed to me I doubted we could justify it in the eyes of the world. If the world should blink, however...

Jack had his hands full. We found ourselves calling him that despite our attempts at his given name, Everett. Jack he had been to us before, as Jack he had impressed us, and Jack he would always be, or at least until another name impressed us as much. With Malcolm it had been different; we had known him for years as Malcolm before he Awoke. We had no trouble with the name.

Yes, Jack was up to his eyelashes in police work, yet he had managed to get himself assigned to us through his connexions within the Yard who were also within the Order, and we confirmed our desire to have him with us as a personal liaison. His work on the assassination became secondary to his work with us, but he still devoted several hours of his day to what he could do from the Tower, most of which consisted of using the Interpol uplink installed in Stephen's day and modified the day we moved in.

The Tower was familiar territory to us all, each of us having lived and died within its walls on more than one occasion. The changes over the years had not marred the original spirit of the place, though the Roman wall which had originally defined its area had fallen during the last century's earthquake and its loss left but the bottom row of stones upon which it had stood and a commemorative plaque which hardly did it justice. The ravens had been back for nearly a hundred years, this time of their own free will and with their wings unclipped, a sign that we were doing something right at last. The yeoman warders once again lived within the castle walls pretty much as they had through the generations before the sale of the place to German bankers in the mid twenty-first century when the entire area had been converted into hotel. When Stephen II had restored the place they returned, but their ranks came to be drawn from the Order of the Sword and the Rose, as they are to this day.

It was three days after we moved into the White Tower, the oldest part of the castle, that we contacted Parliament about the succession, informing them of Kieran's marriage and expectations of a child and our decision that I should reign alone with him as my heir designate until I should marry and father a child of my own. It was another three days before they responded: Gwenna had herself been secretly wed to Duncan of Scotland on the eve of his brother's death, was also expecting a child, and contested our succession to the throne on the grounds that our birth was unnatural and unprecedented. Since there was no clear-cut method of determining which of us had the right of primogenitor, let alone which of us would actually wear the crown on any given occasion, we should be set aside in favour of her. Further, since by ancient law a king wounded in the thigh could not reign, we should be excluded, for we had been joined at the hip, and we had been "wounded" by the surgeon's laser when we were separated, although there was no scar which remained. To top it off she added that the scars we bore for the Order made us "blemished" and unfit to serve, we had both been branded by those scars as King-Killers and so there was a conflict of interest in either of us being crowned, and that we had an unnatural love for each other which was an abomination to not only our Gods, but the religions of all who called themselves English.

No wonder they had chosen not to stay with us at the Tower.

We would have laughed had Parliament not considered the charges worthy of investigation.

The odd thing about Parliament in the mid twenty-second century was that no matter how liberal its members were when it came to passing bills and running the day-to-day functions of the nation, when it came to issues of the Monarchy they were all to a man and woman totally conservative. What charges, if any, were true?

There was no way to tell which of us had a definite right to claim the rule of primogenitor. Had the obstetricians who delivered us tilted the head of one of us a fraction of an inch higher as we were removed from our mother's womb, and had it been noted in the reports, it might have been taken as a confirmation of firstborn, but such had not been the case. Even if it had been, there was so much trouble identifying us before we made the decision as to which of us was which that such a crucial moment would not have carried much weight, for who could remember which of us had been which then? Point one was conceded to Gwenna.

Point two suggested that we might try to defraud the people of England as to who actually wore the crown, insinuating that we might trade off, one of us pretending to be the other. This we had no intention of doing and answered the accusation by saying so. As for point three, "wounded in the thigh" had been a polite euphemism for castration, and we would be glad, we said, to prove to Parliament as they sat or individually in private that we were both still anatomically whole. I am told this delighted at least three female MPs and one openly homosexual male MP, but the offer was rejected in favour of an affidavit from our physician attesting (pun perhaps intended) to our wholeness. I suggested to Kieran that Eleanor could also affirm (pun definitely intended) that we were both fully functional and had no problem performing a Great Rite, discounting her last point that our love of each other was somehow "unnatural", but I reminded him that our relationship with Eleanor was not what most folk would consider natural either.

As to the whole "wound" concept, the incision was not a wound at all, but a surgical procedure to correct, not create, a deformity, and the hip was hardly the thigh. The wounds we had obtained by sword were wounds of honour, such as Edward Longshanks, most of the Henrys, and at least the first two Williams had. Would they have denied the throne to any of them, especially William Rufus, himself a Sacred King? As for the oaths to the Order, they were to the Lady and the King, not to the Order, and since we both carried the Tyrell blood as well as the blood of Kings our sacred duty was doubly confirmed, whether it be to kill or be killed. Since the matter had already been decided between us at any rate, it did not concern Parliament, for the Land would be sustained, and an heir had already been provided, with one of his own on the way. By tradition I was already, at the death of my father and with my brother's consent, King of England, and for the added security of the nation in these troubled times I decreed the first Coronation would take place upon Glastonbury Tor at Summer Solstice, the second at Westminster Abbey at Lammas.

A week later Parliament informed us they were taking the matter under advisement.

Our reply this time was not so gentle, especially considering our beloved sister. We suggested that her marriage to a foreign prince without permission of Parliament or King Geoffrey, who had been very much alive at the time and her pregnancy by said prince would compromise the Sovereign status of England should she become Gwenna Regina; she, not we, should therefore be excluded from the line of succession to the throne.

Her reply was direct, and to us. The child she carried was not Duncan's. She had been impregnated by artificial insemination at a clinic in Edinburgh with a frozen embryo, the sperm and egg donors of which had impeccable lineage: our great-great grandfather Richard Windsor and his mistress/sister-in-law Kathleen O'Conor. She, in effect, carried the very much younger brother of Stephen II and Anastasia, Duchess of Cornwall.

We wondered if Mother and Father still lay as we had left them.

"And she calls us unnatural!" thundered Kieran.

"It's all perfectly legal," commented Jack." A bit twisted, I'll agree, but not legally incest and there are enough generations in between that it would hardly produce a genetic abnormality had it been so. It's been done before. A man in Carlisle had been plagued by the obsession he would die at an early age, and persuaded his wife that they should have embryos frozen in case she ever wanted a child after he was gone. He died soon after, just as he had predicted. She was impregnated with one child in this manner but decided against any more. The embryos remained. His granddaughter, a woman living in Edwinstowe, was so taken by a portrait of him and the story that she bore her own genetic great uncle, hoping to see the same likeness produced in him that she had seen in her grandfather's portrait."

"And did she?" I inquired.

"Close, but no closer than any two brothers who are not twins. She eventually died, having never married, leaving her entire estate to the lad."

"How do you know these fantastic stories?" I asked.

"Scotty Taylor, the lad in question, married my daughter, Anne. They're living up in Edwinstowe, if you want to speak with them."

Malcolm looked at Jack with new interest.

"So you have a daughter."

"Two, actually. Elaine, the other one, emigrated to New Zealand about three years ago to study Maori art. She's quite the artiste herself, you know."

"You and your wife must be proud."

"I am. Betty passed on several years back."

"Oh. I'm sorry."

"Don't be. We had a good life together. I'm sorry to hear of your loss, though. You didn't have the eighteen years we did."

"No. Nor the children. But perhaps it is all for the best. Yours are grown, and you are relatively free, as I suppose the King's Men must be if they are to truly serve him."

It was true, for the Companions needed to be able to come and go at the King's wish, unencumbered by the pressing needs of family. In the old days, when knights were frequently away for long periods of time this had not been a problem, but in a modern society which expected home and family to take precedent such a style could be too restrictive, especially if either the King or his surviving Companions were forced into exile or death.

If Gwenna won the contest for the crown, such exile was a definite possibility for us. With Malcolm in better grace with his mother and elder brother than Duncan, we might all retreat to Scotland and live at Stonehurst, technically since the reign of Stephen II as much a part of English soil as the Tower, but lands owned privately by Kieran and me, deeded as such by Father, and irrevocable by Gwenna. If the death of the King was called for and we were unable to cross back into England, the grounds of Stonehurst would do just as well as a killing ground, although I had always expected it to be back at Stonehenge.

Cumbria isn't far from the border, Neil. There are a lot of stone circles up there: Castle Rigg, Long Meg and Her Daughters, Swindon, all beautiful. I'd be content to die in any one of them.

Perhaps you'll get that chance. Perhaps I'll come back and slay you in twenty-five years or so.

Now that's a comforting thought. I've always wondered what would happen if we'd worked it out wrong this time and I was the one intended to die. Will you promise me that?

If it will keep you alive to carry on after I'm gone, I will promise you that; may the Gods allow me to carry it out.

Even if we are right this time I hope you will.

Why?

It seems fitting somehow.

If we're right this time you won't know it's me, and I won't know either. It will be an act of regicide, like the assassination of our parents, not the sacrifice of the Sacred King. It will be an act of hatred, not of love.

You're wrong. I'll know you. There have been other times we've recognised each other.

But we didn't act on them. We didn't kill each other. We just knew, and shared the memory fragments we were allowed to see.

Promise me that much at least, Anmchara.

If it's within my power.

Power. That was what it was all about. For Gwenna it was the power of the Crown of England, yet although she could wear the crown the real power was something she could not use but only pass on to a male descendent. The blood within her was shed monthly, woman's blood. It could create life within her body, but it could not heal the Land. As a woman she was venerated, for she could be filled by the Presence of the Goddess in a way no man could, but the Lady was the Land; She did not die for it. That duty belonged to the God, the Young Lord, the lover of the Goddess who impregnated Her and shed His life's blood in Her service, to be reborn of Her again.

It was that macrocosm which expressed itself in the microcosm of this world. Both Lady and Lord were immortal, though the Lord gave up his physical form at times, as we did. We had impregnated Eleanor, the Lady's Priestess, and would one day return through our descendants, as we had always done, no matter how distant the relationship. Serial immortality, we called it, the same immortality shared by those who slept and did not Awaken to their totality.

The big question to us was how much did Gwenna remember? We wondered exactly what had been triggered in her the day Kieran's sword very nearly ended the debate about the succession before it had begun. Was all this merely a reaction, or did she know, consciously, of her past misdeeds?

It was something which seemed to fade in and out of her. At the funeral she had been the soul of sorrow, weeping uncontrollably as the coffin had been lowered into the ground. Duncan, too, seemed upset by it, comforting her so closely we should have imagined they were already husband and wife. But why should she choose to give birth to the child of her great-great-grandparents instead of one she and Duncan created together? There was no sense in it. Others had a much closer claim to the throne should ours and hers fail; our family abounded with cousins of this generation, and both of Father's brothers were still alive. Uncle Edward was next in line after the three of us, and his brood, and theirs, then Uncle Julian and his children.

It made no sense to us.

There was nothing we could do but wait to see what Parliament would do next.

Or what Gwenna would do.

Chapter Eighteen

*T*he Tower was everything Windsor Palace was not; its dark foreboding corridors were our history as much as England's, and though it seemed to others a place too sombre in which to make a home, to us as to our great-grandfather the whole shadowy aura of the place was peaceful and comforting, unlike the garish golden baroque flourishes of Windsor.

The Tower was older by centuries than the castle from which our family had taken its name, and touched on mysteries which pre-dated even the traces left behind by Rome, mysteries to which we were heir in a way which could not be contested. Within its sturdy walls we were surrounded by death. It had always been with us, always on our minds, reinforced by the chain of unforeseen bereavements which had plagued both us and the Scottish court in such a short period of time. So much royal blood had already been spilled, yet it was not the right blood, the Sacrifice the Gods had prepared for Themselves.

Each day we walked past the spot where the boy-King's blood had been poured by James Tyrell. The place had called to us since our first visit there as children. We had known its history then, at least the official version, yet even at that age we had been aware there was more, and somehow it concerned us directly. Fragments of memories had returned like phantoms to haunt us each time we had passed by the Bloody Tower, although the feelings they had impressed upon us were not of terror but of sorrow. Finally, one day we made the short pilgrimage to our own past, hoping to understand it more fully. We climbed the stairs to the small, dark room where Edward V and his brother Richard had met their end.

We were our own ghosts as we sat upon the bare wood floor gazing at the slit of light which streaked across it from the narrow window set into the four metre-thick stone walls. Kieran's eyes met mine and he took my hands as we began the backwards flight through time, letting the scene play out within us once more as it had occurred that June night in 1483.

The young King knew Tyrell was coming for him, waited anxiously to be liberated from his cell in the only way he could be freed. The ravens had sung to him all day of the welcome fate which awaited him at the hands of his one true friend, the friend who had always been there for him when the time came.

It was in the darkest hour of the night that he appeared with the three others, the Kings Men, ready to ransom England with the King's own blood from the feuds which blossomed with the red rose and the white. The Plantagenet line would end with Richard of Gloucester, the Usurper, and he would be blamed for what took place that night. Edward waited patiently for the key to turn in the lock of his door, smiling at the sight of the fair-haired man who entered the tiny cell, fell upon one knee before his King and bowed his head.

"Arise, my Jamie," he whispered. "There is no need of that between us. We've known each far too long for such a show. Look at me."

James Tyrell looked up, tears blurring his vision of the blue-eyed youth before him, and slowly drew to his feet, wiping his own eyes upon a burgundy velvet sleeve.

"My King."

"Your Edward. Come. Find joy in this night. We serve the Land and you set me free from this cramped cell. Is that not enough to make you smile? The wars which drain the blood of our people will soon be over and the land will heal."

"It will take time. A generation at least."

"So little time in the scheme of things. We must cease shedding our own blood when there are so many others who would shed it for us. We must not allow our nation to grow weak while those who would conquer us grow strong. Let my blood be the end of it, or at least the beginning of the end of these battles. Our Lady cares not for the colour of the Rose, only that it is protected by sword and thorn."

His smile was enigmatic as he spoke, his eyes much older than the thirteen years his body owned, eyes which looked deep into the heart of his friend.

"My Uncle will be greatly vexed that he cannot control my life any longer."

"He would be doubly vexed if he knew you kept the Old Ways."

The lad smiled broadly.

"Ah yes. Truly pious man that he is, he will go to his Christian Heaven and not find me there. We will be far from him, safely here once more in different form, yet we will know each other, as we always have, as we always shall."

Tyrell returned the smile.

"I shall look forward to that day."

"As shall I. But now, my dearest friend, are the others here too?"

"Yes. The cell is too cramped to bring them to you. They await without."

"Good. I was not mistaken in your intent, then."

"No."

There was a long pause as the other boy turned restlessly in his sleep.

"I have no wish to disturb him."

"No. I promise to make no sound."

It was a difficult moment for Tyrell, asking the next question, the one which would lead to the final litany.

"What is your wish in the manner this is to be done?"

"It is of no importance to me. The body will feel no pain. It never does with you. You are good at what you do, my Jamie. Your blade is always keen and quick and sure. Just let me look into your eyes as always as I pass. Feel me in your heart and there I shall be for as long as you walk this earth."

Tyrell nodded, reaching back into the corridor for the flask of wine which began the ritual. He passed it to the King, who drank and passed it back to him. Tyrell drank the warm claret, its taste still heavy upon his tongue as he passed the flask back to the others. He drew in his breath deeply to strengthen his resolve, then exhaled slowly to relax to his work at hand.

"The signs are given," began young Edward in a voice not much above a whisper. "The time has come when I must fulfil the promise of my birth. As the seed is sown, so must the grain be reaped for the nourishment of all."

The litany was familiar, yet trimmed, subtly altered to fit the circumstances. There was no sword to pass between them, merely a long dagger, keenly edged and sharply pointed, which hung at the knight's side. Tyrell clutched its shaft tightly as his part of the litany began.

"Why do you come unto this place?" he began in a voice so low it could be heard only by the boy.

"To give up my life that the Land might be healed"

Edward's eyes were fixed upon Tyrell's, seeing more than just the man before him. Tyrell's voice wavered for an instant, but he caught himself and steadied it as he went on.

"Why do you come unto this place?"

Can you hear me in your mind, Jamie?

"To give up my life that the Land might be healed."

Yes, my King. How goes it with you?

"Why do you come unto this place?"

Can you not feel it yet? The peace, the wonder of it all? Feel it, my Jamie. Feel the joy of it.

"To give up my life that the Land might be healed."

The feeling took him by surprise, for it was warmer, more intense that he had remembered. He had to work to keep his balance as its beauty swept through him. He smiled at Edward with the King's own smile.

I understand.

"Why do you come unto this place?"

Yes. I feel your heart. May it always be as full as mine is now.

"To give up my life that the Land might be healed."

Lady bless you, Edward.

"Thrice asked, thrice answered. And by what right do you claim the honour to be the Blessed Sacrifice?"

And you, my Jamie. We're almost through it now.

"I am the son of Kings, and bearer of the blood which heals. This vessel must be shattered that the bounty within might return to the Land to nourish it and its people."

Be nourished, Jamie. Remember only this beauty, not the ugliness it may appear to be later.

"And do you do this of your own free will?"

I will be quick and true, my King, straight through your heart.

"Before the Gods and of my own free will I offer you my heart's blood. May it run as freely as I offer it."

Catch me as I fall then, and hold me until you're certain I'm gone.

"So Mote It Be, then, Sire."

"So Mote It Be, and may the Gods grant us Their Grace to do this well."

Tyrell embraced the young King as if he had been his own son, no, more tenderly than that, for the bond between them was far stronger. He held him for what could never have seemed long enough, then kissed him upon the forehead as he released him and drew his dagger.

May the Gods keep you safe and filled with that joy you have shown me, my King, my Edward, until next we meet.

I am with you always, my Jamie, by whatever name you are called, with whatever face you wear.

The thrust was quick and true, as Tyrell had promised, and dealt as their eyes still held each other. Edward's smile spread as he felt the dagger unlock his heart, freeing the emotion and the sacred fluid it contained. The same feeling flooded Tyrell as he caught the small form in his arms and watched the light fade from those eyes, eyes which he closed gently, kissing the lids as if the boy merely slept.

Then the only feeling was emptiness.

Tyrell lifted the body of the King, so light, so small, and carried it to the doorway. He set upon the floor as tenderly, as lovingly as he could, retrieved the flask from the Companions in the corridor, and went to work quietly catching as much blood as he could in the container so it might be spilled on the ground of the courtyard, back into the earth of this most ancient hill, sacred to the Old Gods for as far back as any could remember.

There was a noise in the corridor; the other child stirred from his sleep. Without thinking Tyrell reached for his pillow to stifle any scream from those young lips, then realised that once he had begun the process there was no turning back. The grey-blue eyes of the boy stared at him in horror, then as the pillow was moved to cover his entire face he stared no longer at anyone. His struggle was slight; he yielded to the smothering almost as easily as the King had yielded to the knife, but without the knowledge, without the will to give his life for a higher purpose. With the King it had been sacrifice; with the prince it had been murder.

The room tilted under us, spun all around us as Kieran and I clung to each other. The memories had been so strong in that place where it had all happened, so sweet between Edward and Tyrell that our own eyes were wet, so guilty between Tyrell and the prince that we both trembled at the thought. We knew those eyes only too well, had known this all before as Kevin and Stephen had seen it and forced themselves somehow to forget it. They were the eyes of Francis Eddings-Roth.

They were the eyes of our sister.

Whatever she had been, whatever she had become, our own actions had begun centuries before, in the very room in which we sat.

Chapter Nineteen

*I*t was some time before either of us could move or speak, so intense had the experience been, a combination of watching the scene play out before our eyes and living it, both parts of it, all at the same time. The elation, the grief, the heart so full it might have burst on its own unaided by the steel which pierced it, the heart so empty at the end that it felt as if it would implode, and the soul-wrenching guilt at the death of the second child, all of them still flowed within us, cascading over our own temporal emotions and leaving us somewhat less than grounded.

Gwenna.

Yes, Gwenna.

We've wronged her, Neil.

And she's more than paid us back for it already. What she did to Richard when she was Frank.

Fitting, somehow, as that was her name in 1483.

And what Frank tried to do to Stephen.

"Wait a minute," I said out loud. "Listen to us! Frank murdered Richard, tried to murder Stephen."

"Yes. And several others who just happened to get in his way."

"But Richard and Stephen and his father were the King, not the Knight. They had been Edward, not Tyrell. Why would the person who had been Prince Richard who died in the Tower try to kill the person who had been his brother, the King, instead of taking his revenge on the man who had killed them both, Tyrell, or Kevin as he was in that generation?"

"Kevin was only three when Richard Windsor died. He wasn't Awake, and Frank had no way of tracing him. Perhaps he felt a resentment at being abandoned by Edward. Did he even know his brother was dead?"

It made sense. The little prince could not have seen his brother's body from where he lay, and must have assumed Tyrell was rescuing the older boy, intending to leave the younger there imprisoned. When he had been caught in the act, the younger child was murdered to keep him from crying out. His heart had been broken at the thought that his beloved brother would allow this to happen. He had been betrayed by his father who had died, his uncle, who had imprisoned him, and his brother. He had no will to survive. He gave in to the hand which held the pillow over his face without a struggle.

"And so we are equally guilty to that mind which had no idea of what truly transpired here," I concluded. "Wonderful. How do we put this to Gwenna and set it all to rest at last?"

As I said it I knew the answer. We didn't. Things had already gone too far for mere words to go any farther than her ears.

Don't say it, Kieran, I know. It will take more than words.

Malcolm and Jack found us there, still sitting on the floor in very much the same positions we had taken before we had let the timestream wash over us.

"Are you two all right?" Malcolm asked.

We answered that we were, and then had a difficult time proving it. Muscles, locked in the same position for how long only the Gods knew, refused to cooperate with our attempts to stand. Both my feet had gone to sleep, and Kieran found only one of his would support him.

"Oh you're in great shape," chuckled Jack as he and Malcolm helped us stand and remain in that position until the blood flowed once again at the proper rate to our extremities.

"Better than we've been," I said, the past not that distant from my mind. "Remember this place?"

"I'll give you a hint," said my brother. "It was night. We were inside and you were in the corridor."

Malcolm's face contorted in pain.

"Oh Gods. The children. The young King and his brother. I'm glad I didn't have to watch that one. It's hard enough when he's grown, but that one was just a child."

"We heard it though, the whole Litany, and the silence afterward, though you spoke it in such a low voice our ears had to strain to catch the words."

Jack, too, was shaken by the memory.

"Men, it's not so bad, I promise you. We're here, now, both of us, and we just went through it all over again."

My brother nodded.

"When you see it from both sides it's not nearly so traumatic."

But they didn't hear it all, Anmchara, only the spoken part.

The other was private, between us, Kieran. They were not meant to hear it then, nor should we share it with them now.

You're right of course.

"No, not nearly as traumatic as it was to the other child."

Kieran and I related the whole story to them, except for the private exchanges that had taken place between us, ending with our speculations about Gwenna.

"But Kevin and Stephen didn't forget the incident," Malcolm remarked. "It's in Kevin's journal. Don't you remember? It made enough of an impact on both of you, according to the journal, that you had a falling out about it and didn't speak to each other for at least a day and a half afterwards. Emma had to intervene."

We looked at him in disbelief. We had lived through the incident, found it important enough to let it come between us for more than a day, one of us had written it down in a journal, a journal we had both read many times in the course of the last few years, and yet neither of us had recalled any of it until we had confronted it on a personal level this time around. It was almost as if we had been ordered to forget it, but by whom?

"Do you remember what Emma said, or did, to reconcile us?"

"As I recall it was not just Emma. The Lady told you through her to more or less let it be. She had plans, and you had no right to question them."

And the plans, it seemed, had to do with Gwenna.

"What would have happened," Jack mused, "if Tyrell hadn't smothered the other one?"

"The boy would have probably shouted, alarmed the guard, and we would have been caught and disposed of in a very unpleasant manner," answered Malcolm.

But that was just the point: that was the way things usually went. The Companions were generally caught in the end and killed, sent from a world which no longer mattered to them to await the next tour of duty with the King, or to experience inconsequential lives while they waited. Once the King was dead and the blood spilled their job was over, and the spilling of the blood from the flask to the ground outside in this case couldn't have taken more than a minute. What had prompted this sudden worry about survival?

"No, you're right," said Jack after the discrepancy had been explained. We've never been really cautious for our lives afterward. I think if Owen and I hadn't had the bond we did and given our word to look after the Queen and the Duchess we would probably have hit the stones with the two of you."

"What happened to Ian, do you know?"

Malcolm shook his head.

"Not exactly. He left as suddenly as he came. Perhaps the bond between the two of us left little room for him. He stuck around for perhaps a month, then off to Ottawa or Toronto or somewhere across the pond. There were too many reminders for him here. He'll show up again, though, when the time comes."

When the time comes. That phrase had been bandied about throughout the generations we remembered, by all of us. It was a comfort, a curse, and everything in between, expressing no sense of urgency, only a polite waiting period during which we were supposed to prepare ourselves for the inevitable and do as much quality living as we could squeeze into an indefinite period of time. It also reminded me that now we were four, which meant it was doubtful if twelve more months would go by before we would be five, and then shortly they would be four again and I would be...I would be somewhere else.

The thought was not really disturbing, it just, well, it just was there, always in the corner of my mind, waiting to cross it as I waited with a certain amount of eagerness to cross swords with my brother.

Neil?

What?

Let it be. It will happen when it happens.

I know.

You want it too much.

I know. After what we've just been through how can I feel any other way?

How can I?

What?

You may have to really fight me for it in the end.

I will if I have to.

I know. I'm counting on that.

Let's make it real, then.

Are you serious?

Perhaps.

Make it real and let the Gods decide?

"Hey you two. Back to this world for now; if I have to keep you both on a short lead to keep you here I will."

Malcolm always had a way of putting things.

"The point is, lads, that we didn't behave as we normally do."

"It's happened before. The three of you helped the killer get away after the rapier duel," I said.

They looked at each other.

"Yes, we did. But he was dead before the night was over." Malcolm argued.

"But the girl was with him, and the girl was pregnant."

Jack was right. Therese had been pregnant, though whether it had been the Knight's child or the King's neither knew. Still, it was a good cause for self-preservation in either case, for as long as it had lasted.

"I know because I helped her get to safety in Scotland," he continued. "and the child she bore became an ancestor of Francis Eddings-Roth."

We all held our breaths for a moment. It was too much of a coincidence. It was not just a matter of a pregnant woman, Gods knew, because both Emma and Anastasia had been pregnant when Stephen and Kevin had hit the trilithon at Stonehenge; hardly an instinct for self-preservation on the part of the Duke, although Owen had remained alive to see the children grown, and Jack's death that time had been entirely accidental. Besides there had been no pursuit of them in the first place.

No, it had something to do with Richard, the prince in the Tower, something which traced through Frank and was here again with us in Gwenna. The same soul had killed the King before, by garrotte and by arrow, both on sanctified occasions, with the four of us present and willing that it should happen that way.

The fifth had always been male, but did that mean it always would be? What if this time it was not Ian we awaited, but Gwenna?

The very thought churned up the bottom of my stomach, and I realised we had not eaten since the morning meal.

"Do you think we could finish this discussion sitting down to several plates filled with food and glasses filled with something civilised? I'm not sure we can all think well on stomachs as empty as I know Kieran's and mine are."

Kieran grinned.

First sensible idea you've had all day.

Besides, if we don't move around a bit we'll never get the kinks out of our legs.

The walk back to the White Tower was short and quick, and the misty air felt good upon our faces. It was somehow good to be alive there and then in those bodies, young bodies, except for Jack, with old souls. It was the twenty-second century, nearly a full seven hundred years since the incident we had just relived. Six-hundred and seventy-two years to be exact.

I've already thought of that. It is divisible by seven. Ninety-six times the seven year cycle of sacrifice. But we haven't followed the formula exactly in centuries.

I know. I just wondered.

You're looking for signs

I'm looking for excuses.

When the time comes you won't need any. What you need right now is a way to ground. Food will do you good.

He was right. It was easier to think with food in our stomachs and a glass of Irish in our hands. Eleanor joined us, for the matter concerned her as much as it did us.

"Have you thought of what would have happened if the boy had lived?" she asked.

"He would have raised the alarm and doomed us all." Kieran answered. "That's just the point. Ordinarily we wouldn't have cared. Why this time?"

"No, Kieran, that's not the point at all. That's not what I meant. What if he had survived? What would have happened historically, not to you, but to England?"

Perhaps we had all missed that point. Had Richard lived he would have been the rightful King after his brother Edward. How would the death of his brother have been explained? Not so easily. The Old Ways had been kept by fewer in each generation, and the Usurper was not one of them. We would have been dispatched slowly, painfully, unless we could manage to find a way to die in the interim, but then the public would have cast a wary eye upon the goings on in the Tower and the little prince, the rightful King, put there for his own protection. Richard of Gloucester would have had to have been very cautious in his movements. Yes, the child might have survived long enough for a faction to have championed him, not believing he had been illegitimate.

And so the Wars of the Roses would have begotten the War of the Richards, yet another civil war to suck dry the marrow of the people. Bosworth Field might have happened in the same way, but after how much more suffering, how much more blood shed by the innocents of the Land? Perhaps one young life had been their price, sacrificed for them. Two Sacred Kings, not one, for at the instant of Edward's death his brother Richard had become King, though he did not even know it had happened, and then he died, with barely a struggle. No blood had been shed, but perhaps, just perhaps, the blood of his brother had been enough.

The messenger came with a note for Chief Inspector Dodd before we could weigh all the perhapses. Jack read it twice, rubbing his eyes between readings.

"Gentlemen, it seems Alejandro Locasta is, as the Argentine government has claimed all along, not theirs. He is Venezuelan by birth, and Locasta is not his real name. Interpol calls him Carlos Ybarra, but he's also known as Benito Marcos and Joaquin de Sandoval. He's a mercenary, with ties to the petroleum cartels, notably OBP."

OxyBritPetrol. The merger between the two largest petrol conglomerates in the world half a century before had raised some eyebrows to be sure, for their combined forces had made the exploitation of the Antarctic Pool feasible and had kept technology bound to the petrochemical industry far longer than anyone would have predicted. The corporation was almost a sovereign nation unto itself, with an intelligence corps and paramilitary wing larger than that of some of the European countries. Indeed, governments had been both made and broken by them, even before the merger.

"You think he was working for them?" Kieran asked.

"It's a possibility."

"But why? To start a war between us and Argentina?"

"What good would that do for anyone?" Eleanor asked.

"Well, I may be cynical, but war is good business," suggested Malcolm.

"No," I said. "I think it's more involved than that, some wickedly intricate plot. Don't ask me why, but I have that definite feeling."

Neil?

Wasn't Frank in intelligence for BP?

Oh Gods! You're right.

"Jack, have you made any attempts to trace communications incoming or outgoing from Gwenna for the last month?"

He looked surprised at the question.

"Gwenna? Why? You don't think she..."

"I don't know what to think yet. Just please let's be thorough in this, even if it's to make certain she's not threatened."

Before he'd had a chance to say anything there was another message, this time from Parliament. They had decided to allow me to be crowned at Glastonbury Tor. The nation needed a King, and as Kieran was willing to take the back seat to me in this, they were willing to accept me in the role.

Had this news come a day earlier there would have been jubilation unbounded, but with everything else we had to consider all we could do was to breathe a prayer of gratitude to the Lady and hope we could put together a coronation which would not be a target for terrorism.

Well, I guess this makes you official.

Not yet it doesn't.

I will swear fealty to you, Anmchara, with no reservations.

As I would to you.

But no, it's your right.

Suddenly I had my doubts. It had been little more than a coin toss with a fifty per cent chance I'd come out the winner. Would it matter so terribly much if I were wrong? He'd be king, and we could do it all over again that way, but we'd have to wait for my return. Could the Land wait? It had waited for Richard to come again as Stephen, waited for Kevin to be old enough to handle his task.

The Land was eternal, Her sense of time totally different than even the serial immortals who were bound to Her. She would wait until the time was right and then make Her desires known in ways which could not be denied.

Kieran chuckled.

Don't be so serious, Anmchara. Neither of us will get out of this alive.

Perhaps we should just let Gwenna do us both in.

It would have been so easy, but it would have been wrong.

Chapter Twenty

*I*t is in the Celtic nature to take things in threes, and despite the Norman and Saxon blood which ran through us, we were Celts to the core, not just the Tudor Welsh, the Scottish Stuart or the Irish O'Conor, but Cornish, Breton and Manx also by soul experience as well as blood, and roots which went into the soil of this island to a time before Boudicca's rebellion against Rome. It was therefore merely a matter of waiting for the third harmonic to fill in the nature of the crisis at hand. It came within the hour: Gwenna's response to Parliament's decision.

She declared us all illegitimate, including herself, all the way back to Stephen's and Emma's son, Kevin. There had been no witnesses to our great-grandfather's handfasting to our great-grandmother, and no proof that when she showed up in Glastonbury several weeks pregnant that Stephen had fathered the child he later recognised. We were all bastards, all of us, and had usurped the throne. Nor should the crown go to descendants of the Duchess of Cornwall, Stephen's sister. If succession always went to the male ahead of the female, the child in her womb was the only true king of England, for he was Stephen's younger brother, and would be named Richard after his biological father.

"This is preposterous!" shouted Malcolm.

"No, it's tragic, somehow flawed, just like she is," I said as I read further. "And she and Duncan will of course act as Regents."

"Bloody hell they will!"

We put in a call to Derek and Robin in Glastonbury to see what the Archives had on the question, only to have her accusations confirmed. The legal records showed the registration of their marriage had taken place 22 December 2065. Our grandfather had been born 29 July 2066, of a proper weight and length to indicate he had been the product of a full-term pregnancy. Queen Emma had been pregnant when her legal status as Stephen's wife had been registered.

We knew all that. We also knew that the account of her pregnancy and how it had come about was in Kevin's Journal. No matter, said our men in Glastonbury. In this case, no matter how contemporaneous it seemed, the Duke's testimony was purely hearsay and after the fact. He had not even met Stephen at that point, and certainly had not been at Stonehurst when the handfasting had taken place; nobody had witnessed it but the participants, both of whom had failed to leave any proof in writing.

What about the whole story in Stephen's own words, as we had channelled it? Inadmissible in a court of law. Not written in his hand. Impossible to determine if it was really him, although the Order knew bloody well the whole thing was genuine. Even if it had been admissible, the fact that Emma's whereabouts were unknown from the time the union had been consummated until the time she had arrived in Glastonbury left a lot of room to suppose the child may have been fathered by someone else. In fact, the most amazing thing about the whole accusation was that no one had ever brought it up before. Kathleen O'Conor Tyrell, Dame Protector to the infant King Kevin had certainly done her job.

There was little way of proving our case, it seemed, except by digging up Stephen's remains and our father's for genetic testing, as King Kevin's had been cremated and scattered from the top of Glastonbury Tor. Somehow I didn't think either was feasible. The nation was still mourning the loss of our parents, and the grave of Stephen II and the Duke of Cornwall was sacrosanct. Besides, there was no guarantee the specimen they would choose would come from the King and not the Duke, for their bodies had been found so intermingled and bloody it was impossible to tell for certain what had belonged to whom.

We did a good job of it, didn't we?

No regrets.

No. None.

Good. Now what do we do?

Pray that Parliament will never admit to allowing the Coronation of the wrong person in the past, let alone two of them in a row.

We switched on the screen to see if the media had launched into the wicked origins of our family, but found to our surprise no trace of the story. Instead we saw long lines of our people filing through the gates of Windsor Palace to pay their last respects to their late Sovereigns. The Union Jack still flew in defiance of the Abolition of Union so long ago, but its place on the pole had slid halfway to the bottom, just above the black bunting which had been draped beneath it. We were a nation in mourning, and even the press had the decency to wear black.

We turned the channel over fifty-three times, expecting to find some mention of Gwenna's proclamation on at least one station, but it was always the same: nothing, as if her accusations had never been made.

"Official Secrets Act?" I asked Jack.

"Could be. National security is very tight right now. No crowned Head of State and all, terrorism in the midst of the supposedly secure Palace, a possible act of war against this sovereign State...I don't think Her Highness is going to have much to say in public for a few days at least. She will be well guarded, if you take my meaning."

We did. So, it appeared, did Parliament.

The following evening a dispatch arrived from The Honourable Sir Thomas Hubley, our Prime Minister, asking us for an audience. We, of course, were delighted to receive him in the antechamber to our private rooms on the White Tower's second floor.

The antechamber had not existed before the last century; it had been a part added by the hotel, but it suited us well as a sort of common room between our sleeping quarters. Eleanor had been pleased to adorn it with tapestries and heraldic devices which not only warmed the stone walls with colour but also kept the heat in. The furniture was bulky, carved from heavy dark wood to maintain the sombre look of the Mediaeval period we so appreciated. It tended to magnify the raw pomp of the whole building, warning modern politicians of their relatively insignificant place in the order of things when weighed against the bulk of our nation's history. A cheery fire burned against the far stone wall, its smoke cleverly directed upwards and out of the building by a series of vents and fans almost entirely concealed in the stonework. Upon the left wall our rapiers hung between banners bearing our arms and that of the nation; we never moved our residence without the swords since the pact had been made between us. Before the tapestries on the right wall stood two suits of full armour plate, one belonging to the Black Prince, the other to Great Harry, symbols of the ideals of chivalry and the practicalities of Empire.

The cushions on the oversized chairs were of forest green and burgundy velvet; whether anyone outside the Order knew of the significance in that was doubtful. Other chairs were cushioned in velvet also, blue, russet, grey, and black, but they stood against the far wall, two by two on either side of the fire and did not appear to be for general use. The chairs set out for visitors were of the same wooden design, but their seats and backs were of woven strips of leather, comfortable enough, yet pointedly more plain than the other chairs.

They were not new, but left over from the original refurbishments Stephen II had ordered several weeks before his death. For three generations they had sat there unused, waiting for us to make of them what they were intended to be, sort of his modest version of the Round Table. It took us a moment to remember the black chair had been there for the King's sister, should she be so inclined to visit, for it was through her that the blood link between Stephen and Kevin had been originally forged, the sister of the King wedded to his Knight by the hand of the King himself.

Stacy. How we had loved Stacy, each in our way, loved her as Therese, loved her as the unnamed Edwardian lady with the pearl and garnet earrings, and loved her now as Eleanor. She had always been there, somewhere, and deserved a seat with the other fixtures of our lives, for were not the male mysteries always conducted by a Priestess?

I loved her still, with all the passion I had known with her that Samhain night at Wookey Hole Caves, and every waking hour was filled with the perfume of that memory, as real and dear to me as the memories of all my lives and deaths before, yet I had given her to my brother in trade for the glory of the crown and the rose-adorned sword which pierced it, the banner of my great-grandfather and the destiny which went with it. I had seen them wed upon the sword at Stonehurst, and though they had both sworn to me that it was for the sake of the child she carried alone and changed nothing between the three of us, I had resolved in my own heart that it should. From that night forward I had slept alone.

Sir Thomas arrived just before the ancient ceremony of the Keys, and was shown to the antechamber only moments after Eleanor had retired. I must admit my mind and eyes wandered to the door to the chamber in which she slept more than once during the preamble to our conversation with the Prime Minister, but I don't believe he noticed, although Kieran, who sat next to me, would have been blind and no longer functioning telepathically to have missed it, and I soon heard him in my mind letting me know he had not.

She misses you, Neil. We both do.

I must not.

Where is the harm? The child is just as likely yours as mine.

There must be no question of parentage or legitimacy. She must be undoubtedly your heir as you are mine, at least unless and until you have a son.

"Sir Thomas, how can we help you and the good people of England?"

The man was fairly young as PMs went, at least for our century, in his early forties, yet his kinky dark brown hair had been considerably touched by grey, possibly the mark the stress of his first term in office had left upon him. His eyes were a very light brown, almost amber, and hard to read, as was his face. It was an interesting face, the product of two cultures, for his mother had been the favourite daughter of the Indian Ambassador and he had taken in the subtleties of diplomacy with her milk.

He hesitated, possibly weighing the rank by which I should be addressed, as such would be telling as to how the scales were tipping in the matter of the succession.

"Your Majesty," he nodded at me.

Victory!

Perhaps.

"Your Highness," he nodded at my brother. "At least tentatively I may call you that."

I warned you.

"As you know, these are profoundly trying times."

"Yes. We are very much aware of this. They are times which both trouble us and make us grieve."

"Just so. And we of England grieve with you. You have, no doubt, heard of your sister's claims."

Ahhhh, here it comes.

Confront him right back.

"You mean the preposterous notion that we're all illegitimate?"

"That is the allegation, yes."

"I'm sorry, Sir Thomas, but our parents were quite married at the time of our births, and so were theirs."

Nice.

He remained almost expressionless as he looked back and forth between the two of us, then settled his gaze upon me.

"We have no doubt of that."

"Good."

"It is a previous generation which remains in question."

I fixed him with the iciest stare of which I was capable.

"Sir Thomas, has there been any fault in the manner in which our late father or his father before him governed this nation?"

His expression remained unchanged.

"No. They both wore the crown with grace, dignity, and impeccable judgement. There is no challenge to that."

"Then what, sir, is the challenge?"

"Whether or not your grandfather was legitimate."

He had fallen into my strategy.

"Sir Thomas, are you aware of who built the castle in which we are sitting?"

A change of expression: surprise, curiosity.

"William the Conqueror, I believe."

"Correct. He had another, less flattering name, however. William the Bastard. He was illegitimate, yet that made no difference in his ability to take and keep England's crown, nor in passing it to his sons. I suggest you consider that the primal precedent in this case."

A bit of a smile came to the corners of his mouth, but only briefly. He rose from his chair.

"It is well noted."

"I also suggest to you that in these 'troubled times', as you have named them, a strong man upon the throne with another to back him up as heir, an heir who has an heir of his own due at Samhain, seems to me at least to indicate a stronger kingdom than a vacant throne which waits upon an unborn King with no immediate heir himself, and Regents who would discredit the family and possibly have designs upon the Scottish throne as well."

Very nice.

Thank you.

"Your friend and confidant, Prince Malcolm, is, I believe nearer to that throne than your brother-in-law, is he not?"

On the other hand, perhaps you should have left the Scottish throne out of this.

"Yes. He is at present the second in line, until his brother produces an heir. However, there have been unfortunate deaths in the Scottish royal family recently. Who is to say what Duncan's station may be by the time his mother's reign is over?"

"Quite."

He nodded his head and made his move to leave.

"With your permission?"

I rose also, as did my brother.

"Of course. Chief Inspector Dodd should be just beyond the door. He will see you safely outside the gates."

"Thank you. I will sit with Parliament in closed session in the morning and discuss this matter. You will know the wishes of your people as soon as they have had a chance to make them known to me."

With a final trade of bows he was gone.

"Well?" asked Kieran.

"I think he went for it. Now if only Parliament will."

"No, not that. I know how that went. I mean about Eleanor."

Eleanor, the most enchantingly beautiful and seductive woman I'd ever known in any life, whose body had set my soul on fire. My former mistress. My brother's wife. Eleanor.

"You know how I feel."

"That's just it, Neil. I do know how you feel. So does she. And you know how we feel. I will have a full lifetime with her after you've gone to your glory. Is that fair to you? You know she loves you as much as she does me. Is it fair to her to deny her your company just because we gave in to your desire to see us married?"

"Neil?"

I turned around to see her standing before the fire, backlighted in the diaphanous white robe she wore. Her early weeks of pregnancy had made her even more desirable, for there was a gentle softness about her face and breasts, a roundness there and in the curve of her abdomen which had replaced the girlishness with the full bloom of womanhood.

"There is no one here but us, no one to know what goes on in our private apartments. Malcolm and Jack do not disapprove, and they are downstairs anyway. You spoke of precedents to the Prime Minister."

"You heard?"

"Of course I heard. It was wonderful. But the precedent here is just as valuable The pact we made at Wookey Hole Caves was between the three of us and the Gods, Neil, and preceded the marriage vows Kieran and I took at Stonehurst. For months we were lovers. I need you as much as I need him."

I trembled as she approached me and took my hands in hers, my resolve in the matter melting like snowflakes before an inferno. Her eyes looked more deeply into mine than anyone's had ever looked before, anyone's but Kieran's that is, and his voice was soft and loving in my head.

Take her, Neil. Take her while you can. Things are in enough of a mess that there's no way of telling how long we all have left together. Don't deny her love, or the love I have for both of you. Besides, you outrank me, my King. You should have demanded prima noctem at Stonehurst."

I had no choice but to smile at that one, and smiling was the beginning of everything. My brother was right. She was right. I had been living as if I had been already slain. For it to be truly a sacrifice on my part I should have to give up not only my life but all the joys that went with it, and the chiefest of those joys would always be her love. If it was the flesh I was to lose, it should be the flesh which experienced the pleasure of that love.

I yielded, unquestioning, to her kiss, sweet and warm upon my lips, and to all that it promised.

"May I join the King in his bed tonight," she whispered, "or will he enjoy me in my own?"

"I promised to make you a Queen, did I not?' I said, returning her kiss with the passion she had newly rekindled within me.

Will you share in this Kieran?

I already do, Anmchara.

Chapter Twenty-One

I awoke late the next morning feeling as if there existed nothing I could not master. I was the most fortunate of all men anywhere, the very darling of the Gods, and if my death was the price for such happiness, it was a paltry price indeed. Not even the matter of the succession troubled me that morning; in the eyes of the Gods I was already King; if in Their wisdom I should not be seen so by the eyes of man it did not really matter. I'd gone to my death uncrowned by human hands before and the Land had accepted me just as readily.

Or perhaps it had been Kieran.

Well, we'd let Them sort that one out too.

It was about noon when we eventually tossed back the covers and prepared to meet the world, deliciously exhausted from a night well spent. The bedclothes were fragrant with her, making me long for just one moment more before I had to leave their warmth, but even warmer was the realisation that Eleanor was still just as much mine as she was Kieran's. They had both been right all along. The legality of their marriage had changed nothing except the legitimacy of the daughter she carried.

We took breakfast in our antechamber, four of us including Malcolm, and wondered where Jack had gotten off to, as it had become a custom of late for us to share most meals. About halfway through he appeared, looking quite irritated, even anxious about something, refusing to sit and not interested in so much as a cup of tea or coffee.

"It's not bad news from Parliament, is it?" I asked as I buttered my toast, for I could no longer stand the speculation.

"No. Good heavens no. Not that."

"What then?" asked Kieran between bites of orange-yolked eggs.

"Our prisoner, whatever his real name was, the last of the assassins."

"What about him? You said 'was'. Has something happened to him? Has he escaped?"

"I suppose you could call it that. He was found dead this morning in his cell."

Memories of the death of Francis Eddings-Roth spun through my head. He'd hanged himself, supposedly. Well, he actually had done as much, but with a little assistance from his then-wife, Kate, who had first given him strychnine and then offered him the choice between a slow death in convulsions and a quick one. She'd even helped him make the noose, but her involvement had never even been hinted at.

"How?" asked Kieran.

"It seems he choked to death on his supper."

"What had he eaten?" I asked.

"A banger. Tried to swallow it whole."

It was one of the strangest methods of suicide ever to come to my attention.

"Had there been visitors?" I inquired.

Jack shook his head.

"None beyond the usual prison staff and investigators from the Yard. Not even his legal counsel. They all checked out. I'm afraid it really does look like suicide. I can't believe it was accidental. At any rate, the other three managed to kill each other or themselves before they were caught. It's suicide all right."

"Which means?" asked Eleanor.

"Which means we have less of a chance to finding out who was really behind the whole assassination. It will probably be the cause of speculation and controversy for years, like the celebrated Kennedy case in the twentieth century. Oh, by the way..."

He cast a hesitant look in Malcolm's direction.

"Genevefa hadn't been taking any medication her personal physician didn't know about, had she?"

Malcolm's face drained of colour at the mention of his late wife.

"No. Absolutely not. There was nothing wrong with her. She took calcium pills and some typical vitamins you can find at any chemist's. That was all."

"Interesting. That's what Dr Riordan said. It certainly doesn't explain the levels of helotuprine that were found in her blood scans."

Malcolm rose slowly from his chair in disbelief.

"Helotuprine?"

"Yes. In a mild dosage it's a blood thinner. In the dosage she seems to have taken it, it can be lethal. It would explain both the miscarriages and her haemorrhaging."

There was shocked silence, broken abruptly when Malcolm's fist slammed into the table.

"Why now? Why after the fact? If they had found it before could they have saved her?"

The greyness in his face had been replaced by red as his anger and sorrow combined. The tears in his eyes were of both emotions and he made no attempt to staunch their flow.

"Unlikely, Malcolm. I'm sorry. It's a subtle drug, found in some more exotic herbal mixtures. It has been used in the Orient for lowering blood pressure, but it gets into the system slowly, and like lead or mercury it stays there, and can build up to a lethal level unless it is discontinued for about a month between doses. The levels found in Genevefa's blood samples indicated she had been taking the stuff for about three months without a break. There is no antidote, other than letting it wash out of the body naturally."

Eleanor, our lovely Eleanor, put her arms around Malcolm and did her best to comfort him, sitting him down again and rocking him back and forth until he calmed. It seemed a natural instinct for her to soothe pain, just as it had been when Stacy and Owen had mourned the loss of Jack Beaudry. I wondered if the slightest recollection of that time went through their minds as his arms slipped around her waist, yet there was no jealousy in my thoughts, only curiosity.

The thought had crossed my mind as well.

If something were to happen to the both of us do you think history would repeat itself?

Why not? It usually seems to.

"Your brother Robert asked for further tests on the cause of Genevefa's death after the assassination of Geoffrey and Katherine, figuring there were just a few too many royal deaths on this little island we share. There were still some tests not run on her blood, as there had been no suspicion of foul play and no thorough autopsy. That's how they found the helotuprine. Any idea of how it got there?"

"Three months back."

"That would be Yule," Eleanor suggested. "Did she get anything for Yule that she might have eaten over a three month period? Sweets or something?"

"Tea. Someone gave her a tea chest filled with tea from Tibet or Sikkim or Nepal, one of those unusual places. Oh Gods, she drank it every day. I tried it once but couldn't stomach it. I've always thought tea should taste like Typhoo, not herbs. But she had it every morning, even that morning she died."

"Who gave it to her?"

He shook his head and buried his face in his hands.

"I don't remember."

"Malcolm, wouldn't her secretary have kept a list for thank you notes and all?"

"Brilliant, Eleanor. Where is her secretary?"

"Yann went back to Breizh after the funeral, but I'm certain he can be found. Mother's secretary would have his address on hand. Come to think of it, Lady Graham-Douglas may have the other list as well. Mother always wanted to know what was going on. Shall I ring her, or do you want to make it official business, Jack?"

"It already is official business. I'll take care of it. You don't need any more grief right now. Just remember, lad, we've been through worse, and will be again, but there's a reason for it all, even if it isn't apparent right now."

He nodded, accepting what he knew in his heart to be the truth.

"Some days are worse than others," he sighed. "I thought I was over it until this dredged it all up again. I suppose I should just look at the whole picture and stop trying to live one life at a time."

He took the Chief Inspector's hand, squeezed it and sighed, smiling at last.

"It is strange, though, Jack, to have you fussing over me instead of the other way around."

We finished our meal in much better spirits then, and Jack settled down to the task he'd taken upon himself. It took several hours, but at their end the list was in his hand. About half way down it, in Yann's clear, bold handwriting was the notation: one teak and brass Mongolian tea chest filled with assorted herbal teas from Her Royal Highness, Princess Gwenna of England.

"And there is not one bloody thing we can do about it either," remarked Jack. "There is no way to prove she knew the effect of the herbs in question upon Genevefa. The labelling requirements are not the same in Mongolia as they are here, so there would be no warning on dosage, or the fact that pregnant women should not take this."

"But she must have known," Kieran insisted, "Herb lore has been her passion since before she began her priestess training."

"Still, it would be impossible to prove what she did or did not know. For one thing, the herbs in question are not native to these islands or any of the rest of Europe for that matter. For another thing, she did not force Genevefa to drink the tea. Even if she had sent her a bottle of cyanide, unless she forced her to take it or administered it to her by stealth it would not be murder."

"No, wait. Something I remember. Genevefa said that there had been a card in the tea chest. Something about the teas having a beneficial effect during pregnancy, toning the body for birth or something."

The effect of Malcolm's words upon Jack was almost electric.

"Do you think the card might still be with the box? If so, that's tantamount to administering a lethal chemical by stealth."

He shook his head.

"No. I don't think so. I don't even have the chest. Robert's wife was quite taken with it, so I sent it on to her."

"Was there any tea left in it?" Jack asked.

"Some. Not much. Enough for eight or ten pots of the stuff, no more."

"Not enough to be deadly, to be sure. Well, perhaps we cannot pin this to your sister-in-law, but we know the truth; that will keep our eyes open wide for any mistakes she makes from hereon in. Sorry, Malcolm."

"No need. The Gods will deal with her in their own time, in their own way. We have our own work to do, and that is to protect Kieran and Neil from harm. I just wish there had been one witness to what really happened when Alexander died."

The thought was not far from the mind of any of us. Just as Stephen had known for some time of his uncle's treachery but could not prove it, so had Kieran and I sussed out the darkness within our fair-haired sister. The same mark had been upon the two of them, identical in design, and yet for some reason this time the acts seemed aimed against our entire fellowship instead of merely one of us. Why Malcolm? Because as Owen he had thwarted the attempt to kill Stephen in our last round? Or had Gwenna leapt from Frank's rendition of Claudius in Hamlet to Lady Macbeth? Truly, Duncan had increased his chances of becoming Scotland's King several times over since his liaison with her. There were only two brothers between him and the status of Tanist where once there had been three brothers and potentially the two children of one of them.

"Jack, can you get records of any trunk calls placed by Duncan during the last few months?"

Venezuela, perhaps?

Possibly.

"If I can piece together his itinerary."

"He was at Edinburgh most of the time between Samhain and the day Genevefa died, the Isle of Skye afterwards with Gwenna, and before all that he spent time with Gwenna at Glamis," said Malcolm.

How appropriate. No Cawdor?

You've been in my head too much. I wonder if that's where and when they got the idea.

Too much? You wound me, sir.

Sorry. I didn't mean it that way.

I know.

"Exactly what are we looking for?" Jack asked, a little confused at the speed the direction of conversation had changed and the momentum it was building.

"Calls to Gwenna. Calls from Gwenna, if you can get them too. Calls to South America or anywhere those terrorists might have come from."

He was quick to defend what he could not accept.

"But surely you don't think..."

"Jack, that little sister of ours is Frank, and every bit as ruthless as he was before. It's just that this time a sweet, beautiful young blonde face disguises it so well."

He looked back and forth between the four of us, reading the truth of it in our faces. It was there, all right, that truth and the rest we had been ourselves trying to run away from.

"And somehow we're responsible for everything he or she has done."

Chapter Twenty-Two

*I*t was less than a week later, the following Tuesday, if I recall correctly, that Sir Thomas Hubley reported to us the desires of our people. For the sake of the nation's security, my Coronations would go on according to the timetable I had set up, but without the great lavishness accorded to previous Coronations, as the country was still officially in a state of mourning. It reminded me of Act I, Scene II of Hamlet, for as in Claudius's marriage to Gertrude, our Coronations would be "with one auspicious and with one dropping eye".

It would be a tight squeeze to put it all together in the time remaining, but not impossible. Stephen's Coronation upon the Tor had taken place at midnight on the night of Winter Solstice, and preparations for it had not begun until after Samhain. This time it was not yet Beltaine and the Coronation had been set for Summer Solstice at noon, as befit that season. We had three weeks longer, at least, than had been available to the planners of that Coronation, and although theirs had been under the rose and ours would be public, we at least had precedent by which to go. The ritual had been repeated twice already in daylight, with cameras mounted to the top of the ruins of St. Michael's Tower for broadcast of the event.

One of the problems that faced us was who would take part in the ritual. The High Priestess of Chalice Coven, Ruth Margate, was a lovely lady, but she was eighty-two years old and had retired from the position in all but name. The person who had been hand-picked to replace her when she finally did step down in title was our Eleanor, who had been away from Glastonbury for several months and would be halfway through her pregnancy at the time chosen, and who had been seriously realising that she should step down herself and let the group find a new HPs who intended to stay in Glastonbury where she would be needed.

My brother reminded me that it was technically possible for both ladies to function at the ritual, for it called for three. They could both retire afterward. Then who would be the third? Unfortunately, public sentiment would probably call for Gwenna. Would she do it?

"Not a doubt in my mind," said Kieran. "What would make her look more innocent than to be one of the three to officiate at her brother's Coronation?"

Malcolm was concerned for our safety, but Jack assured him it would be difficult for her to get much past a worldwide live audience under the noonday sun, with as much security as would have to be provided for such an event so soon after the assassination of the last crowned heads.

"Besides," he added, "if she's asked to participate she'll have no idea we have her marked. If she isn't, you may have the uninvited fairy godmother from Sleeping Beauty on your hands."

It was agreed then. Eleanor had no problem with the idea; she was very comfortable in her pregnancy and could see no reason another nine weeks would change that appreciably. Ruth Margate assured us she would be delighted to perform the actual placing of the Plantagenet crown upon my head.

That left Gwenna.

She seemed surprised at the call, caught off her guard. Yes, she had received word from Parliament that her claims had been rejected. Yes, she had been disappointed, but understood their political needs to maintain the illusion of the continuity of the dynasty. And yes, for the good of the nation and to heal the rift between us she would act as co-priestess in my Coronation.

As she agreed I could tell there was more on her mind than healing the rift. She would be up to something, to be sure, but we would be one step ahead of her all the way.

She was under surveillance and had been for some time. Although she knew two men had been assigned to her "for her own protection" since the assassination, she never saw the other two Jack had set after her the night we'd discovered her connexion with Genevefa's death. Nor had anyone suspected the tail he had set upon Duncan, only to find Malcolm's elder brother Robert had done the same, convinced of his youngest brother's complicity in the supposedly accidental death of Prince Alexander.

There was something truly mediaeval about all of it, something right out of Machiavelli. Not since the Wars of the Roses had so many shenanigans gone on within one family; not even the Tudors could boast of so much intrigue. Had it begun between us then, or did the beginnings lie even further back, to a time we'd all but forgotten? The Druid who had tightened the garrotte had seemed sane enough; there had been no hatred there at the time, only sacred duty. The grey archer in the forest had actually seemed sad at his task, though later thought projections from Frank had shown both memories distorted in his mind. The incident in the Bloody Tower had been the next after that chronologically, or at least so it seemed to us, although that had left a span of more than three hundred years for which there was no accounting for the whereabouts of any of us.

What if the whole thing had hinged upon a sleeping life, one into which we were all thrown, unaware of our pasts? What if there had been an incident between us and him/her, remembered by only that spirit which now was our sister because of some deep traumatic effect the rest of us did not feel?

Let it be, Neil. The Lady told us that once before. Don't question Her reasons. Just do Her bidding.

What if we can help Gwenna by knowing?

What if knowing would undo all the good we can do by not knowing? Let it be.

You sound like the Old Testament. Here we are, forbidden to eat of the fruit of the Tree of Knowledge.

We are the Old Testament, Anmchara. Older than anything written down. Brother slaying brother.

As it has always been, as it will always be. No matter our blood relationship you will always be my brother.

My point exactly. Think of it, Neil. Why do we always do this?

Because it is our duty.

You can do better than that.

Because it is Her will.

Better still.

I don't know.

You've never asked.

No.

And we shouldn't, anymore than we should ask those things She's told us to leave alone.

Why?

You're asking, Neil.

I know.

All right. What would it do to you to find out there was no reason?

A test of faith, then?

No. Absolutely no reason at all, not even a test of faith.

I was stunned. The thought had never crossed my mind. No reason at all, no reason to give up the continuity of life, the love, the sunshine and the moonlight and the taste of good Irish whiskey, the sound of the wind on the Tor whistling through my hair and often as not chilling me through and through, the sensation of a hot shower restoring me from that cold with its massage of insistent wet needles bringing my body temperature back to normal, the smell of bangers and eggs cooking in the morning...

I thought so. Now what would you think if I told you there was a reason.

I would be greatly relieved.

What if that reason was purely selfish on our part...to ensure our own immortality and return in the bodies born to wealthy and noble families?

That's not always true for either of us. You know that. And you hate the killing. You always have. It hurts you so much you have died yourself rather than face the rest of your life without me.

Ah yes, but then we both enjoy the dying, don't we, safe and secure in the knowledge that it's not the end for us? It feels so good, doesn't it, the shuffling off this mortal coil? We can control the pain, and we have no fear.

He was right. Death had become an addiction to the Awakened, for it gave us a chance to sleep again for a little while, to lose ourselves in oblivion for a time until we next played the game of life and rediscovered what we had known before. Each time the surprise and delight were the same, but each time, toward the end, it had become more and more attractive to knock over the board and let the pieces fall, for in that fall was the most seductively blissful sensation of them all.

Now forget everything you've supposed. None of it is true, though some of it is real. There is a reason, a purpose for everything we do, for every breath we take, for every drop of blood we shed, and it's not for our benefit, but for Hers.

But you were right. It is a selfish reason on our part.

No more selfish than orgasm, for by that pleasure mankind perpetuates the species. Do you think we should have no reward for what we are asked to do?

If it is for Her benefit we should ask none.

Nor do we. She is bounteous in Her way of rewarding us for a job well done, that is all. And for not questioning Her motives and methods.

You mean about Gwenna.

Yes. We may try to stop her rampage through the royal courts of England and Scotland, as we stopped Frank last time, but as for the rest...

I know. Leave her to Heaven.

His smile was wry, the very echo of the way I felt.

Or to Hell.

Neither of which we believe in.

Exactly.

I sighed.

"You two are at it again, aren't you?" asked Malcolm as he poured himself a cup of tea.

"How can you tell?" I replied.

"It's too damned quiet in here, and I know you both must have a lot to say to each other. Just please, once in awhile do it verbally. It's too bloody eerie to be around your private conversations. At least Eleanor doesn't let you get away with them."

Kieran chuckled.

"Sorry. I suppose she doesn't, which is probably why we've taken advantage of her nap to have one. But as I recall there were times you and Jack had a few profound silences yourselves."

Jack stood, slapped the printout of the London Times onto the table and peered over his reading specs.

"Oh rubbish. We never had all that much to say. The 'silences', as you call them were just that, silences, no more. You're trying to make something more to it than there was."

"A bit touchy on the subject, aren't we, Jack?" I asked.

Malcolm burst into laughter.

"Yes he is. Oh come on now Jack, there were silences. We did communicate during them. You were a lovely lad then, and there's no point in you being an old curmudgeon about it now. No one outside these walls will ever know a bloody thing more than they knew five minutes before you Awoke, I promise."

The older man looked down at his highly polished black boots for a moment, shifting his balance back and forth between feet.

"After all, what would Mother think if she knew her second son had once had a love affair with a young man in Nottingham? Of course it was ninety years ago and they were both different people then, literally, but then one can't be too careful now, can one?"

It would have been funny had Jack not had tears in his eyes.

"No," he sniffled. "One cannot."

"Well, it certainly didn't keep Richard Plantagenet off the throne," I said, trying to make light of what was potentially a very emotional experience.

Too late I realised my mistake.

Stash it, Neil. Can't you see the emotions are still there? We've been through this one, remember?

Yes, and Malcolm is still going through it too, but Jack is too set in his ways to admit it out loud.

Perhaps if we were to retire?

No. I have another thought.

The link? It's easy between us, I know, but we've not tried it with them in the same way.

"Jack, give me your hand," I said.

"Why?"

"Just do it. Malcolm, take his other hand and then take Kieran's with your other. Kieran, give me your other hand."

We don't need to touch.

It will amplify things for them. Trust me.

He took it, and we began running an energy ring through them, projecting a feeling of peace and trust so vibrant it became almost a tangible thing, for with each round it made through us it spiralled, winding around us and through us like the coil of copper in a step-up transformer, increasing the surge until we were engulfed by its power. Kieran added the strongest wave of love he could emote, and I completed it with joy, the kind we both knew so well at our journey's end.

Any resistance in its path was blasted by the force which had become undeniable, any negative blockage swept away in its ever-increasing current. When we felt we could no longer hold onto the feeling without losing the flesh, we reluctantly set the energy free to do its good elsewhere, then collapsed together into a pile on the floor.

There was silence between us for awhile; words would have been useless and the afterglow was delicious. I don't know if Kieran had ridden my mind or I had let him carry me, for we were somewhere in the pile together, linked to the point that even thought had become unnecessary. We were. That was all. We were, as we had been before our birth. We were joy, we were love, we were peace, we were trust, we were the pattern She had created and She danced within us.

And She danced within us all.

Some vague time thereafter a body stirred, an arm or a leg, something made of flesh, and the spell was broken.

"Any questions?" asked Kieran.

"No. I'd forgotten what it was like. Thank you."

"Are you two all right with it?"

Jack looked up at Malcolm.

"Yes. I'm sorry. I never really forgot anything, you know. I just didn't remember how to express it before."

"Perhaps that's what silence is for."

Chapter Twenty-Three

Glastonbury was a welcome sight, the scene of so many treasured memories of both recent and distant past. Robin and Derek were overjoyed to see us and to meet our Jack, hoping, I think, to pick his brains on certain details of their own childhood, should such mundane remembrances ever pop into his head. I think we were all sort of a walking museum to them, and the feelings between us were very curious, curious because Kieran and I were at least spiritually their fathers as well as physically their cousins. Relationships for the Awakened were seldom simple.

At any rate, I suppose they had their reasons for curiosity, as we had arrived for Beltaine, and it had been upon the same night eighty-nine years before that they had been conceived upon the Tor, the seed of the Green Man being sown in a ritual of fertility older than mankind could remember.

"Will you be going to the Tor this evening?"

Eleanor asked the question matter-of-factly as we sat down in the chambers we had occupied before as student princes. It was probably her seeming lack of emotion in its phrasing which caught us by surprise.

"Why ever would we do that with you here?" I answered.

"Because you are the sons of the King, Priests of the Lady, and it is your duty to do so," she answered in a tone which seemed to indicate she believed every word of what she was saying.

"But what if we'd just rather stay here and love you?" asked my brother.

"Cheeky. I'm already quite fertilised, thank you. And I don't think either of you would actually mind a romp on the Tor with a lovely young lady who wants nothing more than to jump the flames of the Beltaine fire and then your bones."

Kieran pulled her down to him and silenced her for a moment with kisses, then rose and pulled her over to his bed.

"Oh no you don't," she laughed as she wriggled free. "You'll need to save your strength for tonight, both of you."

She was serious. We were amazed.

"It really is your duty, you know. If it weren't for Greenwood Marriages the blood would have been lost many times over. I'm carrying a girl. What if the Need should come in the next generation and I never bear a son? Would you chance leaving no one in your stead, no male to come back through should you both die and be needed once again before this unborn child herself carries a child?"

That was what it had always been about, the perpetuation of the bloodline of the King, the original concept of Prima Noctem too, in which the King could claim the right to deflower any woman in his kingdom on her wedding night, hoping his seed would be spread far enough to guard the kingdom should his dynasty fail and the next one not have the blessing of Lady Sovereignty to carry on in the bloodline. Too bad that the Normans found a way to pervert the custom into a method for asserting their hated authority over those they had conquered by extending the privilege to anyone to whom they had granted a title. Like any family, there had been ancestors of whom Kieran and I were not proud.

"You're right, of course," I said as I kissed her. "But if we do our duty may we come back and celebrate the rites with you?"

Her smile was a mixture of imp and angel.

"If you truly do your duty to the Beltaine maidens you won't be home until sunrise. If you still have energy left, my darlings, I'm all yours."

She retired early, kissing both of us goodnight in a manner designed to ready us for the duty which called us into town and up the green hill we knew so well, even in the darkness of night.

As we walked from our vehicle toward the Tor we realised how many had come to celebrate with us the season of growth and fertility at the node of the year in which the Veil again parted, this time to welcome life into the world instead of to bid it farewell. Beltaine had become a Masquerade since Stephen's day, its celebrants wearing disguises so no one would know who lay with whom. Much fuss had been made after the fact that the girls with whom the King and Duke had lain had recognised the fathers of their children, and so the horned masques had become fashionable. Ladies, then, began to dress more seductively, appearing in filmy gowns which showed their bodies more upon the Tor than many would prefer to show in the privacy of their own homes, leading the majority of them to wear masques also so their identities would not be revealed along with their boldness.

Due to the popularity of the ritual, celebrated not just in Glastonbury but around the world, the livestock which roamed the fields surrounding the Tor at other times of the year had been penned up that day and night, and the fields raked to rid them of animal droppings and any tourist trash, for actual room upon the Tor was limited and the surrounding meadows would hear the pleasured moans of the celebrants until the dawn.

The path to the Tor had not changed in centuries, up Chilkwell, past the metal gates designed for humans to pass but restricting the movement of the four-footed creatures who usually made the fields their home, through the meadow and up the stone steps which climbed the hill and switched back upon themselves. We could smell the green of the meadow, in its freshly cut grasses, in flowers which bloomed, and knew even in the darkness that the Tor itself was alive with that life-magic of which we were only a small part.

We were fortunate; we were early enough to make it all the way to the top ahead of the throng just arriving in the streets below, some with candles, others with small torches to light the way we knew without seeing. The flickering glow they carried would be swept away by the winds which whipped around the Tor like the breath of a Banshee, but the sight was splendid while it lasted, reminding us of the torches which had lined the streets on the way to Stephen's Coronation.

As the circle began to fill in around the spot upon which he, our grandfather, and our father had been crowned, we felt the energy build within the hill itself, for the White Spring which found its source beneath the Tor carried the charge between the worlds and encouraged its amplification, much as we had amplified our own energies with Malcolm and Jack back at the Tower. We stood together, male and female alternating until there was no more room. The others formed a circle outside ours and waited for the fire to be ignited at the centre of everything, where the Kingstone would be placed in six and a half weeks' time, and upon which I would ache anxiously until the stone should declare me King.

The High Priest was one of ours, for as he removed his shirt I saw that he bore the scar in the same place as all Knights of the Order, and then as all the men responded by removing their own shirts I counted ten more Knights, apart from Kieran and myself. Malcolm was among them, across the circle from us, and Jack not too far away, for no one who could physically take part in the rite was barred due to age.

No wonder Jack had not made a fuss about security; over half the men there had in essence sworn fealty to me at their consecration as Knights.

The High Priest and High Priestess consecrated the cup by plunging a black-handled dagger into the liquid it held, a gesture which always took my breath as I recalled the times it was the King's heart and not the chalice into which the blade had been thrust. A portion of the contents of the cup were poured into a large silver bowl adorned with cunningly wrought stags' heads. The rest was poured over the unlighted wood, an action which seemed odd to many of us until the liquid began to sputter and boil, and we saw the brilliance of the phosphorus flare into its white heat, kindling the wood and setting it ablaze within seconds.

"May the light and heat of passion fill you on this holy night," said the priest as he passed the silver bowl to the High Priestess. She nodded, drank from it, and handed it back to him.

"May Love and Life spring from this night as the Horned Lord brings pleasure to Our Lady and Himself, and may we share in their love and happiness."

She offered the bowl to the High Priest, who drank deeply and returned the bowl to her to pass it on to the nearest man in the outermost circle, instructing the celebrants to pass it around. The High Priest pulled a very familiar looking sword and held it above his head, turning slowly at the circle's centre and casting energy to its farthest boundary and beyond into the night.

"It is all hallowed ground," said the High Priestess as her partner scribed the circle into the air, "all sanctified, for it is our Mother, Whom we love, from Whom we are born, to Whom we bring back the Mystery of fertilisation, and to Whose womb we return to be born again. Let this Circle extend beyond this place, to the hearths and homes of all the Mother's children as Her love extends to them, that tonight may be blessed and blissful to all. So Mote It Be."

"So Mote It Be," we all answered in one voice, breathless as we felt the Mystery begin to unfold once again.

"Every man is the Green Man, the bringer of the seed," began the High Priest.

"Every Woman is the Mother," his partner responded, "in Whose body the seed is nurtured and from Whose body it will spring to give life to the Earth again, and to the Green Man in His season."

The bowl worked its way through the outer circle on back to the inner, as those who had sipped from it were led spiralling inward by the High Priest and Priestess to jump over the fire. It had dwindled from its first brilliant flash to a size which could be leapt by anyone present who had the will to do so, and it seemed as the participants filed by in its direction that everyone had chosen that option.

Hand in hand they approached it, then dropped their hands so the women could lift their skirts out of the flames' way as they jumped, often lifting them high above their waists to show fancy undergarments or the lack of any beneath. The night was for the celebration of the flesh; no one who carried any prudish ideas belonged upon the Tor on such a night. As soon as they had jumped they began to pair off and find a place in the night shadows of the hillside or the meadow below in which to take their pleasure of each other. Even before Kieran and I had taken our turns over the fire the unabashed giggles of disembodied voices began to punctuate the night in counterpoint to the sensuous moans of those who had already begun their physical invocations of the Green Man and the Lady.

The tall red-haired woman who joined hands with my brother as he cleared the fire wasted no time in slipping her hand down the back of his pants, and I could feel his response sweep emphatically through my mind as I watched the slender young blonde jump before me. There was something about her, her youth perhaps, which seemed almost out of place there on that lusty night, but the warmth of her smile, a mixture of innocence and knowledge, compelled me to take her hand; I led her to the far side of the ruined tower where I knew the winds were gentler and the grass softer than anywhere else.

The night was warmer than it should have been, probably a mixture of a glamour and an enchantment, for the Priestesses of the area had set great store by weather magic to ensure nights such as Beltaine would have optimum conditions. The young woman with me was not shy as she opened her lips to my kisses and gave me her own, sweeter than the mead, yet there was behind the wet warmth of her mouth an innocence which made each kiss even more precious. I pulled back her long silky hair and kissed the nape of her neck, working my mouth toward her ear.

"How old are you, my pretty one?" I whispered.

"Sixteen tonight, My Lord. Old enough to celebrate the rites at last."

She was old enough indeed, and had yielded up her will entirely to the night. Her body was no longer that of a child, but not yet fully that of a woman, though the desire which burned there was as strong as that of any woman who had leapt the flames. She pulled me closer to her and drew my hands beneath the loose white garment she wore. Her skin was as soft as that of a child, and her breasts small, but I could feel her tremble with delight as I touched them.

"Do I please You, My Lord? I have wanted to for so long, ever since I was old enough to make a woman's blood. I have wanted You to take me and fill me with life, to change me from Maiden to Mother."

The magic of the night had begun to work its way upon us, for in her eyes I was no longer a man, but the personification of the Lord of the Trees, the Antlered God who in His young aspect was the Green Man. Even I felt His presence within me as her eyes and lips invoked Him.

"You please me very much indeed," was all I could manage to answer, for the night and the God had claimed me.

"I always wanted the first time to be like this, at Beltaine, upon the Tor, and with the Green Man."

Her beauty was so delicate, the purity of her body and spirit so sweet that my heart ached for her as much as my body did. I covered her with kisses, arousing her as gently as I could, wanting to fulfil her dream completely, to bring her into womanhood with as much pleasure and as little pain as possible. She was a flower, opening slowly to my touch, yielding to the hot thrusting of my flesh with as much ecstasy as I would one day yield to the cold metal of my brother's sword. The two events were intertwined as they had always been, the dance of life and the dance of death, for without one the other was impossible.

She held me tightly, gasping ever so slightly, ever so triumphantly as the veil within her tore in response to the tearing of the Veil between the worlds, her pain brief as the Green Man and I turned it to pleasure, rocking with her and within her until I could no longer hold off the tide which swept me up with it and poured its gift of life into her.

The world was still for a very long time thereafter, only the sound of her heart and mine racing breaking the silence we felt within ourselves. I held her close to me, my breath warm upon her, my arms aware of how fragile she was in their embrace, yet how strong she also could be. After a time I stroked her face with my fingers and found it wet.

"Have I hurt you badly, little one?"

"No. It was beautiful. All that I had ever prayed for."

"So young in life to have your prayers answered."

"That's half of why I'm crying. I will never again have this to look forward to. It has become the past now."

"And the other half?"

"Because I am so happy."

"Shall I help you down the Tor, My Lady?"

"Might we stay here for a few more minutes?"

I stroked her hair, silky, soft, bright as the moonlight, then cradled her once more in my arms.

"For as long as you'd like, My Lady."

The horned mask upon my face became unbearable, and I lifted it to the top of my head as she snuggled against me and we drifted off into a short slumber.

I was quick to dream, or perhaps it was not a dream at all, for too much of it had been familiar, too much real.

I do not know for certain the century or the country, but the light was a yellow-white upon whiter sands and the sea the same shade of blue I have always associated with the Mediterranean. It was before our lives in Britain, I'm sure, but there were once again the five of us, and once again I cannot be certain if it had been my brother or myself who wore the crown, for I have all his memories and he has mine.

Suffice it to say this King had been granted the position for seven years and then his turn to die was set, by the date, not the Need of the Land, for the ritual was repeated anew each seven years and the Land never thirsted for long. It was the night before his reign was to end, and as was his right, he had been allowed to choose from among the Vestal Virgins one to share his bed, one who would thereafter be separated from the other Priestesses. If she had conceived from that night she would be supported by the people and live a life of plenty, but the child would be taken by the Priesthood for schooling and she would not be allowed to raise or even see it again. If three months passed and there was no sign that she had conceived, she would be strangled by the next ruler and her body thrown into the sea.

The woman chosen by the King was young and beautiful; no more than half a year had passed since she her initiation, no more than a year since the moon had begun to change her body with its phases and cycles, yet this had been one of the reasons the King had chosen her. There was some talk of refusing his choice because of her age and the probability that she would not conceive as easily as a woman whose cycles were established. One of the biggest protests came from the girl's father, a wealthy merchant who had never wanted her to leave his home in the first place.

The elders among the Priesthood decided that the King's choice was undeniable, for he would himself die the next morning, a horrible death, but one necessary for the fulfilment of the Land's requirements; he would be flayed alive and his skin donned by his successor. His last request must be honoured.

It was a splendid night for the King. The girl was lovely and he enjoyed her to the fullest, hoping she also enjoyed him. She seemed to, for she made no protest to the ways in which his body joined with hers, whether for duty's sake or the sake of her own pleasure. Her smiles were genuine, for she had secretly loved this man since the day he had first sat upon the throne, and her child's fantasy of his one day returning that love had led her to the Temple of the Vestals, there to be chosen by him or to live out her life without ever knowing a man.

The night seemed too short, and when the sun rose they were parted by the Priests, he to be bathed ritually before his sacrifice and she to be bathed and dressed in the manner of a Queen, though her reign would be a short one. When the sun was high in the sky he saw her last, a delicate figure in reds and purples and golds, seated in a fine chair before the tree to which he would be bound. He kissed her one last time, not upon the lips, but the top of her head, and gave himself up to the four priests.

When the crowd had gathered, they brought out to him a massive golden bowl to draw the name of his successor. Each male who had undergone the rites of passage and whose body was unscarred was eligible for the honour, for an honour it was, even if the end was grisly. For seven years the King ruled almost as a God. Only the vilest coward deliberately marked his body to escape the lottery.

As the hand of the King drew the tile each man held his breath, some praying his name would be found, others that it would not. Whatever the prayer in the heart of the girl's father, the Gods saw fit to choose him.

He staggered up the pathway, unable at first to comprehend why he had been summoned and all that it entailed. When he saw his daughter he nearly fell, for the total realisation struck him; he was to be the new King, and if the Gods had decreed she did not carry the child of the King who would die that day he must kill her with his own hands.

In tears he allowed the Priests to strip him of his robes, then watched as they stripped the King naked and drank the last toast with him and led him to the tree. The King was bound to the tree with ropes about his waist, not because he resisted his death, but because he might fall and tear the skin they cut from him, the skin which must be worn intact by the merchant to transform him into the new King.

The King flinched only once, at the first cut. After that he was beyond pain, smiling as he looked into the blue eyes of the Priest who sliced his skin from his flesh. How long he was still alive there was no way to tell, for the separation of his spirit began with the first cut, and the expression on his face remained long after the heart had ceased pumping his blood to the ground below.

The bloody skin was wrapped around the merchant's naked body with great care to keep it intact, and the merchant was led to his throne by the Priest who had done the flaying. The Priest knelt before the new King, and everyone else followed in the action. As the Priest looked up at the face of the new King he saw confusion in the grey-blue eyes, sorrow, and the seeds of a hatred which would spring up in full bloom millennia later.

Neil?

I could hear my brother's mind even in my sleep.

Neil!

More insistent, pulling me back.

Neil, where are you?

Here, Anmchara.

For a minute I was worried. I've just had the most interesting dream.

Chapter Twenty-Four

*W*e were still discussing the implications of our shared dream the following day over a very late breakfast when Jack arrived with a bundle of papers in his hands and a worried look upon his face.

"You two were out rather late. Dare I ask if the sun caught you on your way home?"

Kieran grinned wickedly.

"Not that it matters, mind you. I see you had a pleasant evening. By the way, have you seen Malcolm? He's not in his room."

We both shook our heads.

"No," I said. "We didn't see him on the Tor when we left, although we weren't actually looking for him. Perhaps he let some lovely lady lead him home."

"Lead him astray is more like it," he grumbled.

"Oh come off it, Jack," my brother scoffed. "Let's not be too much of a hypocrite. We know you were there too; even with the masque you're well known to us. Don't pretend the evening wasn't good for you."

For the first time I can remember I saw him blush, a quiet rosy pink at first, blossoming into an utter red as the final flush crept up his neck to the top of his head.

"I was only doing my duty."

"To us, to the Gods, or to that pretty brunette who stood in circle at your right?" Kieran taunted.

"All of the above," he admitted.

"And?"

"All right, Kieran, or is it Neil?"

"Neil."

"He's sending you up, Jack. I'm Neil," I said.

"I thought so. Kieran's humour is a touch madder than yours. At any rate, yes, we enjoyed ourselves immensely if you must know, although I believe it's between us and the Gods. So you have no idea where Malcolm is?"

"No," I said. "Something wrong?"

It seemed there was, and Malcolm wasn't going to be thrilled with the news. His darling brother Duncan had made several calls to Venezuela, the Cayman Islands, and Switzerland during the weeks preceding the assassination of our parents. Over half of them were to Juan Ignacio Portalez, a Senior Vice-President of OBP in Caracas. The interest of OBP in the petroleum fields off the Scottish coast, an interest Queen Alexandra and her three eldest sons had refused to consider, the fact that Portalez's brother-in-law was Antonio Velasquez, a well-known figure in the South American underworld who was believed to have headquarters in the Caymans, and the fact that the calls to Switzerland had been to one of the three banks implicated in the earlier scandals but allowed to remain open due to lack of evidence indicated young Duncan might be up to his chopable neck in a conspiracy.

I asked him if he'd been able to find any witnesses to Alexander's "accident".

"No, he said, "but we've not stopped looking. There were several tourists in the area, but we've not been able to track them all down yet. Fortunately for us the bed and breakfasts keep fairly good records of their guests. Most of the lot that day was from across the pond, although there were one set from Nottingham and another from Belfast, one lady writer researching the Ulster Cycle and taking copious notes on Dunskaith as the place where Cuchulainn trained at arms under Scathach. She's probably the best bet, as she was shooting everything she could for reference."

"Still," said Kieran, "It would be difficult to prove a picture of them holding him under the water wasn't showing them dragging him from it."

"Unless, of course it was a vid and the action was apparent."

THE SWORD OF THE KING

We turned at the sound of Eleanor's voice.

"Well good morning, love. You're the early riser, then, aren't you? Where've you been?" I asked.

"Off with Malcolm. I had to make a run to the house for a few things. You know it's a good deal more comfortable there than it is here at Tyrell House. Why don't we all move operations there?"

"Security, dear." Jack and the rest have no problem guarding this place; it's set up against invasion. Your house is set up for what it is, a bookstore with living quarters upstairs and a huge underground room for rehearsals, circles and classes. Not very defendable. So, Malcolm, how late were you out last night?"

I did not miss the glance between him and Eleanor.

"Not very. I was the last to go over the fire and there were bloody well no women left by then. I figured you were well enough guarded without me so I came home."

Well it wouldn't have been the first time.

I wonder if he wore the masque.

I hope he had the sense to remove it. It was damned uncomfortable.

Besides, it's not as if she were going to get pregnant by him.

Do you think they'll ever speak of it?

Probably not.

Then neither should we.

Eleanor just looked at us with a knowing smile, for the bond between us all was too deep for there to be jealousy. Even without the moon crown upon her head she outranked us all, for she was our High Priestess with it or without, and the representative of the Lady we served. Who would deny Her any pleasure She asked?

Smiles passed between the four of us as Jack looked once again at the papers he had brought with him. After a moment of perusing them he broke the news to Malcolm, who didn't seem surprised.

"There's one problem," he said. "He's a foreign Prince. He can no more be arrested for High Treason in England than Gwenna can be arrested on that charge in Scotland. Conspiracy, yes. Accomplice to murder, yes. But unless you're willing to hear an outcry from Scotland at calling the same charges against him that saw William Wallace hanged, drawn and quartered, you cannot charge him with High Treason here. We've never forgotten that Wallace was not a subject of the King or Kingdom which tried, convicted, and executed him on that false charge."

"Granted. What if we could find proof of his complicity in Alexander's death?"

"Then I'll drag him to the block myself and swing the axe."

"Wait a moment," Eleanor said with an unaccustomed intensity. "Gwenna can be tried in Scotland for High Treason. She and Duncan were married the night before Alexander died. She may be Princess of the Blood Royal here, but in Scotland she is the wife of Prince Duncan and by that marriage a subject of Queen Alexandra. If her role is proven in this she is just as much a target for the axe as is Duncan."

She was right. Gwenna Marie Elizabeth Windsor Stuart might be the first member of the English royal family to go to the block since Charles I. Somehow I doubted the Land would receive her blood with as much enthusiasm.

Then I thought of the dream Kieran and I had shared the previous night.

"Yet somehow I feel responsible'" I sighed.

"For what? Regicide? Or the deaths of Alexander and Genevefa?"

Malcolm had two reasons to hate her; his anger was warranted.

Do you think we should tell them?

We can't. We've been forbidden to bring it up, remember?

It's not questioning Her.

No. It's interfering with what She has set up. Let it be.

"No. I suppose it's just that big brothers are supposed to watch out for their little sister, and we've spent most of our lives hiding away here at Tyrell House, away from her when she probably needed us the most."

I don't know if it was convincing, but no one asked further.

Perhaps she needs to have her head lopped off.

She won't enjoy it.

She's perverse enough, she just might.

Kieran?

What?

Do you know if the merchant had to strangle his daughter?

No. I don't think we lasted three months apart.

We must this time. Promise me.

Yes. I won't be happy, but we've had so much more this time. I can live on that.

And Eleanor.

And Eleanor. And if she and Malcolm should need more of each other's company I can live with that too.

I don't think that will happen.

Why?

He's too close to the Scottish throne. If Robert's wife...what's that woman's name anyway?

Margaret

Of course. If it turns out Margaret is barren, Malcolm had better be able to produce an heir.

What if we both should die? We'd be leaving her in excellent hands.

Now that would complicate things, wouldn't it? Mother to the Queen of England and the King or Queen of Scotland by two different husbands.

Shakespeare would have loved it.

"You two are being rude again. What's going on in your wicked heads?"

As we were about to answer the explosion rocked Tyrell house, sending us hurriedly to the floor and under the protection of the table.

"Oh Gods!" shouted Eleanor as she rolled into my arms and lay there shaking with fear.

Neil?

I'm fine. Eleanor is shaken up, but I think she's all right. How are you?

I think I need to change my undergarments, but other than that I'm fine.

"Malcolm? Jack?"

"Neil?"

"Yes.

The thunder and rumble had ceased, and the building no longer moved.

"We're all right. You three?"

"Half deaf, but other than that..."

The smell of smoke began to fill the place, triggering alarms in every room. We prayed fervently that the Order's own fire-fighters would be able to take care of things before the Glastonbury forces showed up.

"Quick. Downstairs. The tunnels won't burn, and there are several passages to the outside only known to the Knights."

I felt the door first; it was cool to the touch. I opened it and saw the hallway, not as badly damaged as I had imagined, but the smell of smoke was getting more intense. I led them down and to the right, feeling my way along the walls for evidence the fire had spread closer, but found none. There was no apparent door to the left of me, so cunningly had it been fit into the architecture, but it was there all right, and when I pushed upon it in three places the panel slid open for us. The descent was steep but necessary down the narrow passage. Kieran led them down as I secured the door from the inside.

"I seriously doubt anyone can do us harm here, " Kieran reassured his wife. "This is one place even you have not been permitted to go."

The passage led to a series of tunnels. We took the rightmost one, as it led away from what we believed to be the source of the explosion. After several moments of wandering through sparsely lighted corridors, feeling as if we were meandering in a maze of stone, we travelled upon an upward incline for a short distance and emerged through a well-concealed door just outside the stone wall which surrounded what was left of Tyrell House, dismayed at what we saw over the wall.

The police were already there and welcomed Jack to the scene, not knowing he'd been there all along, much too close to the blast. The officer in charge was a member of the Order, and did what he could to make sure no outsiders gained access until things could be somewhat camouflaged. Jack was able to invoke the Official Secrets Act on the grounds that the bomb had somehow been related to the prior assassinations, and things were kept down as best he could.

It was hours before we realised the extent of our losses. So severe had been the explosion that it had collapsed three of the tunnels beneath it, sealing off access to the chambers in which we had taken our Visionquests. Fortunately no one had been below ground at the time.

Above ground it was another tale. The entire west wing was gone and with it passed an age: both Robin and Derek Watson had been taking tea in the west parlour with Sir Edmund de Brecy and Sir John Edward Villars, MP for Nottingham when the bomb had exploded. The Old Guard of the Order had died amid the rubble and fire, their mouths full of scones and clotted cream.

Had we not been so late in getting in the night before we might have joined them for tea instead of meeting in the east dining hall for breakfast, and we would all have met the same fate. Indeed, we had been planning to join the others for a chat when our more substantial meal was over.

There would be questions in any event; there was no way to conceal entirely an explosion this near the city proper, and questions were always a problem for a secret society. Even if the titles and emblems were readily displayed to the outside world, even if some part of our function had been guessed at after the true cause of death of King Stephen II and the Duke of Cornwall had been revealed, there were still many secrets we possessed which the public had no right to know. Now, when we needed them the most, the Archivist and the Grand Knight of the Order were both dead without having passed their knowledge along or, as far as we knew, designating their successors. How much we had lost in losing them was immeasurable, though the vaults below had not been touched; they were in the other wing.

Oh yes, there would be questions. A Member of Parliament had been slain, along with three other Knights. The King of England and his brother and brother's wife, and one son of the Queen of Scotland had been endangered.

We had no time to worry about it until after the fire was out, as we helped our brothers in the Order pull the twisted bodies of our mentors and friends from beneath the splintered beams, pieces of walls and ceiling and fragments of what had been the fireplace, four frail old men who had been giants in their own way. Still choking on the smoke, dust from the debris and the tears of rage and sorrow, we invoked the Morrigan for a triple purpose, to safeguard their passage to the next world, to guide, guard and protect us, and to take vengeance upon whomever had been responsible for the bombing even though in our hearts and heads we already knew exactly who to blame.

Chapter Twenty-Five

*T*he cover-up was excellent: an unexploded German bomb left over from World War II had been found on site by a workman who was an avid collector of World War II memorabilia. He had been convinced he could disarm it himself and add it to his collection. Unfortunately, he had overestimated his own skill and had paid for it with his life and the lives of four others, including a Member of Parliament. Memorial services would be held at St. Paul's Cathedral in London and upon the Tor in Glastonbury. A nationwide wake would begin at sunset, but please drink responsibly: if you wake, walk.

We moved to Eleanor's old home temporarily, assured that the three collapsed tunnels would be repaired quietly and quickly, just as would the rest of Tyrell House, and by members of the Order. John Nigel Windsor-FitzWalter, Duke of Cornwall, would take Derek's place as First Knight of the Order, and Edmund Tyrell Jones, a distant cousin of Eleanor's and even more distant cousin or uncle of ours was next up for the post of Archivist. Both men were in their sixties, and both had served the Order faithfully for more than forty years. The Duke and Duchess would reserve their home in Torquay for the summer and make Tyrell House their main residence as soon as its restoration was completed.

The idea of a woman in permanent residence at Tyrell House was not a new one, but the place had been without a chatelaine since the death of Lady Tyrell, our dear Kate, more than fifty years before. Perhaps a woman's touch was what it needed.

Kieran, do you ever think about Kate?

Of course.

I wonder if we'll ever see her again.

When the time is right.

Do you think she would be able to tell us apart?

If anyone could.

So much had happened and so quickly. So many had died in such a short time, so many who had tied us to this round of life, that it was a bit unsettling. The only people left who were close to us were those who we had known again and again. Only the differences in their current forms remained to assure us of who we were and where we were this time; with our eyes closed they were all as they had always been to us, the same internal energies and bright beings who continued on with us through the ages to make the patterns of our lives complete.

And the one dark blot to make it more complicated.

Gwenna and Duncan had not been in Glastonbury when the bomb had gone off; their penthouse in Kensington had been the scene of a charity brunch that day, hosted by the happy couple to benefit the Hospital For Sick Children. Who could accuse them of the deed?

Jack could. The calls to and from Sinclair House had been monitored since the moment Gwenna and Duncan had taken up residence. The sequence had been just as before: Caracas, the Cayman Islands and Zurich. With adequate preparation there were more than numbers and guesses at who had spoken to whom; there were voices and conversations. Gwenna had, however, been cautious this time. All the voices had been male, and the conversations vague. Duncan could be charged with many things, but the tie to her was not yet absolute.

The picture of her neck stretched across the headsman's block at the Tower of London was foremost of my mind. The axe came down with a mighty blow, cutting through skin, flesh and bone in a single stroke. The blood spurted and pooled from the red fountain of her neck as the head tumbled to the ground and rolled to my feet. Her face was set an expression of mocking laughter, and those grey-blue eyes stared at me, unblinking and accusing, their victory complete.

"We can't use any of this, you know," I said to Jack.

"Why not?"

"You've already invoked the Secrets Act. You can't just drop this in the lap of the nation after having told them it was an old German bomb that blew up in our faces. We must prove they murdered Alexander and let Scotland take care of the matter."

He nodded, agreeing.

That's not the real reason, is it?

No. We can't have that blood on our hands again.

We didn't last time.

We did, even if Kate carried it out for us.

It was self-preservation.

It was revenge. The courts would have convicted him. He would have been punished by the people, not us.

You're awfully sensitive in this matter.

You're not?

No. Perhaps I've become immune to blood. If I have to kill you later I can't worry about who chops off the head of a repeated regicide. She must be stopped, for the good of both our nations.

I was stunned. We had never been so far apart emotionally on any issue. Perhaps I was letting my own dislike for the method of execution influence me in the matter. Hanging was actually more pleasant, I recalled, though I had been quite drunk at the time, or had that been Kieran? The memories were still so jumbled. so tangled between us I couldn't be sure, but whether they had been my own or his it didn't matter. They were mine now, and as I remembered it there had been an exquisite feeling as all the vertebrae of a bad back had been jerked at last into alignment, a rush of electricity up the spine as the neck snapped which quite outweighed the struggle against strangulation. Pity, custom decreed that royals did not hang, but spilled their blood in death, a good tradition if one would get off the supposed humanity of beheading and just run the person through with a piece of pointed steel; pike, spear, sword, pole arm, knife, even arrow, it did not matter.

The thought of it made me giddy.

Not now, Neil.

I know.

"And Jack, let's not close in until after Coronation. She will be a part of it whether she wants to or not."

Why, Kieran?

Politics, pure and simple.

???????

Even if she is convicted she can't be executed until after her baby is born. That's pretty much the law in every civilised country now, just as it was here hundreds of years ago. That child is going to need a family, especially if both parents have kissed the chopping block. I want him to be looked after as if he were our own, for Kate's sake if nothing else. He is our brother and our son, Kieran, Richard's son. Stephen's brother."

Suddenly nothing Gwenna had done mattered more than the birth of that child.

"Jack, if something happens to Gwenna, who gets custody of the child?"

"Duncan, I suppose."

"But it's not Duncan's child. They've already admitted that. Parliament knows the real parents, nicely documented by the doctors in Edinburgh. Besides, Duncan is liable to have something happen to him too."

"And if it's clearly not Duncan's child, as they both have testified, Scotland can have no claim on him, nor can he have a claim to the Scottish throne. We should be able to make him a royal ward, should we not?"

"I'm only a member of His Majesty's Police, not a Wig. You'd have to ask someone with more knowledge of Crown Laws which might apply, but there's no reason I can see to stop you, especially if he's born on English soil."

"If a cat had kittens in the oven they wouldn't be biscuits."

"What?"

Kieran laughed.

"Something I remember one of our ancestors was fond of saying. If a cat had kittens in the oven they wouldn't be biscuits. It's the old English law that gives you citizenship according to the citizenship of your parents, not by where you were born. Richard Windsor was definitely an Englishman, and he, not Duncan, was the father of this child. We have proof."

"Trust in Allah, but tie up your camel," I said.

"What?"

"A line from an old Sinbad vid we used to watch when we were children. Keep Gwenna here until after the child is born."

"What if they try to extradite her?"

"Malcolm is not without his influence."

"You can say that again," he said as he rounded the hall corner and plopped a viddisc on the table. "Play that."

"What is it?" I asked.

"Just play it," he said, his voice shaking slightly.

I slipped the disc into the side of the box and switched it on. Before us the screen leapt to life with tones of brown, green, white and blue, then focused in sharply. There were several small white houses with gravel paths to them, very rustic. The shot panned to the hogs in the pen at the side of one house, very large, very fat hogs, a detailed study of an enormous black and white cat skulking, then leaping after something which moved by too fast to see, several sheep...

"Past this point; run it by."

An old woman in a dark blue dress waved frantically and moved ahead in a jerky motion at a speed no human could have moved. Clouds rolled by overhead as a small herd of sheep galloped down the narrow street. A lone red letterbox zoomed in and out at us...

"All right, it's next."

I pushed another button to bring the speed back to normal.

The coastline was rugged, large dark rocks jutting from the land like the teeth of some impossible sea monster. The land itself was craggy, tide pools filling in the crevices, the salt of the water not seeming to interfere with the growth of whatever green plants clung tightly to them. In the near distance was what appeared to be a large pile of dark rubble silhouetted against the grey sea and almost blue sky.

The photographer must have walked while shooting, for the scene travelled in a manner which suggested it was not a zoom, as the letterbox had been.

"Is there audio?"

"Yes. Mostly birds and wind and waves. No point in switching it on just yet."

The pile of rubble proved to be the ruins of a castle, Dunskaith or Dun Sgaith, or several other versions, depending on who was writing it down. There were no signs to mark it, but Kieran and I had been there as children, climbing it despite warnings of its danger.

"Here. Look in the background."

As the shot showed the left edge of the ruins, approachable by the water, it also revealed a small boat on the water. There were three people in that boat, two men and a woman, and the boat was coming toward shore.

"So they were there," said Jack.

"It gets better."

The picture moved from that side, panning the entire castle, treacherous stone steps and the area which had once been a drawbridge or at least the frame for one; the wood had long since rotted away, leaving a nasty six metre drop into what might have been a moat below. The stones which jutted upward through the opening would be as hard on a body from that drop as had been the trilithon at Stonehenge upon which we had landed, although the shorter fall indicated a longer span of consciousness and pain before everything would go away.

There was a gap in the shot while the photographer found a way over the narrow ledge to the castle, for the next shot was a reverse, looking back at the drawbridge from the castle side, then up to the top of the castle itself.

"Now, hit the audio."

Seabirds called against the whistle of the wind, and the waves lapped against the rocks below. The view showed the green overgrowth atop the ruins and what appeared to be the castle's well. The view of the ocean included the far side of the little bay to the left, and then the hazy sky meeting the sea. Out there were shadows, perhaps Rhum or Aigg or one of the other Inner Hebrides, but as the audio continued it no longer mattered.

"What are you doing?"

It was Alexander's voice; that curiously gruff yet nasal sound could have been mistaken for no other.

The shot panned down from the castle to the left, to see the coracle within perhaps ten feet of the shore, its occupants unaware there was anyone else near. The girl sat at the forward end, the rower in the centre, and the second young man was at the aft. The second man had left his seat and was holding the rower's arms behind his back.

"This isn't funny, Duncan. Let go of me."

"Do it, Gwenna. Now, before he gets away."

"Gwenna?"

The woman pulled a knife from beneath her coat.

"Gwenna! Put that thing away. You're not going to kill me, are you?"

"No, Alexander. That's Duncan's job. This is mine."

We sat there holding our breaths as she plunged the knife through the skin of the coracle.

"You're mad!"

"No. Just theatrical."

"Mary, Jesus and Joseph!" came a whisper over the scene, evidently the photographer's. Her brogue was thick, her voice soft and filled with fear. "What should I do? Blessed Mary, what should I do? I'd never get down there in time to save him. Forgive me, Jesus. I leave him in your hands and pray for his soul. The best I can do now is catch the culprits."

The focus zoomed in on the coracle and its occupants.

Smart woman.

Shhhh!

I didn't say a thing.

You think too loudly.

There was no denying the faces, our sister and Malcolm's younger brothers. We all leaned forward in our seats, watching in a mixture of horror and gratitude for the truth as the little boat took on water quickly.

"Help! Somebody help!"

"That's good, Alex. Make it loud. Make it very loud. It will sound better when they find us. Help! Help us!"

"Should we be calling for help so soon? What if they see us?"

"They can't see a thing out here."

She climbed over Alexander and helped Duncan pin his arms back.

"I have him. He can't move. Now grab the rock and do it."

"Why are you doing this?"

"You're in our way."

His voice was chilling, emotionless.

"Do it, Duncan!"

The rock had been beneath his seat. He fumbled around for a moment and found it, pulled it up, and brought it down hard upon the right side of his brother's head once...twice. Alexander toppled over forward, limp and bloody, just as the boat vanished beneath them into the water.

Malcolm sat back in the chair and let out his breath slowly.

"God have mercy upon his soul, in the name of the Father, The Son, and the Holy Spirit, Amen", whispered the Irish voice.

"So Mote It Be," added Eleanor. "She has a good heart, this photographer."

"There's more. Keep watching. It's all there."

They dragged his body through the water, face down. It was unclear at that point as to whether he was dead or merely unconscious. They scrambled up the rocks with him in tow, slipping back several times.

"Do you think he's really dead?" Duncan asked.

"Hit him again to be sure, in the same place."

"Again? I dropped the rock."

"There are plenty of rocks. Oh never mind. Just drop him. I'll hold his face under until we're sure."

She positioned the head face down in the water and sat on him.

"How did it feel, Duncan, killing him?"

"It felt powerful, like being in bed with you."

"In the old days the King was killed by his brother. Did you like killing him, Duncan?"

"Yes."

"You still have two more brothers. You can feel this way again."

"I know. When can we have our wedding night for real?"

"Not until after we go to Edinburgh. My first child must be from one of those embryos. I can't risk getting pregnant by you. After we know for sure I'm already pregnant."

"It's going to be hard to wait."

She undid his pants and began to fondle him.

"It's better when it's hard," she said as she moved from Alexander's body to cover Duncan's phallus with her mouth. She came up for air a moment later.

"I have two brothers also, remember."

"Are we going to kill them too?"

"Perhaps. But not until we've made them suffer. You've taken care of everything else?"

"Yes. The money was transferred this morning."

"I love you Duncan."

Her mouth covered him once again as the shot streaked away from their tryst.

"I can't shoot such filth," came the whisper. "Blessed Mother, if there is justice in this world let me be a part of it."

The screen went blank and silent.

"As she would say, Amen," said Jack.

We all let out a sigh.

Malcolm was shaking, his face white.

"I've seen it twice before, but it still gets to me."

"I don't think he suffered much. That first blow seemed to take him out of it."

"Yes. I know. But it's the sense of betrayal I heard in his voice, his little brother doing that to him, for no apparent reason. It's not like the two of you. There was no reason, no love, only the cold logic of him being in the way. Not even hatred. I can kill Duncan with ease, because all that I loved in him and all that I loved in Alexander now rages within me as hatred."

"Let it go, Malcolm. They will both be dealt with by the law. We have the evidence. Where did you get it?"

"It's been sitting on a desk in Sleat for weeks. They didn't know what it was and they didn't have a vidplayer new enough to use this size disc. That woman had evidently intended to turn this over to the authorities, but when she found out what she had, she became too frightened to do it in person. She returned to Belfast and posted it back to Skye, to the local constabulary, thinking they had jurisdiction. Robert's people found it, and he sent me a copy."

"So he's seen it," I assumed.

Malcolm nodded.

"Has your mother?" asked Eleanor.

He shook his head.

"No. It would kill her. Her health has evidently not been good since the funeral. Her heart is already halfway broken. This would break the other half."

There was more that he wasn't saying.

"Malcolm, how is she really, between us?"

Eleanor had a way with her, a way of soothing with the tone of her voice, and of getting at the heart of the issue with her straightforwardness. Add these to the bonds already forged between them and Malcolm could hold nothing back. He rubbed both hands through his ginger beard, staring fixedly ahead at nothing as he unburdened himself completely those closest to him in the world.

"Robert will be on the throne by the year's ending. Her heart is weak, not just broken. Very weak. She's been on medication for two years, in ever increasing doses. Her lungs fill with fluid because her heart can't pump fast enough or strong enough. She has pleurisy now, possibly pneumonia too, from standing out so long at Culloden, and the latest I heard from Robert she may have endocarditis. She is in constant pain, and the medication they are giving her for that is making her heart worse."

"So we can do nothing about any of this while she lives."

"What can we do, Jack? One dead princess who has miscarried two potential heirs to the throne, one prince dead in an alleged accident, a Queen of Victorian proportion in the eyes of her subjects at death's door...do we dare to add the scandal of murder by her youngest son? How much can Scotland bear?"

"The King and Queen of England assassinated by his hired help with the aid of their daughter, the same combination attempting to kill the male heirs to the English throne and the second in line to the Scottish throne, namely you, blowing up Tyrell House and killing the Grand Knight and Archivist of the Order of the Sword and the Rose, one MP, and a legendary philanthropist. How much can England bear?" I countered.

"It has to end, Malcolm, and end while there's something left in both Kingdoms to salvage. Unless you're willing to have them transported to the Sagan Colony, they must both die, legally executed, not murdered."

Malcolm did not look at Kieran as he spoke, but continued to stare off into space, stroking his beard and rubbing his eyes.

"You know, once Mother is gone we'll be down to equal odds: two brothers, one evil sibling apiece, two royal wives and two babies on the way. No, we can't send them off to trouble those poor colonists; they'd be no match for them. I'll speak to Robert. If we can keep them at bay until he's on the throne I'm sure he'll have no objection to an execution."

It was a relief to us all.

"What about your sister? There's enough on that disc to convict her on either side of Hadrian's Wall."

We thought about it between us for a few moments, agreeing at last.

"We separate them after my Coronation. We lock her in the Tower until the baby is born. She dies there, on the block, by my hand if necessary. Do you have a safe place to keep your little brother until Robert is King, a place your mother won't hear about?"

He thought about it for a moment.

"We have many strong castles in Scotland," he answered.

Chapter Twenty-Six

*T*here were no more chances for Gwenna and Duncan after that. Word had somehow gotten back to their South American connexions that if they had any hope of ever tapping into the petroleum fields off Scotland's coast they had better cooperate with the Tanist to the Scottish throne, as the whole wretched conspiracy was known to Interpol, the Yard, and the Board of Directors of OxyBritPetrol, none of whom were amused. The phrase "heads will roll" was uttered more than once, and it was not to be taken figuratively.

Their calls to Caracas were never completed, nor those to the Cayman Islands. In Zurich the bankers were suddenly unable to make transfers without the physical presence of the account holders. Still, when it came time to rehearse the Coronation our sister and her husband acted as if nothing was amiss in their rapidly shrinking world.

The actual date came at last, cloudy and cool, and we climbed the Tor in the same order of procession as our great-grandfather, our grandfather, and our father before us, yet to us there was a difference: we recalled the first time, the night at the opposite end of the year when Stephen had made his pact with the Land and sealed the legal marriage of his sister and his Knight with a royal handfasting, surprising them both by investing Kevin as Duke of Cornwall.

The memories of that night were sweet as we climbed the long stone steps in our heavy robes, repeating it all with friends of different names and faces. When the actual litany of Coronation began I called to my brother to share it with me, for his right to the crown was as undisputed as mine.

This way we are both crowned. We are complete.

Almost. At the end we will be complete.

Ruth Margate stood before me in robes of white embroidered with threads of gold and silver. Her hair was as white as the robes she wore, hanging long and loose beneath a silver circlet which bore a crescent and decrescent moon separated by two round moonstones, one above the other. Except for the face well etched with the lines of age she looked for all the world like a Christmas angel posed in the window at Harrods for the December shopping season, only the effect was real; the beauty and wisdom of her heart shone through the wrinkles and charged the air in a way no plaster angel could. I held out my hands, palms upward to her, and she placed a rose in each, one red and one white.

And with them comes the promise of the black rose.

Kieran?

Remember?

"I place the care of all England within your hands," she said.

"And this charge I do readily accept and bear, my lady, to love, to protect, and to defend Her with my life, my soul, and my sacred honour."

It was as if Kieran spoke the same words in my mind as I spoke them aloud.

Ruth took the roses from my hands and gave them to Gwenna, who performed her duties mechanically, not a shred of emotion betraying her inner thoughts. Eleanor handed Ruth my sheathed sword, Stephen's sword, which she placed in my hands.

"And how will you defend Her?"

I pulled the sword from its sheath.

"With my sword, with my word and with my heart's blood I will protect and defend Her."

I smiled with an inner peace as his voice filled my head, as my voice filled the silence of the Tor. It was his Oath, too, one he would take on his own here when my heart's blood had indeed been spilled.

She took the sheath and handed it to Eleanor as I placed my left hand upon the blade of the sword.

"And upon what do you take your oath?"

"Upon the Stone and the Sword of the King, the flame of the Sun, and the Chalice Well."

The ritual had been changed slightly from what we recalled to fit the time of day. If the Sun itself could not represent fire in the daytime as well as the torches represented it at night, what could?

The sheaf of barley was handed to Ruth, as it had been handed to Gwen Jones in the past, and once again the most emotional part of the ritual took place. As she placed the barley between my hands I felt Kieran's hands within my own, and with the double vision of our shared consciousness we watched as the Plantagenet crown was unveiled. She held it before our eyes as Gwen had done nearly ninety years before, and the same thrill went through us as we gazed upon it and all it meant, a thrill which had been a mere glimmer as we watched our father's Coronation. It was perhaps the oldest relic of the monarchy still in active use except for the two swords, Stephen's and Rufus's, something which spoke to us of the endurance of ourselves and the Land. As she held above our head the joined metal plates with their great cabochons of precious and semiprecious stones we broke the sheaf of barley into pieces, remembering with a quiet joy the meaning behind the gesture. Rolling the grains around in our palms and letting them slip through our fingers as freely as we had let slip our lives we said

> "I am the Seed and I am the Harvest
> I am the Stalk and I am the Grain
> I am the Sheaf which must be broken
> And laid in the Earth to rise again."

If they only knew.

It is enough they believe.

Together we scattered the grain, and together we felt the weight of the crown descend upon the head which housed for that moment the essence of both of us.

Thank you for this, Anmchara.

You will feel it in your own right soon enough.

Perhaps. But it will not be the same. There is one King between us, and one Knight, but not necessarily each divided so distinctly into two bodies.

"Neil Andrew Edward George of the House of Windsor, by the right of blood and the oaths you have taken, by the will of the Gods and the people before you and with the consent of your brother, I do proclaim you this day our crowned and rightful King Neil, the first of that name to rule over us. So mote it be. Take up your sword and rise, my Liege."

The Priestesses fell to one knee as we stood, sword in hand, anxious as to the response the Stone of Destiny would give us. We were one in that body, and if Kieran's supposition turned out to be true, that should be enough for the Stone. For a moment there was nothing.

Are you sure about this, Kieran?

Feel me in your heart. Feel me in your mind. Feel me in your hands and feet. Pull the energy through the sword and send it down into the Stone. I know what to do, Neil, but it's your body we're using. Concentrate with me.

I looked across at his inert, kneeling form wedged between Jack and Malcolm, wondering for the first time if I had been hasty in deciding which of us was to wear the crown.

A fine time to worry about it, Neil, It's on your head now. Let's make it work.

How?

Relax. Merge with me, more than the normal link. Yield yourself as completely to it as if it were the death you crave. Remember how it felt as we fell through the sky? And at that very last second? Hold that feeling in your mind.

I closed my eyes and felt the blue tranquillity surround me, the surge of joy, the utter clarity of it all as there was no barrier at last between us, but only that one pure emotion, stronger than life, death, or the flesh which tried to isolate us from each other. The lightning shot forth from my heart again, the white hot fire of the stars, the sweet soothing cool light of the full moon. The physical forms shattered, releasing us into the brilliance where we existed as harmonics of the same note, pure and clear and strong, needing nothing but to exist as a fragment of the song upon the lips of Our Lady.

As if in resonance to that note we were, the Stone beneath the feet of the body designated Neil began to vibrate, slowly at first, the vibration growing faster and more intense until it became audible. The humming sound of it began to grow louder and louder and higher and higher in pitch until it reverberated throughout the entire Tor, ringing out below our feet.

Somewhere in the Milky Way a small planet took its turn around its central star in such a manner as to make the yellowish star appear to stand still for an instant in the heavens. It was the moment of the Summer Solstice

Yes! We've done it.

So we have. Hold on to the feeling Anmchara.

I will never let it go.

Nor I, but I must withdraw. Malcolm is having to keep our other body from falling over.

Have you ever considered leaving it entirely and just staying here?

Or the other way around. If I'm going to kill you I'd better have a body to carry the sword.

Oh that.

That. Gods Save the King.

And I was alone once more within my body, wearing a crown, and wondering what to do next.

I looked around. Gwenna was pale. I'd forgotten this was probably the first time she'd seen and heard the Stone in action. Frank had arrived after the main show was over, and it had been some time since we'd had access to a true Kingstone. Perhaps she sensed a Power behind all the ritual, a Power stronger than she could ever hope to be. The Queen was the most powerful piece in the game of chess. It was her goal, but she was playing for the wrong side, for the Great Queen controlled our board, and one novice Priestess of a Princess was no match for Her game.

No one saw the Knights of the Order whisk her from the Recessional Parade into a waiting car, nor another group of the same grab her husband Duncan for the same purpose. Only Malcolm knew where the second batch was headed, but Kieran and I knew just the room at the Tower of London which would house our fair and wicked sister, a room she had known before.

Chapter Twenty-Seven

Queen Alexandra did not last until Lammas. On the eve of our Coronation at Westminster Abbey she expired in her sleep, a fact which was kept from Malcolm and the rest of us until after the ceremony was over, in deference to the importance of the day and his role as my banner bearer in the procession. It did not matter; he knew she was gone and told me so before breakfast. He'd seen her in his sleep, looking much like her early portraits and warning him that although Alexander was very much all right, Duncan should be dealt with harshly. According to Malcolm, she thought a public execution might not be a good idea, but a private one should be recorded for posterity so the historians knew the truth and could reveal it when the time was proper. The evidence against him should of course be made public at the same time. She would take matters into her own hands once he'd been dispatched.

If William had been the Lion of Scotland, Alexandra had certainly been the Lioness.

Kieran watched behind my eyes during the second Coronation, but it seemed more a matter of tradition than an actual transference of power; the cold marble halls of a manmade Abbey, no matter how ornate, gilded and ancient could not hope to compare with the canopy of the sky and the green earth beneath our feet, for it was from those elements as well as the waters beneath the earth and the fire in the sky which conferred the true crown, the one worn not upon the head, but within the heart of the King.

Neil? Would you like to rest here with Henry V, Great Elizabeth and Mary of Scotland and the others?

Rest? We never rest long.

But have your bones laid here for the tourists to gawk at?

We'd be in good company. Poets' Corner and Isaac Newton and all.

And in bad. I never cared for Mary Tudor.

Nor I.

Still, perhaps we should make it a habit to be laid to rest at Stonehenge.

I could feel him smiling within me, the warmth of it flooding through me like sunshine as we knelt upon the cold marble floor.

I like that. Shall we have the duel there as well? It will be like going home.

It will be going home.

Such was our mood when the news arrived. We made quick provisions for the next few days and journeyed with Malcolm, Jack and Eleanor to Edinburgh Castle for the funerary preparations.

Robert had been strained to the limit. Though only five years older than Malcolm he looked to be fifty, his dark hair streaked liberally with silver which had not been there at Alexander's funeral. He embraced his brother warmly and wept, not only at his mother's absence, but at Alexander's and what must be done about Duncan.

"He must die, Robert. If you won't hire an executioner I'll do it myself."

"He's our brother, Malcolm."

"No. He killed our brother. You've seen the disc. He was plotting to kill us as well. That monster is no brother of yours or mine."

"What would Mother have thought?"

Malcolm took him by the shoulders and told him precisely what the good Queen had thought about the situation. Robert's posture began to change. He stood straighter, held his head higher, even relaxed a bit more.

"All right. The only question is when and where."

"That's two, but I'll answer them. Here. Tonight. Mother always wanted a funeral pyre, a big blazing bonfire, she said, to light up the whole sky. We lop off Duncan's head tonight and toss the body on the same pyre."

"And the head?"

"If I had my way it would be on a pike, but we can toss it on the pyre as well."

Robert thought, dark thoughts to be sure. How many years had it been since a Stuart had been beheaded? Perhaps too many.

"Robert, he engineered the deaths of the King and Queen of England, the head of my Order and it's Archivist, a member of the English Parliament, and the man who built and paid for eight free day care centres in Scotland and twenty throughout the rest of these islands. Most of this mayhem he did while he was trying to kill me, the current King of England, his brother, his brother's wife, and a Chief Inspector of His Majesty's Police. Not to mention he killed our brother with his own hands and was instrumental, along with that she-wolf of a wife of his, of causing Genevefa's miscarriages and death by slow poison."

The last accusation hit Robert harder than anything else. He grew tense, not quite believing what he heard.

"What? How?"

"Those herbal teas. They contained something which over a period of time killed both the babies and her. Gwenna sent the tea chest to Duncan, Duncan delivered it, knowing exactly what was in it. Two more potential heirs to the throne knocked off the list, and me so upset I might have tried to do anything until Kieran and Neil pulled me out of it. And Jack and Eleanor, too."

I noticed his eyes sparkled a bit more when he mentioned Eleanor's name than any of the others, and it made me glad. She was a very special lady and deserved special treatment.

"Herbal teas?" asked Robert.

"From Mongolia," Malcolm replied.

"She sent some herbal soaps or something to Margaret. I wonder if they have anything to do with her frequent "female troubles" as she calls them."

I could stay out of the conversation no longer.

"Anything's possible. Get her to toss them out immediately, man. Anything Gwenna touches seems to be poison."

He began to pace back and forth before the neatly arranged fire, like an animal who has been caged too long, or like a man trying to find his way out of something he fears is a trap.

"Neil, what are your plans for your sister?"

"Execution, by all means. No one I know personally is safe while she lives."

"When?"

"As soon as she is delivered of the child she carries."

"A child? Kill her first man! What kind of monster would those two spawn?"

"No monster, really. She's not the mother, nor he the father."

I bade them all sit down while I told the story of the innocent within the womb of the guilty, and Robert agreed the child had no part in it, nor a claim on the throne of Scotland. He was ours to rear as we saw fit and although his relationship to us was odd indeed, there was no indication he would be anything but a healthy normal child, at least as normal as Stephen and Anastasia had been.

"When is she due, then?"

"December. Richard, as she wants to name him, and I can't see how that can hurt since it was his real father's name, Richard will be handed off to a wet nurse as soon as the doctors allow, and Gwenna will kiss the headsman's block at the tower soon after."

"She cannot escape?"

"The Yeoman Warders are all Knights of the Order. She will not get by them," Kieran assured him.

There was a silence as black as the Tower ravens. Robert rose slowly, paced back and forth once, his hands behind his back and his eyes reading the patterns of the floor. Finally he stood as tall as he had previously stood.

"Yes. Tonight then. I want it well documented. Let history see this time exactly what it looks like when a Stuart's head comes off. Neil, I want you to show it to your sister. Show her what happened to her husband, and what fate awaits her."

Some good that will do. She'll probably enjoy it.

Perhaps we should take her the head.

The idea was deliciously medieval and well suited to the melodrama of her life. She was imprisoned in the Bloody Tower, this time for her misdeeds, not for the political intrigue which had placed her there as a child all those centuries ago. It was tempting to us both to confront her in the dead of night in that thick-walled chamber, holding out to her by its hair the head of her executed husband, severed neck still gory and eyes open wide in terror, yet somehow we held ourselves to be too civilised to do so. Besides, what was the point? What happened to Duncan's physical form once he'd left it would be of no great concern to him, and I had the feeling from watching the viddisc that her love for him extended only so far as his ability to feed her ambition.

Malcolm would have been content to haul Duncan from his cell and behead him at once, but Robert insisted on more formal proceedings, and that Jack record them all. His youngest brother was brought in chains before him that night, and before a panel of his peers, Malcolm, Neil and myself he denied vehemently any knowledge of the assassinations, the bombing, or that Alexander's death had been anything more than a tragic accident. He remained calm and unconvinced as recordings of his long-distance conversations hinted at his complicity in the matters.

Then Malcolm popped in the viddisc. From the moment Duncan saw the outline of the ruined castle his demeanour changed. His eyes stared, unblinking, and he leaned forward in his seat to watch the horror unfold. He winced as he saw the image of himself strike the blows, but in his fascination he could not bear to turn away from the scene which damned him as well as doomed him.

"Duncan William Douglas Stuart," Robert began with as little emotion as his young brother showed, "you have by these actions condemned yourself to death. You have murdered your brother. You have committed High Treason as well, for by this action you have tried to place yourself nearer to the throne than your station has called for, and you have openly conspired to do so twice more, by killing both Our Tanist, Malcolm, and Us. It is Our judgement that in return we shall take from you your life this night by merciful means of the headsman's block, and not by torture as Our early forbears would have ordered. Have you anything to say before sentence is carried out?"

"You can't do this. It isn't legal. Mother will never let you get away with this."

Robert looked long and hard at his youngest brother before speaking, searching his face for a sign of remorse or repentance; when he found there nothing but hostility he hardened his own heart.

"We can do this. We are now King in Scotland. Our mother died two nights ago, Duncan, and We set this death also upon your head, for it was her grief for Alexander's loss and the illness caused by her exposure to the cold and damp at his funeral which killed her."

The King of Scotland motioned to Malcolm to fetch the block and axe. In a moment he was back with them, an old blood-stained piece of wood which had tasted the lives of countless victims, some guilty, some as pure as flame, and an axe ground so fine at the edge that it flashed as he set it carefully against the wall. The block he set purposefully directly before his younger brother, making sure it was something his eyes would be unable to avoid.

"Malcolm, do you still wish to do this yourself?"

Our friend, our Companion for so many lives looked from brother to brother, the face of one resigned to what must be done and the face of the other still disbelieving. He ran his fingers through his beard, then sighed and picked up the axe.

"Yes," he said quietly with a nod.

There was terror upon Duncan's face.

"No, Malcolm. You can't do this. I'm your brother."

"Alexander was my brother. Genevefa was my wife. We nearly had two children. You and your wife saw to it that I have none of them any more."

His voice was strangely even, controlled, although we all knew the emotion which had torn at him for weeks.

"Malcolm, that was Gwenna's doing, not mine."

"Yes. That was Gwenna's doing, but you aided in it. Had she not had cause to plead her belly she would be with you now, to die at your side. As it is she will follow you as soon as the child is born."

Duncan squirmed in his chair, cowering as Malcolm reached for his shoulder.

"Malcolm, I'm sorry about Genevefa. I truly am. Forgive me."

There was a trace of genuine regret there in his voice, only a trace beneath the fear he felt at the prospect of what awaited him.

"I will forgive you, Duncan, as soon as your head rolls onto the floor."

"No!" he shrieked.

"Duncan, have some dignity. This is being recorded for the historians. You are a Stuart. At least have the grace to die as one."

They say blood will tell. There must be some truth to it, for to his credit he managed to pull himself together at the reminder of his station, and asked that we at least remove the chains so he would not appear to die as a slave. Robert could not deny the request.

The chair was moved back to the wall, and Duncan went to his knees before the block without aid or direction from anyone else, and removed his white silk shirt.

"No point in getting this all bloody," he said, and tried to pull his long hair away from his neck. "This either. It's going to get in the way."

He stretched his neck over the block, still pulling his hair forward to keep it off his neck.

"There. You're right, Robert. I can at least die like a Stuart if you won't let me live like one. I hope Gwenna does as well. She was right, though, you're all illegitimate. All right, you bastards. Get it over with."

Malcolm positioned himself and raised the axe, and the world seemed to spin out of control within me as I watched it come down hard, slicing through the skin, bone, spinal cord, flesh, oesophagus, trachea, carotids and jugulars and all else in its path in one dizzying stroke. The whole thing passed before me in slow motion, the arced spurting of the blood, the soft muffled thunk of the metal hitting the wood at last, the half-turn the head made in its roll as the blood-soaked hair caught it and stopped the motion, the involuntary twitching of the body before it slumped and collapsed altogether.

I thought for I moment that I would be ill, for the memory of what he was experiencing at that moment triggered a sense of psychic nausea in me. He was still alive within that head and would be so for several seconds more, seconds which stretched before him like helpless hours of dizzy disorientation. For the first time I pitied him.

Neil?

I'm all right.

No you're not.

I will be in a minute, once I know he's completely gone.

It really affects you this much.

Yes.

Another subtle difference between us.

It doesn't bother you?

Not than much. More like a ride at Alton Towers or Blackpool.

I never quite thought of it that way.

Don't worry. I promise to leave your head attached, Anmchara.

Malcolm picked his brother's head up by the hair, closing the eyes which stared at him in defiance more than terror.

"Now, Duncan. Now, as I promised. Now I forgive you."

Chapter Twenty-Eight

*A*lexandra's funeral pyre glowed red-orange against the blackness of the midnight sky as the raging fire returned her physical form to the elements. No one was any the wiser that it also engulfed the remains of her executed son, nor would many actually care.

One copy of the viddisc was sealed in a vault within Edinburgh Castle, the other came with us to the Tower to be shown to Gwenna and then to be sent to the Archives of the Order in Glastonbury, as it was vital to the history of England's crown as well as Scotland's.

Although Gwenna seemed more than a little distressed at viewing the evidence against her, she seemed less interested in the account of Duncan's somewhat succinct trial and summary execution. I couldn't bear to watch the axe fall again, so I watched her face instead as she viewed it. There was none of the grief, none of the disgust or fear one might have expected from one suddenly widowed in that manner, only an expression of detached amusement which intensified slightly at the end, almost as if she had been sexually aroused by what she saw.

"Strange," she said, then drew her tongue over her lips, "I would have expected him to have bled more."

She rubbed her hands over her rounding belly.

"Well, I'm glad you know the law. I do plead my belly, and you cannot touch me for months. A lot can happen before this baby is born."

It sounded like a threat and I told her so. She merely looked at me defiantly and laughed.

"You know you'll never let anyone chop my head off, Neil."

For a moment I was afraid she was right. How did she know my secret revulsion at even the thought of decapitation? It was something only Kieran knew, something I had never spoken of louder than in my thoughts. Suddenly the memory of a conversation with my brother came to my mind, one of those non-verbal conversations of which there had been so many. This one, though, had been on the day of our consecration as Knights, the day I first began to suspect our sister was more than the sweet flower of our lives. I looked into her grey-blue eyes as I recalled the day of it and the way of it, and the whole uncomfortable feeling echoed within me once again as a fragment of that mental conversation transited my consciousness.

That's the same look Frank had when he tried to kill me the last two times.

Kill you?

Me, you, us, Richard, Stephen, whomever. The memory is the same for both of us. There's no point in splitting hairs as to which of us it was. Remember looking into his face just before the knife slit Richard's throat. Remember the face Stephen saw down the length of the sword at his throat as he lay on the floor of Nottingham Castle.

God's Hooves, Neil. Gwenna?

Yes.

Then close your mind even to me, Anmchara.

Why?

Remember that Frank was also a telepath.

Had Kieran been right, and our diversion with Eleanor caused us to forget the initial warning?

Neil?

Yes?

Are you all right?

Perfectly. Do you remember once suggesting Gwenna had Frank's telepathic abilities?

Yes, but I doubt it now. She and Duncan would have never allowed themselves to be captured so easily. Besides, if you're worried about it why are you thinking to me?

The face didn't look as if she'd tuned in on anything. It was a cool masque of annoyance through which an occasional ember of hatred burned. Perhaps it had been a coincidence. Perhaps there had been no reference to anything in the past. Perhaps she had not even been Frank, as we supposed, but merely a rotten apple on her own. I looked into her eyes again, those steely eyes so cold they made me shiver, and I had to steady myself against what I saw.

There may have been no telepathy, but there was something behind those eyes which demanded to be acknowledged. There was some measure of power, but a tremendous appetite for more, an old hunger which yearned to devour all in its way. It was a hunger which had nearly consumed me once before, one that knew me and knew that I had recognised it once again and given it a name.

Frank.

Yet I heard my sister's sweet voice telling me that I would never let anyone chop her head off, and I saw in my mind my good friend Malcolm with the axe in his hands and watched it swing through the arc which left his own brother a headless corpse upon the block, and once again I swallowed hard to keep from retching at the thought of the sensation I had myself known upon a similar block more than once.

At least the decision was not one I had to make immediately. Her child was not due until Yule or thereabouts and we had one of our own to worry about.

The months passed swiftly with no one even questioning the whereabouts of Gwenna and Duncan, and a good deal of our time was spent preparing with Eleanor for the birth of Princess Emily Rose Victoria. Eleanor carried her well, seeming to have little discomfort even into her eighth month of pregnancy as we attended the September Coronation of Robert at Scone, delighted to hear the song of the stone beneath his feet. Its ring was not so loud or pronounced as ours had been, but the Tor itself had been responsible for the resonance which the slightest vibration from our Kingstone had produced. Still, there was no mention of Duncan's absence from the occasion.

The one awkward moment came when the Great Lairds including Malcolm, as Tanist, were asked to swear fealty to their King. It was an old custom in which the sovereign took the hands of the noble between his as the noble knelt to make his oath of fealty. Robert knew this was something his brother could not do as his fealty had already been sworn to the English crown, yet it was something which must appear to take place, at least in the minds of his people.

Malcolm approached, unsure of what to expect. As he drew near his brother and prepared to kneel, his brother stopped him and bade him turn outward to face the crowd.

"Prince Malcolm, Our brother, shall not in any manner kneel before Us, for he is Our Tanist, who shall succeed us upon the throne unless and until Our wife Queen Margaret is blessed with children. If she is so blessed he shall be their guardian and Protector and give judgement and laws in their name until they come of age. He has made his oath of fealty to his rightful King even before the crown was set upon Our head. Malcolm, before these witnesses We ask only that you reaffirm upon your sword all that you promised in your faith and duties to your Sovereign Lord and King as you have already sworn."

Malcolm smiled at his brother with more love in his expression than I'd ever seen before in the Stuart family and drew his sword. His eyes met mine and his expression became totally serious.

"My Liege Lord and Sovereign King, upon my sword and before the Gods and these people I do reaffirm the oath I have taken."

He kissed the rose upon the sword's hilt and slipped it back into his scabbard as Robert turned and winked at me. England and Scotland never had known so strong an alliance as Malcolm had brought between us, nor so much respect for each other, despite all the attempts of Duncan and Gwenna to destroy the families of both kingdoms.

Confident in the ability of Parliament to cope with the affairs of State for a few weeks we all settled in at Stonehurst for a well-deserved holiday, our last having ended so abruptly with the assassination of our parents. The beauty and peace of the place was like a tonic to us all, and in the afternoon of Samhain Eve, the anniversary of the death of our great-great-grandfather and the birth of our grandfather we saw our daughter Emily Rose Victoria come into this world in the same bed which had seen the births of so many of our family.

She was perfect, the delight of our lives, tiny and helpless, and Kieran and I didn't care which one of us was the father. She was our daughter, Eleanor's, Kieran's and mine, and although legally she was theirs, spiritually she was ours.

Eleanor was strong and healthy and more beautiful than ever to us, to all of us. Jack, though long out of practice in the care of infants, was well experienced and soon found himself giving advice on every little nuance of the art, while Malcolm found himself overcome with emotion each time he held "the Bonnie Rose" as he was fond of calling her, remembering his own unborn children and accepting the care of ours as a sort of consolation.

Still, the two of them found time for mischief.

"You know, I think she looks more like Kieran," began Malcolm one morning as he held Emily.

"No, if you look closely, especially around the eyes, you can plainly see she looks more like Neil," countered Jack.

"You really think so? Well I don't see it. The nose is definitely Kieran's."

"But the mouth, now that's pure Neil, if I ever did see a resemblance."

And so on, until there was a sudden rush of wet warmth in Malcolm's lap.

"But the plumbing now, that's all Eleanor."

Kieran and I took the joking for what it was, love, and played along. We had lived to see our child born, to hold her in our arms, to see some of what the future would bring. It was the sweetest and most peaceful time I can recall in any of our lives.

We knew it could not last forever.

Chapter Twenty-Nine

I suppose it had started earlier, although we had been so caught up in the birth of our daughter that we paid its importance little attention, besides, who has time to think of dreams when there is a newborn in the house; for that matter, who gets enough sleep to have them?

We all began having them sometime during the first week of November, and as usual, Kieran and I continued to share dual roles in each, the slayer and the slain in all their aspects, though the role of slayer had passed the barrier of guilt and anguish this time, enjoying the bliss of the slain. Such had been Stephen's gift to his Knight, our gift to each other even before we had merged in the blue summer sky above Stonehenge.

They were all there before us, all the doors to the past, opening and revealing old faces, old politics, old loves and the simplicity of their resolution. We were gathered there each time, the five of us, gathered to focus the power and the joy we had carried within us, and dedicated to returning it to its Source. All was as it had been, yet subtly changed. All was subjective and objective at the same time, everything perceived from all sides as a matter of we or he/we/I.

At the stone circle with the others watching the bloody gladius did its task once more, the cold blade bringing its ultimate release to a thankful King. This time there was understanding in the eyes of the slayer, and the final breath passed between us in peace.

"It is time," said the voice to the slayer some days later. "Your work is done. Come home".

He/We/I climbed the yew tree, tossed the noose around his/our/my neck and leapt.

The time changed, the places and the bodies, but the eyes remained unchanged, knowing all that had gone before and ready to reprise their roles as the Lady directed.

The litany was spoken in hushed tones and manic euphoria as we dressed for the occasion, adjusting each other's rapier carriers to just the right angle, and for this one occasion we exchanged swords.

"The signs are given," said the King, as solemn-faced as he/we/I could manage. "The time has come when to the appointed place I must travel to fulfil the promise of my birth. As the seed is sown, so must the grain be reaped for the nourishment of all."

"Why must you go unto this place?" asked the Knight, his/our/my eyes twinkling at the secret we shared.

"To give up my life that the Land might be healed."

The sense of anticipation between us was sweet, the foreplay which led to the final ecstasy, though the Knight was eager for the thrusting to begin.

"Why must you go unto this place?"

And why must we waste time with these questions? The moon has already risen.

"To give up my life that the Land might be healed."

Patience, Raoul. The steel won't rust while we take the time to do this right.

"Why must you go unto this place?"

I am sorry, mon ami. You are right. We have only one chance this generation. Yet it is your life's blood which matters, not what we say here.

"To give up my life that the Land might be healed."

What we say here is part of what we do here. We must be focused on what we do, although I must admit, my impatience is as great as yours.

"Thrice asked, thrice answered. And by what right do you claim the honour to be the Blessed Sacrifice?"

You know as well as I it is the steel which will focus us.

"I am the son of Kings, and bearer of the blood which heals. This vessel must be shattered that the bounty within might return to the Land to nourish it and its people."

The steel and Her will.

Her will. Of course. Think carefully before you answer the next question Armand. Answer it not with your mind but your heart, for I am just now being able to answer it myself.

"And do you do this of your own free will?"

Oh yes, Raoul. With my heart so filled with love for all of you that if you don't pierce it, it will surely burst on its own. And here, in the midst of those who have no idea they have built their great estate on our most sacred land.

"Of my own free will I offer you my sword in assurance that I do."

Strange, but I feel it too. Perhaps for the first time there will be peace at my end of this.

"So Mote It Be, then, Sire."

So Mote It Be, Raoul. When this is over go with Therese. She will need to comfort you as much as you will need her comfort. We will not be separated long, I promise.

"So Mote It Be, and may the Gods grant us Their Grace to do this well."

We spoke no more to one another as we took our places and began to feel the temper of the ground upon which we would stage our last fight in those bodies. The grass was mercifully dry; the chances of slipping upon it were slight, and it would quickly and thankfully drink in Armand's blood. We drew our rapiers and the crowd began to gather around us, the sleeping crowd who walked through what they thought was life, unaware of what went on around them, of what life could truly be.

The night was clear, extraordinarily clear and black but for the silver beacon of the full moon which hung a hand's breadth high over the eastern horizon. Yves in russet held the King's jacket and waistcoat, Michel as he had always done wore blue, and green-eyed Guy in silver and grey held the goblet of wine and made light talk of the season and the harvest as we prepared for what was to appear to be a fencing match.

The torches flickered, their light glancing from the rapier blades as we two, Armand and Raoul circled each other, smiling. The clash of steel upon steel kindled our blood with fire brighter than flame. We were alive, so alive, so filled with the moment and the purpose that we thought we might burst from the joy of it, the reason for it, and the private joke we played that night upon the Pagan-hostile world in yielding up the precious blood of the King in the midst of those who would burn us at the stake for our impertinence.

After a few heated exchanges Guy stopped us for a cooling drink of deep red wine. It was the last toast, the final salute, and the five of us shared it in love and gratitude for our time together, and to hail our next meeting. The goblet made its round and what we had not drunk was poured out upon the ground. It mattered no longer to us whether or not the grass was slippery, for as long as Armand died well and swiftly by Raoul's hand Raoul's life was unimportant.

From our viewpoint the whole dance of death occurred in slow motion. Each breath, each position of foot, hand and sword was anticipated, met, and played to as if it had been rehearsed, which it had not. There was no need for that, for our minds were linked in those final moments to the rhythm of the tune She called. Our purpose was sealed and could not fail. The clashes, the clangs, the dazzling flourishes of our swordplay were all for show; Armand's body held the spirit as delicately as fingertips might direct a foil in practice play. The little smile, the slight nod of the head, and the opening was there for the rapier.

He/we/I felt its welcome pathway through the flesh, cold against the heat of the blood which rose to meet it, felt the sturdy blade slide across the ribs, running true to course, felt both in the hand which held the sword and the body which relaxed and yielded gracefully and completely to its demand. Raoul pulled the smiling shell of the dead man off the rapier and closed the blue eyes as he/we/I laid him gently in the pool of blood, then with the help of Yves, Michel and Guy, ran to the carriage where Therese waited. He/we/I noticed in passing the face our friend Guy wore had changed slightly. His hair was now auburn, but the eyes were, as they had been on so many occasions, green.

Back in her quarters our lovely Therese held Raoul, sobbing, and once more they/we made love, lonely for Armand's demands to move over and make room for him in the bed we had frequently shared. Even the sweetness of filling her could not compare to the ecstasy he/we/I had felt in that brilliant flash of steel as the flesh had embraced it.

There was a noise; I/we/he dressed hurriedly and slipped out the back. The streets were wet cobblestone, the air was chilled, and a low fog had filled the blackness in which the moon stood overhead as the only illumination. From behind him/us/me came the sound of steel being drawn; how he/we/I had missed the other man's footsteps will always be a mystery.

The man was dressed in brown and tan, had sandy hair and blue eyes, a face too round for the shape of his moustache, and a rapier coated with fast acting poison. Before Raoul could engage him the blade had pierced his/our/my shoulder and the poison had begun its journey through Raoul's body.

"It is time," said Armand's voice in his/our/my head. "Your work here is finished, mon ami."

"But Therese..."

"She will be cared for. Come."

There was a surge of warm light which filled him/us/me, then sweet coolness, darkness, and a dazzling brilliance which the living senses could not fathom, but he was there and I was there, and the world of men no longer seemed to matter.

I awoke refreshed that morning, more refreshed than I had been in days, kissed Eleanor and the Bonnie Rose and embraced my brother the way Armand and Raoul had embraced the night they had died. It was in his eyes as well, the understanding, the remembrance.

Neil?

It was more than a dream, Kieran.

I know.

I've never had their names before.

Nor I. Only Therese.

He's Awakening.

Yes.

We don't have long to wait now.

No, Anmchara. Does this make you sad?

No, merely impatient.

To have it all end?

To see how it will all begin again, perhaps.

We were both still smiling when Malcolm called us to the kitchen.

"I hope you know we're nearly out of tea and biscuits," he said shaking the tea caddy. "Why do you always send the staff away before they've had a chance to do a proper shopping?"

He must have caught our expression, for he stopped his blustering at once and set the caddy down.

"You too? Well that seals it. Jack was on about it this morning. That's the third or fourth one for him this week, but this one was detailed, names and all. I wonder how long it will be until we hear from our green-eyed man?"

"Perhaps we should go back to London to wait it out," I suggested. "We're nearly out of tea and biscuits here anyway."

Chapter Thirty

*L*ondon was much as we had left it. Gwenna had grown larger with the child she carried until we thought her body could expand no more but it was only mid-November; she had a good six weeks to go. Her face seemed more angular against the roundness of her body, and her sunken eyes were as full of hatred as ever.

"Is there anything we can do to make you more comfortable?" I asked her.

"Haven't you done enough already?" she responded. "The bed is comfortable enough. The food is nutritious. All you can do for me now is die and take the rest of the family with you so my son can take his place on the throne."

"Your son?" I countered. "I thought he was the son of Richard Windsor and Kate O'Conor. You, my dear, are merely a vehicle to bring him into this world."

"He will outlive all of us, Neil. Or are you Kieran pretending to be Neil? Neil was never so cynical."

"No, I am Neil. I'm afraid the decimation of the royal houses of Stuart and Windsor has made me cynical. And you did almost succeed in starting another war with Argentina."

She smirked at me, her face no longer beautiful in my eyes.

"No, not I. That was Duncan's idea. The one bright idea of his life, actually, other than marrying me. He was a dolt otherwise."

She stared at me even as I stared at her, though I did not feel her gaze pierce me as it had done long ago.

"Who are you, really?"

"Your loving sister," she replied in anything but a loving tone.

"Sorry I asked."

The venom in her voice was mixed with honey; it dripped slowly from her mouth and clung to each word of her confession with a sickening sweetness tinged with a mild hysteria.

"No. You've been working on that one for a long time. If it will make your job easier I'll tell you. Yes, I was Francis Eddings-Roth, the brave Knight of the Order and loyal, trusted friend to Richard Windsor. How do you think I found out about the embryos? I thought having the child of my former wife and the friend I murdered to get her would be the last stroke of irony. How does that make you feel? The real irony is that the child will keep me around long enough to know you're dead."

The look I gave her must have been one of mild surprise.

"Oh yes, you'll be dead soon. Don't think I can't feel the cycles of the Land. We've been through them before. I've killed you three times already, and you've been a part of my death at least that number. Frank made the mistake of not counting the people he tied up and forgetting there had been ladies present. Richard of York was in the wrong place at the wrong time, and Skarios, well his name was the one you drew."

I didn't recognise the name or the inference and told her so.

"Remember I once said that I had a memory, or Frank did, of Richard or whoever he had been smiling sweetly as the skin was peeled from his bleeding body? That was my Awakening, my dear. The memory of that day my name was drawn to succeed him, and the night before when my daughter was taken from the House of the Vestals to be his whore."

The whole episode came back to me in a rush of colour and sound, of emotion and at last the release of it all into a warm and satisfying oblivion.

Eleanor found me unconscious there a few moments later. Kieran had fainted as well, collapsing in her arms and both Malcolm and Jack had fallen into a similar state. She had remembered where I had gone and decided I might be in danger. The Yeoman Warder assured her there had been no commotion inside the room and no one had emerged, but she reminded him that not much sound goes through four metres of stone.

When they opened the door they found Gwenna laughing hysterically as she sat upon the edge of the bed looking at my unconscious and helpless form. Eleanor, satisfied that I was merely in some sort of trance, held me until consciousness returned, watching as her sister-in-law sunk further and further into what appeared to be madness.

"What are you doing here?" I asked when I was finally able to speak; she told me.

"Go ahead," said Gwenna. "Take your little whore out of here. Do you think any of us have been blind to your affairs? At least I know who fathered the child I bear."

It did not matter to either of us that her charge was true, any more that it mattered to Kieran, Jack or Malcolm. I was about to leave with Eleanor when a nagging question ran through my mind.

"I have just one more thing to ask you."

"I have nothing to hide."

"When you were Skarios and became the King your daughter had slept with your predecessor."

"You know that. You destroyed her."

"Did she conceive that night?"

"No."

"Then you were forced to..."

"Yes. I killed her with my own hands. I put them around that slender white neck, put the thumbs at the hollow of her throat and squeezed and pushed until I felt the little bone in there snap."

She was animated, excited as she babbled the horror to us, her breathing fast and hard as her eyes glowed with the memory.

"I squeezed until her eyes bulged and her tongue was as black as her face, until the nails on my fingers dug into her flesh and blood dripped down my arms, and even after I knew she was dead I continued to squeeze."

She was giddy with the memory, little giggles popping in between her words.

"And I have never enjoyed anything as much, until, of course, I slit your throat, Richard."

She was insane, but she was too dangerous to let loose upon any hospital. Besides, with what she knew she could never leave the Tower alive.

Three weeks later James David Swindon of Toronto, Ontario arrived upon our doorstep, a musician and singer of some note to the youth on both sides of the Atlantic, twenty-three years of age with auburn hair to his shoulders and eyes as green as oak leaves in the spring forest. The wound upon his chest had not yet fully healed and the sword in its scabbard had been drawn but once, in the making of that wound and the taking of the blood oath. His visions as he sat his pre-consecration vigil over his sword on Samhain Eve had been sweet and sorrowful, and had continued each night since, the latest occurring the preceding evening as he was sitting in his studio in Tottenham with a nine-stringed guitar working on his latest composition. He had been so upset that he had rung up Tyrell House for advice.

They had sent him directly to us.

He was some distant relation to us, he had figured, for his great grandmother had been the sister of Kevin, Duke of Cornwall, but other than his insistence at preserving the tradition of the family with respect to the Order he had never thought to make the connexion more than it was. The Gods, it seemed had planned otherwise.

There was something of Clarice, as I recalled her, in this young man, the shape of his face, the nose, perhaps the tilt of her head. I had not thought of Clarice more than once before, when I had been reading Kevin's journal. How odd that our fifth man would also come from so close a family line.

He knew all of it, all our times together, all the joy and pain, and yet he knew more, for he had heard the call the wind makes as it blows through the ruins atop the Tor, and upon that call was Her voice, and Her voice had spoken his name. He had looked up to behold no one there, nothing but the walls of his studio. Then the walls faded away before his eyes and he seemed to be upon a rolling plain. It was parched and withered, its crop of barley left to rot on the stalk. Naked children staggered over rocks, their bodies emaciated and feeble, looking for something to feed them or to at least assuage their thirst. The King arrived in a robe of green with his four attendant Knights in burgundy, blue, russet and grey and together they saw the suffering of the children. The King held out a chalice and a knife and a beautiful Lady with flame-red hair appeared in their midst all dressed in black, desiring to consecrate the cup with the King, but the cup was empty. The King called forth his Knight dressed in burgundy and handed both the cup and blade to him, opened his own robe to the waist, and smiled at the children and the Lady as the burgundy Knight plunged the dagger into his heart, pulled it out again, and caught the flowing blood in the chalice. As the Lady drank Her fill from the chalice the King's blood continued to flow in a stream which turned to pure water as it touched the earth. His body turned to sweet, unblighted barley, some of which was broken off and given to the children; it turned to bread as it touched their hands and they were able to nourish themselves with that bread and the water which had been blood. The rest of the barley was broken off the stalks and planted by the four Knights as the Lady danced with the knife and the chalice. When Her dance had ended there was lush vegetation upon the plain and a cool stream running through it with four wells, one at each of the cardinal points of the Land.

Flame-red hair, hair the shade of a raven's wing, it made no difference. She had many guises, many names, and through time we had learned to honour them all. I felt my heart pounding in anticipation as I listened to each word of his tale, hanging upon each rich image as if I lived it, knowing that soon I would. The time was near. The Land had called for the blood of the King.

Kieran's reaction was the same as mine, a mixture of elation and anticipation. This was our destiny, the reason for which we had been born and reborn, the culmination of all our loves, all our memories, our goal and our purpose. It was our end and would be in that end our beginning. Already we could feel the steel in our hands, cold and deadly, the winter air, Our Lady's breath, cold upon our necks, and Her kiss hot within our blood.

There was so much to plan, so much to do before it all came to pass, and it must come to pass soon; we had been summoned by the Lady and could not keep Her waiting long even if we had wanted to do so. That, however, had never been, nor never would be our intention.

We settled on the Winter Solstice, the next major festival, at midnight, and at Stonehenge. As with so many things of late, we opted for secrecy, for this time we wanted no public scene. It was between the five of us and of course Eleanor would need to know.

The Hierarchy of the Order knew. They would be needed after the fact as well as before, for another Coronation should be staged by Imbolc, and their jurisdiction over Salisbury Plain must be utilised to secure the area for us. Of course Robert of Scotland was told, for the death of the King of England affected his Tanist in many ways. For one thing, it would free him to serve his brother.

I did not need to tell Eleanor; she knew from the moment the fifth Companion had shown up that our time together was short, and accepted it as one who has borne that burden all too often. I also had no intention of telling Gwenna.

The timing was not right for everything, of course. I would be out of the picture nearly a week before the birth of Richard. I would not be able to meet him this round, nor to see his host-mother's execution. The former saddened me, but the latter relieved me greatly; I had no wish to watch another decapitation. What did worry me, though, was Kieran's ability to withstand Gwenna's wiles on his own.

Chapter Thirty-One

*T*he days passed quickly as they shortened; the nights were long and filled with happiness. We had two full weeks together this time, an unusual and welcome departure from the norm. Together it became possible to form a link almost as strong as that between Kieran and me, possible to hold hands in silence and communicate more than words would allow. There was a balance between us, as if the elements had each been perfectly invoked and held at their junction, the blade and haft of the sword and its quillons coming together at the point beneath the rose.

We were merry in that manic way which always preceded the end of it, and Malcolm called for the one thing we had not found time for in centuries: a hunt, a real hunt in a forest with longbows and horses and all. Kieran was mad for the idea; he hadn't had a chance to use a longbow in ages, but he was certain his skills hadn't been lost.

Really? Would you prefer to take me at the tree this time as you refused to do once before?

However you wish it, Anmchara. Although I would prefer to be closer to you, to touch you as it happens. Arrows require such distance.

True. Besides, steel makes such a wonderful sound. I can't wait to hear it echo among the stones.

A lot better than quarterstaffs, remember?

How could I forget?

And yet it seemed as if that Summer Solstice had been not that long ago when I had lain face down in the grass, my spirit flying above the trilithons to see the stone we had marked in our fall from the sky when we had been Stephen and Kevin. Our parents had been alive then, and we had all been so happy, not knowing the strange pathways our lives and deaths would follow, and soon...

Soon Kieran would be all that would be left of that family, Kieran and Eleanor and Emily, the Bonnie Rose of our lives, a new generation of Windsors to lead the healthy nation I would leave behind.

"So where shall we hunt?"

Malcolm's voice brought me back.

"Savernake. There should be plenty of red deer, perhaps a few roe as well."

No boar to tear your leg open, though, Anmchara.

Thank you. It will be a much better sword fight if I have two good legs.

And so it was settled. The last full day of my life would be spent as a King, hunting the King's deer.

With Eleanor's leave we set out the evening before to a small hunting lodge inside the forest. It was amazing to Malcolm that so large a forest could still exist so close to the city, but I explained to him the conservation laws set down by Stephen II and the Royal Grants of Reforestation in which the land had been reclaimed and replanted at a sizable profit to the land's former owners. Money could be coined in a moment; oaks took generations to reach their full height.

The lodge was cold and dusty, unused since our father's fifty-third birthday party when a case of "food poisoning" on the part of the French Ambassador had almost caused an international incident. It had been his own fault. He had claimed to be an expert on wild mushrooms. He should have known the ones he had picked and added to his lunch had been hallucinogenic. Fortunately he had lacked the coordination to pull a bow thereafter, or it might have been more than interesting to find out what "monsters" he had seen and attempted to shoot.

The firewood was only mildly damp, and James seemed to have a knack for getting it started. We kept it going through the night, drinking fine dark ale and Irish, singing songs, telling tales and reminiscing. Just before the dawn we set out, not really caring whether or not we found any deer, just wanting to be one with the forest as we were with each other.

The sun had barely risen, its first red-gold rays peeping through the stark winter branches of the trees, when I beheld the stag, his many-tined antlers blending in so completely with the rest of the forest. His breath was a white fog as he stared at me, unafraid. I reached into my quiver and nocked the arrow, drawing the bowstring back tight against my right cheek. Still he stood there in wide-eyed magnificence, this red King who wore the crown Nature had provided. Neither of us blinked or moved for several seconds, and the tension of the bowstring became at last unbearable, when finally his head dipped slightly to me, a little nod, a little gesture of deference from one King to another, and I let the arrow fly.

I saw it all, Anmchara. Well done.

Thank you. Oh Gods, Kieran do you see this?

Behind the fallen stag another figure stepped from the mists of morning, antlered as the stag had been, but as tall as a tall man and with a man's shape. His robe was vaguely tattered, as if it had been made from the leaves of the trees which stood bare behind him. I fell to my knees before him, for I recognised the Guardian of the Windsors since before my bloodline had worn the name.

Herne.

I do see him, Neil. I am right behind you.

I could not turn to look, for I was transfixed by Him.

"You would bring the Wild Hunt with you?" He demanded, His voice like thunder.

"I would do Your bidding, My Lord, as I do Hers."

He seemed to smile, to look at me, through me, and beyond me.

"Soon. Soon King Stag will shed his human blood. We are all hunters for a time, as we are all the hunted. The prey finds his peace sooner, that is all. Go with My peace. This one was a gift to you as you shall be to the Land."

And then He was gone, as silently, as quickly as He had come.

The others had seen, had heard it all. They were strangely silent as we dressed the deer and prepared to haul it back with us to the Tower. We left early in the day, our hunt more successful than we could have expected.

We all shared the venison roast back at the Tower, including Eleanor, who for some reason was not amazed at the tale we told her of the hunt. It seemed only natural to her. After all, had Herne in effigy not saved us once from Frank's murderous plans? He was always near us, always watching, always guarding.

Where had He been then at Windsor Castle when our parents had been murdered?

"Windsor Forest was cut down long ago," she said. "He cannot live within walls of stone. He fled to Savernake, to Sherwood, to Scotland, to Wales to anywhere the trees grow. Perhaps if you reforested Windsor He would come back."

And perhaps that was why we had always felt so uneasy at Windsor although there was no forest near the Tower either. But then we had the Ravens here, and they were Her birds, sleek and glistening, guardians of not just our family but the whole Kingdom.

"It was supposed to have been replanted nearly a century ago," said Malcolm. "Jack was in charge of it. I suppose when he died the project died with him."

Jack looked up at us sheepishly.

"Will all be forgiven if I take care of it this time?"

We assured him it would.

After our feast I excused myself and retired. Not long after there was a tapping upon the heavy oaken door to my chamber. It was Eleanor, sweet and fragrant and dressed in ice-blue silk with pearls woven into her hair. Her breasts were still heavy with milk, but other than that her figure had almost returned to the perfection it had been our first night together at Wookey Hole as Kieran and I had shared the wonder of her and the Goddess who had filled her soul.

"You've managed all this since supper? I asked as I touched her hair, twirling the black tendrils around my forefingers.

"I hoped you'd enjoy it."

She pulled me close to her and slipped my hands beneath her robe. Her skin was warm satin to my touch, hot silk to my kisses.

"Where is Kieran?" I asked.

"In our room."

"Shouldn't we share this, the three of us, as we did in the beginning?"

"No, my love. I want to be selfish with you, just this once. It's the only time we will have alone."

Don't question her, Neil. She wants this so much.

Be with us this way, then.

Yes. But tonight three bodies would just get in the way of what two can do so well. Enjoy.

The feel of him within my head sharing my perceptions only intensified the sensations as Eleanor and I spent Solstice Eve together, holding, caressing, enjoying each other to the fullest. Every touch trembled with delight, each soft stroke, each tender kiss, each wet trail our tongues made over skin which quivered in their passing, each moment was so vibrant, so full, so alive. Her body had softened from motherhood, but its yearnings had only become deeper, more passionate, more eager to be fulfilled, and I was just as eager to satisfy her every desire.

There was no part of her too hidden to receive my kisses, no part of me not welcomed with her impassioned sighs. Again and again we coupled throughout the long night which preceded the shortest day, each time reaching the delicious reward of our sweet struggle until there was no more we could do but sleep, satisfied, in each other's arms.

Neil?

?????

I love you.

I love you too, Anmchara.

I don't know why I've never said it before.

We've never needed to say what we can always feel between us.

It won't be us for much longer.

It will. Nothing can separate us anymore. You can feel me in you as I can feel you in me.

Yes.

You always said we only really needed one body. I think tonight proved that.

It was wonderful. She is so beautiful.

Yes. I don't think I could have gone on that long without you, though.

We'll have to try it from the other direction after...

I could feel a hesitance, a sadness within his thoughts, one he was trying unsuccessfully to hide from me. I had to reassure him, to remove any doubt within him about the night to come.

No Kieran. It will be wonderful. You'll feel it, I promise. And then we'll be as we are now, only there will be no going back. I'm sorry you'll never have any privacy again.

That's all right. I never did any way.

No regrets?

No, only...

What?

Nothing.

No, it's there.

No, really.

If you don't give it to me I'll search until I get it on my own.

You'll think it silly.

No I won't.

All right. I was wondering what it would have been like for us.

How?

Had we been lovers this time. There is a part of me which clings to that very special feeling between Lucius and Marcellinus.

Yes, Anmchara, it was special, but it was a part of what has made us what we are now.

I just wondered how it would have been between us in these bodies which were once one flesh, and with these minds and spirits which meld so absolutely.

I was silent, even in my mind as the emotion flowed between us, an emotion which transcended life, death and gender.

Exactly.

Awhile later he joined us, a crying Emily in his arms.

"She's hungry, darling."

Eleanor turned over and smiled, sitting up and reaching for our child. As Emily nursed greedily upon the same nipple which had filled my mouth an hour or so before, I realised I was as much at peace as any man could be while he lived. This was life, the meaning of it all, the reason to keep it going, and the reason to let it go cheerfully and lovingly when the time came.

I took my brother's hand.

It will be wonderful.

There were tears in his eyes as he squeezed my hand in return.

As it always has been, as it always will be.

Yes.

The rest of the day was almost prosaic, papers to fill out, letters to be sent the following morning, instructions for my burial next to the other grave at Stonehenge, or within it if possible. We might put together a whole collection of our bones there, although these would not be as broken as the first lot. No need to clutter up the place with markers; we were all the same people. One grave would do us nicely. Just leave room for my brother, please. I would feel better knowing the womb of the Earth held us together in death as the womb of Queen Katherine had held us in life.

Darkness came early. Kieran and I embraced our Eleanor and our child with great tenderness, for it was to be the last time we all would be together in those forms. Eleanor smiled, even as we left her side.

"It is as it must be," she said. "May we remember all this with joy when next we meet."

I kissed her again on the top of her head and did not look back.

It was dark already when we left the Tower, dark along the road, and darker still as we arrived at our destination.

"Ninety years go tonight Stephen made the Tor sing as the crown was put upon his head. Six months later he and his Duke died here," I said. "Ironic, isn't it?"

"How so?" asked James.

"Six months ago I was crowned upon the Tor. The stone sang again. Now I am here to shed my blood again."

There's no such thing as a coincidence, Anmchara. Everything happens for a reason.

Including us.

Of course.

We are the playthings of the Gods.

Then let's put on a show for them they won't forget.

The guards knelt before us and asked our blessing. Odd, though I'd been a Priest as long as I'd been a Knight I don't remember blessing anything but the food and drink. Perhaps it was the blessing of the King's blood they were asking. My brother and I each touched them on the head and thanked them for their service.

Could they watch? Of course, we told them, as long as it didn't interfere with their guard duties, but who would be out on the Salisbury Plain on Yule Night?

They were more than grateful, Knights of the Order assigned to special duty on the night of a Festival, eight men about the same age as Kieran and myself who had been told the reason for their assignment and wished to witness the most sacred of the rites. How could we refuse them the very core of their faith, the reason for the Order for which they had already shed their blood?

We stationed them just outside the great stones and asked them if they would like to hold the torches we had brought instead of us sticking them in the ground as we had planned. They were overjoyed; this would indeed be a tale to tell their sons when they reached the age to make their contributions to the Order. I think they were a bit surprised to learn that the torches were the old-fashioned kind, made of wood and rag coated in a flammable solution, and not the cold artificial light we know today. We wanted to recreate the feeling of that other sword fight so long ago.

This time there was to be no acting, no pretence. This time it was open to eyes outside those of the Companions, eyes of those who worshipped as we did, who belonged to the Lady as much as we did, and knew the importance of what we did, those who knew the lineage of the Kings and the blood they carried and were not afraid to see it shed in this manner.

Our happiness could not have been more complete.

We shared the cup with all of them this time; there was plenty, for the bowl was large, the Irish was good, and the cold of the winter's night had made its presence known. I took one last sweet warm swallow and poured the remainder over the grave. Stephen had always been partial to Bushmills.

Kieran smiled at the gesture as he looked into my eyes and we began the litany, loudly enough this time for all who had gathered to hear it as it should be spoken, in pride, confidence, and in love. It was an odd effect, for in my head I heard my voice along with his and his with mine on the replies.

"The signs are given. The time has come when to the appointed place I have travelled to fulfil the promise of my birth. As the seed is sown, so must the grain be reaped for the nourishment of all."

"Why must you come unto this place?"

Do you hear two voices?

"To give up my life that the Land might be healed."

Of course. How else could we do this? There is so much of each of us in the other that it must come from us both, even as it took us both to make the stone sing.

"Why must you come unto this place?"

Then we must both die.

"To give up my life that the Land might be healed."

Perhaps. Would that be so terrible?

"Why must you come unto this place?"

No.

"To give up my life that the Land might be healed."

You promised me I would share this with you.

"Thrice asked, thrice answered. And by what right do you claim the honour to be the Blessed Sacrifice?"

As once I promised we would always leave this world together. But there is so much yet to do. Eleanor and Emily...

"I am the son of Kings, and bearer of the blood which heals. This vessel must be shattered that the bounty within might return to the Land to nourish it and its people."

You know Malcolm will take care of them.

"And do you do this of your own free will?"

Gwenna will soon give birth. What of her and that child?

"Of my own free will I offer you my sword in assurance that I do."

Malcolm is very good with that axe. He has more reason to kill her than he did Duncan. And the son will make up for the son he lost.

"So Mote It Be, then, Sire."

No, Neil, I think you were right in the first place. Let's make this real and leave it up to the Gods.

"So Mote It Be, and may the Gods grant us Their Grace to do this well."

His eyes glowed with the prospect as we exchanged swords.

Yes, Anmchara. So Mote It Be indeed.

The others did not need to know what we had planned, any more than they had needed to know that only three would come back from the skydiving episode.

Perhaps someday we can repeat that one too.

We saluted each other, locking eyes once again as our rapiers crossed, feeling the power of the night around us. Once again our Companions had dressed in their velvet and brocade coats and waistcoats, Jack in russet, Malcolm in blue, and Jamie in silver and grey. Malcolm held our coats and waistcoats of burgundy and green. In black pants, boots, and white ruffled shirts we were indistinguishable from each other, for even our gauntlets, daggers, rapiers and their carriers were identical. I wondered if even She could tell us apart.

Perhaps not. There is not much which has not been written upon both our souls.

In the torchlight, as before, we slowly circled each other, watching each other's face more than the golden lightning streaks our blades made in their thrusts and parries, feints and counterparries. Sweet was the song they sang to us in their own peculiar tempo, the clash and the scrape as our blades slid together, only to be shoved apart. His rapier came in above my left shoulder; my main gauche was there to greet it. I slashed in at his right; his main gauche met my blade with a clang. He came in at my head; I blocked with my dagger behind my rapier, then dropped the rapier blade and lunged. My blade slid along his to the hilt and we grinned at each other as he pushed me off.

Just like old times.

Better.

We're too evenly matched, Anmchara.

I know.

He began to feint more, to come in from beneath, to try all the tricks of our youth, but my blades were there each time to parry him.

I had forgotten how good you were.

No better than you.

We went at it again, the joy of the fight making us giddy to the point of light-headedness. The euphoria, the mania was there within us both, as well as the adrenaline. Our breath was hot upon the cold night air, puffing out of us into little clouds which hung for awhile before they dissipated. Despite it all there was a clarity of mind, of vision, of spirit which did not fade no matter how hard, no matter how fast we encountered each other.

The footwork around the stones was somewhat tricky, for we had resolved that nothing in the place should be moved for our convenience. Should one of us stumble, should one of us fall, the other was prepared to use the advantage, not with hostility, but with the knowledge that such was the way it must be. In that we had agreed at the beginning.

Suddenly we were both aware of the stillness around us. Not a single human around us seemed to blink, to breath, to have a heartbeat. Only the flames moved, their light dancing across the great stones and the small as we danced the dance of steel, the dance of death we loved so well.

Do you feel it, Kieran? The change in the air? In all that surrounds us?

Yes. As if we were all that lived within this circle.

It is a time without a time, a space without a space, and we never even cast a circle.

It was done long before us.

I feel as if we are in a vortex.

We are. The centre of a ley line system. All the energy we create here is sent out along the lines.

We never missed a beat with our swordplay as we shared our thoughts. The weapons were as beautiful and deadly as they had been when we had begun, but it seemed as if they moved on their own with little effort from us, and then...

Soon, my brother.

Perhaps it was a trick of the light, but his face seemed to glow, and everything from there on in seemed as if it was in slow motion. I felt the wave of emotion as it swept us both, the totally indescribable pouring forth of a rapture beyond any of my memories. As it engulfed us we searched out each other's eyes to share it as we had always shared everything. He gave me the tiniest of nods and that little smile by which I had always known the moment and my blade went out and up and through his heart.

I felt it all then, shared with him all of it until the very last. His smile broadened as the blood began to flow, the fullness of his heart emptying onto the grass beneath him. The sensation had not been of pain; far from it. I saw, I felt the light which blasted through him along the path of the steel, a brilliance which was almost tangible. He was filled for an instant with it, we both were, as his eyes shone into mine, and I felt him there, within me once again. Then his eyes were empty, except for the joy which had left its mark upon his smiling shell.

Kieran!

There was no reply.

Chapter Thirty-Two

I was alone.

For the first time since before our birth, for the first time since we had clung together in the skies above Stonehenge, linked and filled with joy at the knowledge that neither life nor death could come between us, for the first terrifying and agonising time there was only my mental voice searching him out and finding emptiness.

It had been this way before at the end, I remembered, always this way before that last glorious time when I had broken the unwritten rules of the game and stolen happiness for us both. Now, as Prometheus had been punished for stealing fire, I would be punished for my audacity, but unlike Prometheus I would have my heart, not my liver, picked out a piece at a time as payment for the confusion my selfish act had brought to my family and my nation. I had grown so addicted to his fire that its absence was unbearable. And yet...

His death had left me with the crown in my own right. I had my duty. I must suffer this in silence.

I held him in my arms and closed his eyes as I had always done, trying to figure out exactly what to do next. All along Kieran had been the King, not me, though hubris had prompted me to see it otherwise. It had been his presence within me which had made the Kingstone ring, and his blood which the Land had sought, not mine. There had been signs, I suppose, some memories which had been strongly Kevin's which were vague to him, and slight differences of temperament toward the end...

Or perhaps he had been right all along, our spirits were so strongly intertwined that there was Stephen in me and Kevin in him, and with that final thrust all of the King died and left the remnant Knight in the one remaining body. Perhaps I had a piece of him still within me. Perhaps...

Perhaps it did not matter.

The point was, Neil went off to die and he survived. Kieran went off to kill his brother, and he lay dead in my arms, and...

Perhaps it did not matter.

We had chosen which name we would respond to when we were babies. Perhaps I could just reverse that choice and be Kieran for as long as was left to me. Of course I would have to go through the coronation again, and would probably not be able to make the stone sing on my own. Or would I? There was now no question as to who had the right to the throne, unless of course the child were really his...

And Eleanor. Would she know?

Would she care?

Malcolm came to me and set his hand upon my shoulder, handing me the green coat. I could not deceive even him.

"The King is dead," he said. "Long live the King."

Through my tears I looked as deeply as I could into his eyes, trying to see if he knew, wishing with my very soul that I could speak to him in the same thought talk I had used with Kieran.

Kieran!

As loudly, as insistently as I could I thought to him, hoping, praying for a response from somewhere.

You said we'd be together. I felt you join with me. Why can't I find you? Tell me what to do.

All that was left of him filled my arms, yet the part that mattered was gone, leaving me empty and aching, hollow inside, another shell, like my brother, only one which could still walk, talk, feel pain, and wish fervently he were someone else so he could take his own life in peace without the thoughts of duty and noblesse oblige which had been ingrained upon him since his birth.

Lady, release me from this as I have released my brother.

"Kieran?" asked Malcolm in a soft and soothing voice.

Only the slightest trace of doubt. Perhaps...

Did it matter any more?

"I have never been alone before," I wept. "No matter where he was I could always reach him in my mind."

"I know. I felt the link break between us all. Come now. We must finish this and leave."

I nodded mechanically and followed his lead. Malcolm was stronger than I. He could face the loss of all he loved and still act as a Prince should, but then that was why he had always been left to pick up the pieces after I had fallen apart, or fallen from the sky, a fall from Grace or to it.

We picked my brother's body up and carried him around the stones, making sure the earth received every precious drop of his blood, then wrapped him in white linen and prepared to take him home to await his burial. Malcolm, Jack and James took care of the rest, as they always had. My duty was over.

My duty had just begun.

I did not lie with Eleanor that night; I went instead to Savernake to watch the sun rise.

"Herne," I invoked. "You placed the burden upon me when you gave me the Stag's life, and I did not understand."

I waited in the darkness, in the pre-dawn gloom, and in the sweet face of the sun, but I heard nothing and saw nothing. I was no longer a Windsor, but a Tyrell in Windsor's clothing, and the Grey Ghost had no bond with me.

I returned to the White Tower, slipping into my own quarters and hoping I could sleep. Eleanor's fragrance was still upon my bed and I wept at the memory of the morning before, from total happiness to emptiness in such swift order. And yet...

And yet I was alive. Death, which had so long been my goal, the whole focus of my life, had passed me by, and I must pick up the pieces of my brother's life and go on.

"Kieran?"

It was Eleanor's voice.

I froze, unsure of myself. Would I be able to convince our Eleanor, my Eleanor, that I was her husband?

She walked into the room and sat beside me upon the bed.

"Oh Kieran," she cried. "I shall miss him too."

"It was so wonderful, and so terrible, Eleanor. His face at the end was glorious, and the feelings he shared with me so incredibly beautiful...we were linked together closer than ever and then, suddenly he was gone and there was nothing."

I could not weep again. I was hollow; I was empty, totally void within myself. She rocked me as she rocked our child and I fell asleep for the entire day and night.

I wanted to dream, hoping against hope that I would find him in that shadow world, but the exhaustion kept me from even that. When I stirred into wakefulness I was alone.

Malcolm came around to see me soon afterward.

"You know of course the oath I took upon the sword and the rose now binds me to you as it did your brother."

I made an effort to smile.

"No, Malcolm. I am not the Sacred King, merely the Tyrell who slew him."

"My duty is to the Lady, the Land, and the King. You are now the King."

"I release you, Malcolm. Go back to Scotland."

He sat down upon the foot of the bed.

"You release me, do you?"

"I've already said so."

"Sorry, lad. Only death can do that. Besides, I won't be Tanist much longer. Margaret is pregnant and Robert says it's a son."

That, at least, brought a genuine smile to my face.

"How wonderful. They've tried for so long."

"They're going to name him Alexander Neil Stuart after...well I suppose you can guess who the names are after."

I wanted to shout that his middle name should be Kieran, but I had to keep my silence.

"Speaking of pregnancies, how is it with Gwenna?"

I told him all I knew, and most of that had been from Eleanor. The doctors had been with her since yesterday; her due date was in two days, and it seemed she might give birth at any moment.

"How long then until her execution?"

"Three days after the child is born. There is some law about her being able to walk to the block or the scaffold."

"Do you still want me to do it?"

"Do you want to?"

He paused, turned away, and ran his hands through his beard.

"She killed my wife and my dreams for a family. It would be justice. If I can lop off the head of my own brother don't think I'd weaken just because she's a woman."

I slept little that night, for soon after I had settled down beside Eleanor the baby cried, and even after she had been changed and fed I could not sleep but had to hold her for awhile, reminding myself that life was sometimes its own reward.

And then the alarm was rung. Gwenna had gone into labour.

It lasted throughout the night, into the following day, and on again into the next night, a total of twenty-six hours, but in the end Richard Stephen Arthur George Windsor was brought into this world none the worse for over a hundred and twenty years of suspension as an embryo in a cryogenic tank.

She was never allowed to see the child or to hold him. Eleanor volunteered to act as his wet-nurse and he was moved into the White Tower next to Emily as soon as the doctors had pronounced him fit.

By the time the evening before her scheduled execution came I had slept six hours of the past seventy-two. Somewhat light-headed from that and all that had gone on in the week before and looking like hell I went to confront my sister one last time.

She actually seemed lucid for once, her golden hair brushed and her face scrubbed, a clean white nightdress over a body no longer heavy with child.

"So you've come to see me at last, have you?"

"Yes," I replied, trying to see in her once more our little Gwenna for whom we would have done anything.

"She's not there, you know."

"Who?"

"Your little Gwenna of the Golden Hair."

I was taken aback; Frank's telepathic abilities were within her after all.

"Of course they are. Somehow the pregnancy dampened them a bit, that's all. I'm no longer pregnant, ergo they have returned."

"You know you're going to die tomorrow at the block."

"Am I? Well that will be something at any rate, a way to get me out of this dreary cell at last. I don't suppose you'll be doing the honours, will you? Killing your brother was more your speed."

"No," I said quickly, trying to keep her mind off that issue, "It will be Malcolm."

"Ah, yes, Malcolm. He has a nice swing with the axe. Poor Duncan looked so surprised at the end. I'm only sorry I couldn't have been there to see it in person. So much lovely blood and all."

She narrowed her eyes at me as if she were probing for something.

"But then you know all there is to know about blood, don't you, Kieran? Tell me, dear brother. How did it feel to kill him, to make his blood run onto the ground? I remember running three men through in a single evening, with a rapier that was a prop from a theatrical company."

She rose from her bed and began to illustrate the technique with her hands.

"Like so: bim, boom, bam. Three skewered so neatly and so quickly they never knew what happened."

"Stop it Gwenna," I ordered as I rose to leave.

"A bit touchy, aren't we, brother? And this is the last night we have to really chat. As I was saying, bim, boom, bam, and I never even knew them, poor things. What was it like to look him in the eyes, our dear brother, and stick a metre of steel into him?"

"Stop it I said!"

"Did you shove it in slowly and feel the metal grate against his ribs? Did you feel a little jerk at the end when his heart beat just once more with the blade already in it, as the auricles and ventricles shredded themselves upon the sharp cold steel you'd poked into them?"

"Curse you Gwenna! Enough!"

I grabbed her by the neck and began to squeeze. She relaxed to my hands around her throat, her eyes filling with delight and victory as her face began to turn red; realising what I was doing I threw her from me in horror and the tears came. I fought them, but they were stronger than I knew.

"I just want to know why you kill a brother and get his crown while Duncan kills one and is put to death by another. Tell me that, Kieran."

There was nothing I could say which would not make it worse.

"Or is it Kieran?"

Her eyes opened like an owl's, wide and keen as she probed the discovery she'd stumbled upon, more jubilant than surprised as her mind chewed upon such a tasty morsel of intrigue.

"No, it's Neil, isn't it? The wrong brother died, or the wrong brother was crowned. Oh what a lovely secret! The key to my freedom, Neil. You must not let them take me to the chopping block, dear brother. There will be witnesses for that. I have a right to my last words and when I tell them what I know it will be your head on the line, not mine, and my son will sit upon the throne of England."

She toyed with me as a cat with a moth, poking here and there with her words before trying to tear off my wings.

"Oh no, Neil. I always knew you would never let them chop off my head."

She laughed at me, mocking me. Daring me.

I grabbed her again and pulled her down upon her bed, my hand over her mouth to shut out the words I could not bear to hear, and then, as I had done before, I put the pillow over her face and pressed down with all my might, my anger dissipating quickly as it was replaced by something else, something which had been there all along, hiding, waiting for me to realise its presence: compassion.

"No, Gwenna. I would not let you go to the block. I hope you can still hear me in your mind and know why. It's not your words I fear. They would fall on ears which do not care. I have been beheaded. It's a horrid way to go."

Her struggling ceased, though I knew she was still alive.

"I would not wish that upon you. Nor would I wish it upon Malcolm to kill you in hate. He must release that from his heart. I do this in love for the sister you once were. I hope you find peace someday."

There was silence, but I held the pillow over her face still, as I had done with Richard of York in the same room so many lifetimes before. After a while I lifted the pillow and looked at her for the last time. There was no sign of pain, no sign she had resisted. Her eyes were closed as if she had been asleep.

I bent over and kissed her goodbye, then left the Bloody Tower and started back to my chambers in the White Tower.

The night was dark, still and crisp, and heavy upon my soul, and once again I could not face Eleanor.

It had all been so much simpler the last time, I thought, remembering the euphoria of falling through the sky with him, our minds and spirits linked.

As they always have been, Anmchara.

For a moment I was too dazzled to move, and then...

Kieran?

Who else?

My eyes flowed as I felt his presence flood my heart, my mind, my spirit once again.

Where have you been? I've been so lost without you.

I never left you. I've been here all the time. You were just too involved with the physical world to hear me.

I thought you'd left me.

I told you we would be together. The King always keeps his word.

And here I thought I was the King.

We were, both of us, together.

I've killed Gwenna.

I know. She was terrified of the axe. She had the same aversion to it you do, and for the same reasons.

Then you are not angry with me?

Why should I be angry? Your work is done now. That was the last of it. It's time to come home.

But Eleanor and Emily...and now Richard...

A ready made family for Malcolm, remember?

I could see the logic of it, the love of it, and was content to let them go.

I have one more thing to do before I join you.

What?

I must travel back to Stonehenge. I must die there.

You're an incurable romantic. It doesn't matter. Our Lady is everywhere, and She waits for you as I do.

It matters to my honour.

I grabbed my sword and switched on the recorder as I headed back to Salisbury Plain to join my blood with that of my brother, and began to make these notations of our lives. My plan: to complete the first step of our next journey together, the first step of our last one also, for the sword upon which I fell as we fenced together so long ago had missed its mark, and my consecration as a Knight of the Order was also fraught with problems.

I have left the recorder on to take it all in. Kieran says Malcolm has followed us, not to stop me, but to bring back my body. He has been so good to us always, the truest Knight, for he has always been there to aid those we leave behind. Eleanor and the children will be well looked after and well loved.

My sword is wedged against the gravestone beneath which we have lain and will lie once more. I kneel before it, stripped to the waist as I did in Glastonbury as I swear my love and loyalty to the Lady, the Land, and the King. I will not keep him waiting long, for he has called me to his side once more and I follow him with an eager heart.

And now...

Lady?

You would steady the sword for me with Your own hands?

Oh Malcolm, hurry! Listen to her sing...

www.ingramcontent.com/pod-product-compliance
Lightning Source LLC
Chambersburg PA
CBHW071137260626
47162CB00003B/822